国学经典英译赏析丛书

丛书总主编　冯奇

白居易诗歌英译赏析

主编　胡雅坪
副主编　唐爱军　张欢

CHINESE CLASSICS

WUHAN UNIVERSITY PRESS
武汉大学出版社

图书在版编目(CIP)数据

白居易诗歌英译赏析:汉文、英文/胡雅坪主编;唐爱军,张欢副主编.
—武汉:武汉大学出版社,2023.12
(国学经典英译赏析丛书/冯奇总主编)
ISBN 978-7-307-24120-6

Ⅰ.白… Ⅱ.①胡… ②唐… ③张… Ⅲ. 白居易(772—846)—唐诗—英语—文学翻译—诗歌欣赏 Ⅳ.①I207.227.42 ②H315.9

中国国家版本馆 CIP 数据核字(2023)第 220336 号

责任编辑:罗晓华　　责任校对:汪欣怡　　版式设计:马　佳

出版发行:**武汉大学出版社**　(430072　武昌　珞珈山)
(电子邮箱:cbs22@ whu.edu.cn 网址:www.wdp.com.cn)
印刷:湖北金海印务有限公司
开本:787×1092　1/16　印张:14.25　字数:291 千字　插页:1
版次:2023 年 12 月第 1 版　2023 年 12 月第 1 次印刷
ISBN 978-7-307-24120-6　定价:48.00 元

序

中国国学指的是中国传统学术文化的林林总总，其中包括经史子集、诗词歌赋、琴棋书画、民歌民谣等各个领域的知识。而典籍则是记录这些知识的书籍，是国学的重要组成部分，是传统文化知识的载体。

作为概念范畴，“典籍”的提法自古有之。最早使用“典籍”一词的文献记载可以追溯到战国时期。在《孟子·告子下》中就有这样的表述：“诸侯之地方百里，不百里，不足以守宗庙之典籍。”这句话用白话文表述，就是说诸侯所管辖的领地应该是百里，如果不足百里，就无法守护宗庙内的经典书籍，也就不能承担起守护宗庙的责任。可见，“典籍”是指古代文献、经典著作等，特指宗庙内的经典书籍或祭祠用的礼典文献。由此也可以看出“典籍”的历史文化地位和价值。

汉代以后，“典籍”一词开始被用作各种书籍的统称。例如在《后汉书·崔寔传》中，崔寔被称为“少沈静，好典籍”；而在《三国志·蜀书·谯周传》中，谯周被描述为耽古好学，以读书为乐，“诵读典籍，欣然独笑，以忘寝食”。这里的“典籍”一词与我们如今泛指一切图书的用法有异曲同工之妙。

“典籍”的概念语义在历史上的产生和发展反映到语言中就是语义的扩大与转移。语义信息的历史沉淀逐渐固化为广、狭两种不同的义项，被广泛地收录在各种词典的定义之中。如在《现代汉语词典》中，“典籍”被定义为“记载古代法制的图书，也泛指古代图书”。其中，“记载古代法制的图书”是狭义的定义；“也泛指古代图书”则是扩大了“典籍”的外延指称范围。在《辞海》中，“典籍”被定义为“国家重要文献，亦统称各种典册、书籍”，也反映了狭义和广义的定义。《汉语大词典》的定义是：“典籍指法典图籍等重要文献。”其中“法典图籍”可视为“典籍”的严式定义，但后面的一个“等”字又扩大了所指范围。《辞源》在《汉语大词典》“法典图籍等重要文献”的基础上，再增加“后作为各种典册、书籍的统称”。无论怎么定义，都没有脱离广与狭的方式，也都反映了“典籍”的重要作用。

和“典籍”的概念一样，典籍的分类可谓同样源远流长，主要的传统分类一般概括为经、史、子、集四大类。“经”包括儒家经书，如《诗经》《尚书》《周礼》《周易》等。这些经书被视为经典，因为它们在历史上被广泛引用和传颂。其中一些著作如《诗经》和《尚书》被认为是中国文学的源头。“史”包括各种历史著作，如《史记》《汉书》《三国志》等。这些历史著作记录了中国古代的历史事件、人物和文化，为后人留下了宝贵的历史资料。“子”包括先秦诸子百家的著作，如《论语》《孟子》《老子》《庄子》等。这些著作涵盖了哲学、政治、军事、经济等多个领域，是中国古代思想文化的重要载体。“集”则包括各种文学艺术作品，如诗歌、散文、小说、戏曲等。这些作品反映了中国文学的多样性和创新性，代表了中国古代文学的精华。

经、史、子、集的分类是中国古代文献分类法的一种，虽然有其一定的合理性，但也存在一些问题。首先，这种分类法以不同书籍的内容为分类的标准，这使得一些书籍难以归类。例如，“史”部中的“杂传”包括了荒诞不经的写鬼神之书，这不符合“史”部的本质；同样，“集”部中的“楚辞”作为总集的一部分，被单独列出来，也让人感到困惑。此外，一些不属于总集的书籍也被错误地归入了“集”部，例如东汉班昭写的《女诫》，这是一篇以封建道德告诫妇女的“箴言”，本应归入其他类别。其次，这种分类法缺乏科学的统一标准。不同的书籍可能会因为内容或形式上的不同而被归入不同的类别，这使得分类结果具有主观性和不确定性。例如，“经”部中包括了属哲学的《周易》、属政治的《周礼》、属历史的《春秋》、属文学的《诗经》，以及属科学技术的农、医、天文等，这些书籍在性质上存在很大的差异，难以统一归类。最后，经、史、子、集的分类法已经不能适应现代文献分类的需求。现代文献分类法更加注重书籍的主题、形式、语言、作者等因素，同时也更加注重分类的客观性和标准化。相比之下，经、史、子、集的分类法显得过于简单、粗糙和混乱。

随着时代的发展和文献数量的不断增加，人们逐渐认识到了这种分类方法的局限性和问题，开始探索更加科学、客观和标准的文献分类方法。如近代传入我国的西方图书馆学分类法就在某种程度上替代了我国传统的分类法。19 世纪末至 20 世纪初，中国部分图书馆开始采用西方图书分类法进行藏书分类，这些分类法包括杜威十进分类法、美国国会图书馆图书分类法、国际十进分类法等。这些西方分类法采用了更加科学、客观的分类标准，如图书的主题、内容、形式、语言等，使得文献的分类更加规范、系统和准确。

此外，20 世纪中期以后，随着计算机技术和信息技术的发展，数字化图书馆成为了现实。数字化图书馆采用了现代化的技术手段对文献进行分类、存储、检索和管理，使得文献的分类更加高效、便捷和智能化。数字化图书馆的出现也使得传统的经、史、子、集分类法逐渐被淘汰。

在编写“国学经典英译赏析丛书”的过程中，我们将努力遵循以下分类原则：(1) 尊重传统分类法，将所选典籍归入相应的类别。(2) 强调现代文献分类法，对所选典籍进行更加细致、准确的分类。(3)注重主题、内容和形式，确保所选典籍能够反映中国传统文化和思想。(4)突出重点和代表性，选取最具代表性和影响力的典籍进行翻译和介绍。(5)兼顾不同读者需求，选取不同难易程度和类型的典籍进行翻译和介绍，以满足不同层次读者的需求。(6)遵循标准化和规范化的原则，确保所选典籍的翻译和介绍符合通用的规范和标准。

中国国学典籍浩如烟海。这就意味着我们这套丛书应该覆盖的范围必须非常广泛：(1)经学。包括古籍经典，如《周易》《诗经》《孝经》《论语》《孟子》等，以及语言训诂学方面的著作，如《尔雅》。(2)史学。包括通史、政事史、制度史和方志等，如司马迁的《史记》、郑樵的《通志》、班固的《汉书》、陈寿的《三国志》、欧阳修的《新五代史》等。(3)子学。包括中国历史上创立一个学说或学派的人物文集，如儒家的《荀子》、法家的《韩非子》《商君书》、兵家的《孙子》、道家的《老子》《庄子》等。(4)文学。包括历史上诸位文人学者的总集和个人的文集，个人的称为“别集”，如《李太白集》《王荆公集》等；总集如《昭明文选》《玉台新咏》等。(5)哲学。包括儒学、道学、法家学派、墨学、名学等主要学派，以及探索人类的智慧和价值观念的相关著作。(6)艺术。包括书法、音乐、戏曲等方面的内容。完善的分类本是好事，可以指导我们接下来的编撰工作。然而，我们却不能按照上述分类来设计这套丛书。我们追求的不是大而全，而是有所侧重的亮点。主要原因如下：(1)中国国学经典浩如烟海，若全面涉及，工程过于浩大。(2)我们掌握的可用资源不足。(3)我们的能力有限，哪怕是国学大师穷其一生，也无法全面涉及。因此，我们只能在自己有限的知识结构体系中尽最大努力选择部分家喻户晓、耳熟能详的优秀作品、译文及其赏析展示给读者。

在评价不同译者的译文质量时，我们将以下因素作为评判译文质量的依据：(1)尊重原作，尽量保留原作的内容和风格，准确地传达原作者的思想和意图。不随意删减或改动原文，更不凭空任意添加个人观点或注释。(2)准确理解原文中涉及的特定概念、术语、典故等，译前进行深入的研究和准确的解读，避免出现歧义或误解。(3)语言流畅，翻译时注重语言的可读性，尽量做到既忠实于原文，又符合现代汉语的表达习惯，以便于读者理解和接受。(4)文化传递，注重传递中国传统文化和思想，尽可能保留原文的文化内涵和特色，以便于读者了解中国文化的精髓和特点。(5)规范统一，遵循通用的规范和标准，对于同一概念或术语的翻译保持一致，以避免出现译法混乱的情况。

中华国学典籍不仅是中国古代学术文化的精华，也是中华民族智慧的结晶，同时还是世界文化遗产的重要组成部分，将它们译成英文对于世界文化的交流和发展有着重要的意义。通过学习和研究中华国学典籍及其翻译，我们可以更好地传承和传播我国的传统优秀文化、弘扬民族精神、增强文化自信。

编写本套丛书的主要目的是为了帮助英语专业学生和翻译爱好者提高国学经典翻译技能，故我们努力遵循系统性、实用性和可操作性的原则，旨在为学生提供较为全面、深入了解中国国学及其英译知识和技能的途径。在编写方式上注重理论与实践相结合，通过大量的名家翻译实例分析和练习，帮助读者掌握中国国学经典英译的基本技能和策略。通过本套丛书的学习，学生将了解并掌握中国国学经典的重要领域和内容以及国学经典英译的基本概念、理论和实践方法，提高他们的文化素养和翻译技能。

本套丛书适用于英语专业本科高年级或研究生阶段的教学，也可作为翻译工作者的参考书籍。希望通过本套丛书的学习和实践，学生能够更好地传播中国国学思想和文化，促进中外文化交流和学术合作。

冯奇

2023 年 12 月

前　　言

唐诗是中国传统文化中的一颗耀眼明珠，其魅力不仅在于其语言优美、意境深邃，还在于诗中所蕴涵的智慧和情感等人文精髓。中唐时期成就最高的诗人当属白居易。他与元稹共同发起了“新乐府运动”，世称“元白”。他主张“文章合为时而著，歌诗合为事而作”(《与元九书》)，强调了诗歌的现实内容和社会作用。他的诗歌语言明白晓畅，在当时广为流传，并远播海外，是中国文学史上负有盛名且影响深远的唐代诗人和文学家。

本书精选了白居易的五十四首诗歌，按照诗歌内容和表达的情感分为六个部分，分别为咏物诗、讽喻诗、送别诗、贬谪诗、写景诗和悼亡诗。每个部分根据诗歌主旨分为三章，每章包含同类诗歌三篇。每篇诗歌都包含诗歌的背景介绍、原文、英文译文、注释和译文赏析，其中英文译文采用翻译家赵彦春的版本。通过同类作品的集中介绍，旨在帮助读者更有效地识别、理解和赏析同类诗歌，进而了解诗歌的分类体系和各自的特征，并习得古诗翻译的技巧。

古诗英译不仅是学生提高英语水平的重要手段，也是拓展中国文化在世界上的影响力的有效方式。英译古诗能增强跨文化传播的贴近性意识，实现文化上的对话，从而有助于中西话语融通，为世界文化发展贡献中国智慧。此外，也可以让人们从繁忙的生活中抽离出来，沉淀心灵，感受中英文字中所蕴涵的文化魅力和价值。本书适合英语专业本科学生、唐诗和翻译爱好者学习和参考使用，也可作为翻译课程的资料使用。

胡雅坪

2023 年 9 月

目　　录

第一部分　咏物诗

第二部分　讽喻诗

第三部分　送别诗

第四部分　贬谪诗

第五部分　写景诗

第六部分　悼亡诗

第一部分　咏物诗

第一章 经世济民

第一节 折剑头

一、诗歌背景

《折剑头》是唐代诗人白居易所作的一首五言古诗。全诗记叙了诗人偶遇折剑头，分析和想象剑头折断的原因，并最终借“直折剑”和“曲全钩”来引申宁折莫弯和不可失节而苟且于世的哲理。白居易以折剑为喻，赞扬了宁折不弯的刚直精神和无所顾惜的决心，并表达了对耿介忠贞之士的敬仰钦慕和对委曲求全之人的蔑视。译者灵巧地运用了语序前置、显性化、整体—部分、具体—抽象等技巧来处理尾韵、无主句、文化负载词、抽象义等翻译难点，使译文朗朗上口、篇幅对称、生动形象。

二、古诗原文

折 剑 头

拾得折剑头，
不知折之由。
一握青蛇尾，
数寸碧峰头。
疑是斩鲸鲵，

不然刺蛟虬。
缺落泥土中，
委弃无人收。
我有鄙介性，
好刚不好柔。
勿轻直折剑，
犹胜曲全钩。

三、古诗译文

A Broken Sword

A broken sword there was I found;
I did not know why it lay aground.
In my hand it looked like a snake[1];
Its edge's serrated like a rake.
Is it because it stabbed a whale[2]
Or once cut off a dragon's tail?
It was thrown to the soil alone;
Such a thing no one would fain own.
I have a peculiar hard trait:
A hard nut outdoes a soft date[3].
Do not despise it for its look;
It's better than a perfect hook.

（赵彦春 译）

◎ **注释**

1. snake: an ophidian reptile, having a greatly elongated, scaly body, no limbs, and a specialized swallowing apparatus, a symbol of indifference, malevolence, cattiness, and craftiness in Chinese culture. 青蛇

2. whale：a cetaceous mammal of fish-like form, as distinguished from dolphins and porpoises. It is a symbol of great ambition, fortitude and uniqueness, and sometimes of an impending threat. 鲸鲵

3. soft date：an oblong, sweet, fleshy fruit of the date palm, enclosing a single hard seed, a symbol of early fertility in Chinese culture. 柔

四、译文赏析

1. 拾得折剑头，不知折之由。
一握青蛇尾，数寸碧峰头。

译文： A broken sword there was I found; /I did not know why it lay aground.
In my hand it looked like a snake; /Its edge's serrated like a rake.

赏析： 原文第一分句组内押韵(ou)，两分句组间押韵(ou)，即"头""由""头"；译文中的两分句组均在组内押尾韵，即 found 和 aground、snake 和 rake。在篇幅的把控上，译文的两个分句组内，两分句的篇幅对称。第一分句组记叙了诗人偶然捡到一段折断的剑头，并深思其折断的原因。第二分句组描写了剑客手握青蛇剑柄，剑身露出几寸铜锈斑斑的剑头，为诗人对剑折断前的想象。为了押尾韵，译者对 there was a broken sword (that) I found 的语序做了调整，将 a broken sword 前置到句首，并将下文"折"译成 lay aground。这体现了译者遵循的语序和语义要让位给押韵的古诗翻译原则。原文"一握"无形式主语，其逻辑主语可能是诗人或剑客，译者选择了诗人，并译成第一人称，有利于译文的生动形象。原文和译文共同呈现了折剑锐不可当的气势。

2. 疑是斩鲸鲵，不然刺蛟虬。
缺落泥土中，委弃无人收。

译文： Is it because it stabbed a whale; /Or once cut off a dragon's tail?
It was thrown to the soil alone; /Such a thing no one would fain own.

赏析： 原文为两分句组间押尾韵，即"虬""收"押韵(iu)；译文则在两分句组内押尾韵，即 whale 和 tail、alone 和 own。两分句组的篇幅较为对称，但第一分句组的句型却变成了疑问句，译者巧妙地用疑问句型 Is it...? 来翻译"疑是"二字。"鲸鲵"指鲸鱼，雄曰鲸，雌曰鲵，可比喻凶恶的敌人或海盗。"蛟虬"中的"蛟"是古代中国传说中能发水的广

义龙类，栖息在湖、渊等聚水处；“虬”指古代传说中一种有角的小龙，可比喻奸臣。“鲸鲵”的译文取其上义词 whale，为与 whale 形成尾韵，译者将“蛟虬”译成了龙身体的一个部分(a dragon’s tail)，并与 cut off 一同生动地呈现了剑斩恶龙的场面。

3. **我有鄙介性，好刚不好柔。**
勿轻直折剑，犹胜曲全钩。

译文： I have a peculiar hard trait；/A hard nut outdoes a soft date.
Do not despise it for its look；/It’s better than a perfect hook.

赏析： 原文为分句组间押尾韵，即“柔”和“钩”；译文则为分句组内押尾韵，即 trait 和 date、look 和 hook。两分句组篇幅对称，具有对偶的诗性。原文描写了诗人生性质朴耿直，喜好刚直而不爱柔弱，并感慨不要轻视这因刚直而折断的剑，即使断了，也胜过保存完好的钩曲剑。“鄙”是高贵义的反说。“直折剑”和“曲全钩”以两种不同形状的兵器来比喻两种不同的人格，分别象征耿直忠贞之士和委曲求全的“软骨头”，在译文中分别为 its look 和 perfect hook，将“直折剑”模糊为剑的外观，巧妙地与 hook 形成尾韵。“刚”和“柔”的翻译最为巧妙，译者分别用“hard nut”和“soft date”做比喻，用具体事物来译抽象的性格，生动形象。

第二节　杏园中枣树

一、诗歌背景

“杏园”为园名，位于今陕西省西安市郊大雁塔南，在唐代为新科进士赐宴之地。白居易担任翰林学士时，尽忠职守，直言敢谏，但宪宗皇帝对他深怀不满，他也深遭权贵的嫉恨。从政愈久，他对权贵豪门专权和贤士才俊委曲求全的现象就愈加不满，于是便写下了《杏园中枣树》。全诗描写了在杏园的各种果树中，唯有枣树既平凡又粗鄙，其树皮像开裂的冻手，树叶像细小的鼠耳，因此枣树未能受到赏识，但庆幸未受到伤害。诗人最后感慨，枣树虽不如桃李悦目美丽，但它是造车的最佳木材。全诗的译文灵活地采用了语序调整、整体—部分、减译、功能对等的策略，来处理人名、地名、押韵和翻译选词的难点。

二、古诗原文

杏园中枣树

人言百果中，
唯枣凡且鄙。
皮皴似龟手，
叶小如鼠耳。
胡为不自知，
生花此园里。
岂宜遇攀玩，
幸免遭伤毁。
二月曲江头，
杂英红旖旎。
枣亦在其间，
如嫫对西子。
东风不择木，
吹煦长未已。
眼看欲合抱，
得尽生生理。
寄言游春客，
乞君一回视。
君爱绕指柔，
从君怜柳杞。
君求悦目艳，
不敢争桃李。
君若作大车，
轮轴材须此。

三、古诗译文

The Date[1] Tree in the Apricot[2] Orchard

As said, of a hundred fruits raised,
The date is common and abased.
Its bark as wrinkled as hands chapped;
Its leaves as small as rat's ears mapped.
Your own status, why don't you know?
Why come to this orchard to grow?
How can you bear all climb and play?
So lucky, free from harm you stay.
The second moon comes to the Bent[3];
No blossoming one can prevent.
Among them the date tree does fade,
Like a crone facing West Maid[4].
The east wind does not choose to blow,
Blowing to all trees that there grow.
The tree will be thick, armful soon,
Having all of natural boon.
To the tourists I would now say
Please look aback or you can stay.
If you treasure what's soft and thin,
You may love willows'[5] smile to win.
To seek what's pleasing if you come,
It will not vie with peach[6] and plum[7].
If you'd like to make a big car;
It is the best wood, here you are!

（赵彦春　译）

◎ 注释

1. date: an oblong, sweet, fleshy fruit of the date palm, enclosing a single hard seed, a symbol of early fertility in Chinese culture. 枣
2. apricot: a tree or the fruit of the tree of the rose family, intermediate between the peach and the plum. Growing, reaping or selling apricots alludes to a hermit who is kind to the folks, just like Feng Tung, who gave free medical treatment to them except that he asked them to plant one to five apricot trees for him according to the severity of their illness. 杏
3. the Bent: Ch'uchiang if transliterated, a royal park of T'ang, located in the southeast of Long Peace, the capital. 曲江头
4. West Maid: a famed beauty of the Spring and Autumn Period. Once a laundry lady in the State of Yüeh, which was then a tributary to the State of Wu. Because of her beauty, West Maid was selected to be trained in Yüeh's palace, and sent to King of Wu as a spy. Immediately, she won the king's affection and favor with her bewitching charm and performance art of dancing. As a result, the State of Wu waned and perished. 西子
5. willow: any of a large genus of shrubs and trees related to the poplars, having generally smooth branches, and often long, slender, pliant, and sometimes pendent branchlets, a symbol of farewell or nostalgia in Chinese culture. 柳
6. peach: any of the plant (*Prunus Percica*), bearing a fleshy, juicy, edible drupe, cultivated in many varieties in temperate zones considered sacred in China, often used as a metaphor for a young woman, as a section of a poem in *The Book of Songs* reads: "The peach twigs sway, /Ablaze the flower; /Now she's married away, /Befitting her new bower." 桃
7. plum: a kind of plant or the edible purple drupaceous fruit of the plant which is any one of various trees of the genus *Prunus*, cultivated in temperate zones. 李

四、译文赏析

1. 人言百果中，唯枣凡且鄙。
   皮皴似龟手，叶小如鼠耳。

译文： As said, of a hundred fruits raised; /The date is common and abased.
Its bark as wrinkled as hands chapped; /Its leaves as small as rat's ears mapped.

赏析： 原文无押韵修辞，而译文两分句组内均押尾韵和篇幅对称，尤其是第二分句组

在句型上一致。原文讲述了在百果树中，唯有枣树平凡和粗鄙。树皮像开裂的冻手，树叶像老鼠的耳朵。为了与“鄙”的译文 abased 形成尾韵，译者增译了 raised，并后置在名词右侧。在四个分句的译文中，最突出和频繁的结构是 *n.*+*v.*ed 结构，如 fruits raised，hands chapped，ears mapped，这种结构有利于减少译文尾韵的难度，而难点在于将语义动词化，如名词“龟手”需转化成动词 chapped(开裂)。

2. **二月曲江头，杂英红旖旎。**
枣亦在其间，如嫫对西子。

译文： The second moon comes to the Bent；/No blossoming one can prevent.
Among them the date tree does fade；/Like a crone facing West Maid.

赏析： 原文两句组间押尾韵，即“旎”和“子”，而译文则在分句组内押尾韵，即 Bent 和 prevent、fade 和 Maid。译文在篇幅上对称，具有对偶性，在音和形上具有诗性。原文记叙了在二月的曲江边上，各种红花随风飘扬。枣树夹杂在它们中间，就像是嫫母对着西子。为使分句字数对称，译者将“二月”译成 The second moon 而非 February，比喻月周期。地名“曲江”的译文 the Bent 还原了地点的字面义和地形特征，但为了押尾韵，译者减译了“江”字。“旖旎”(yǐ nǐ)，本义为旌旗随风飘扬的样子，引申为景物的柔和美丽。其译文 No... one can prevent 虽与“旖旎”的柔和美丽形象不同，但在功能上都凸显了“杂英”的吸引力和美的程度。“嫫”(mó)指嫫母，《列女传》记载了嫫母是黄帝的妃子，长得很丑，但有贤德，其译文 crone(容貌较丑的老妇)采用了部分译整体的思路，用“嫫母”丑陋的特征来译此人。“西子”指西施，是春秋时越国美女，其译文 West Maid 为“字面义+身份”结构，有利于还原西施未婚女子的形象。

3. **君求悦目艳，不敢争桃李。**
君若作大车，轮轴材须此。

译文： To seek what's pleasing if you come；/It will not vie with peach and plum.
If you'd like to make a big car；/It is the best wood，here you are!

赏析： 原文为分句组间押尾韵，即“李”和“此”；译文则为分句组内押尾韵，即 come 和 plum、car 和 are。译文两分句组内篇幅对称，具有对偶性。原文意为“如果您追求悦目的美丽，枣树不敢去和桃树与李树竞争；如果您要造一辆大车，车轮车轴的取材则必须为枣树”。“求”和“若”字分别被译成条件状语 if you come to seek 和条件状语 if you'd like to，但为了押尾韵，译者将 if you come 语序后置到句尾与 plum 押韵。在最后的分句中，译者减译了“轮轴”，将原文的“轮轴取材”译成了“造车取材”，以车的整体译车的部分，最终使 It... are 与 If... car 头尾均押韵，体现了押韵大于语义忠实的古诗翻译原则。

第三节　涧底松

一、诗歌背景

《涧底松》是白居易于唐元和四年(公元 809 年)所作。白居易时任左拾遗，为报答宪宗知遇之恩尽言官之责，作大量讽喻诗，希望宪宗补察时政。《涧底松》便是其中一首。该诗前六句咏涧底松，后十句紧扣涧底松抒写感慨，讲述了松树因身居深山涧底而不被良匠发现和重用的故事，并在最后一句引出了“高者不一定贤，下者不一定愚”的道理。从句式看，全诗以七言为主，间或杂以五言和十言。这种错落有致的句式结构形成了富于变化的节奏感和音调铿锵的诗韵美。

二、古诗原文

涧底松

有松百尺大十围，
生在涧底寒且卑。
涧深山险人路绝，
老死不逢工度之。
天子明堂欠梁木，
此求彼有两不知。
谁谕苍苍造物意，
但与之材不与地。
金张世禄原宪贫，
牛衣寒贱貂蝉贵。
貂蝉与牛衣，
高下虽有殊。
高者未必贤，

下者未必愚。
君不见沉沉海底生珊瑚,
历历天上种白榆。

三、古诗译文

Pines[1] in the Dale

Pines one hundred feet tall, ten arms around,
Grow in the dale low and cold down below.
The dale deep, dangerous, and no way found,
No carpenter e'er comes for timber, no.
A palace being built need beams and wood;
No one knows that there are pines here, so good.
Who can fathom God's will and offer grace,
Using proper things in their proper place?
The rich, the sage are of a different tier;
A herd's coat is cheap, a crown pearl is dear.
A herd's coat there, a crown pearl here,
One is low and cheap, one is high and dear.
The high may not be upraised;
The low may not be debased.
Don't you espy in the depth of the ocean corals[2] grow,
High above in the heaven poplars[3] show?

(赵彦春 译)

◎ 注释

1. pine: any of a genus (*Pinus*) of evergreen trees of the pine family, a cone-bearing tree having bundles of two to five needle-shaped leaves growing in clusters, an important image in Chinese literature, a symbol of rectitude, longevity and so on. 松
2. coral: the hard, stony skeleton secreted by certain marine polyps and often deposited in

extensive masses forming reefs and atolls in tropical seas. 珊瑚

3. poplar：any of a genus（*Populus*）of dioecious trees and bushes of the willow family, widely distributed in the northern hemisphere. 白榆

四、译文赏析

1. 有松百尺大十围，生在涧底寒且卑。
涧深山险人路绝，老死不逢工度之。

译文： Pines one hundred feet tall, ten arms around; /Grow in the dale low and cold down below.

The dale deep, dangerous, and no way found; /No carpenter e'er comes for timber, no.

赏析： 原文第一分句组内押尾韵，即“围”和“卑”，而译文则在分句组间押尾韵，形成 ABAB 结构，即 around 和 found、below 和 no，尾韵密度超过原文，且译文两分句组内的篇幅较为对称。原文描写了有百尺高和十围宽的大松树，生长在地势低和气候寒冷的地方。因涧深山险、人迹罕至，松树老死时也遇不到良工为之取材重用。“百尺”和“十围”为夸张修辞，而非写实，其译文 one hundred feet 和 ten arms 通过直译法再现了这一夸张的修辞。“底”和“不”的翻译采用了增译法来形成尾韵，down 和 below 均能表达“底下”，但为了篇幅对称和押尾韵，译者增加了 below；“不”的译文 no 在句中重复出现了两次，译者采用词语重复的手法来强调松树不为所用的失落。

2. 金张世禄原宪贫，牛衣寒贱貂蝉贵。

译文： The rich, the sage are of a different tier;

A herd's coat is cheap, a crown pearl is dear.

赏析： 译文在分句组内押尾韵，即 tier 和 dear，而原文无尾韵特征。原文有多个文化负载词，“金张”指汉宣帝时的高官金日磾和张安世，二人奢华无度，后泛指贵族。“原宪”是孔子门徒，字子思，为人贤能（见《史记·仲尼弟子传》）。“金张”和“原宪”的译文 the rich 和 the sage 均体现了译者“特指—泛指”的翻译思路，“金张”“原宪”字面上特指具体的人，但在功能上泛指一类人，因此译者将其语义泛指化。“牛衣”指牛御寒的东西，以麻或草编成，a herd's coat 再现了此意。“貂蝉”是古代高级官员头冠上的饰物，配有貂尾与蝉羽，始于汉代武官，其译文 a crown pearl 实现了文化对等，通过在两种文化里寻找对

等的事物来翻译，以西方贵族头冠上的珍珠来译中国高官头冠上的饰物。

3. 君不见沉沉海底生珊瑚，历历天上种白榆。

译文： Don't you espy in the depth of the ocean corals grow,

High above in the heaven poplars show?

赏析： 原文的诗性体现在尾韵和叠词上，但篇幅不对称，即“瑚”和“榆”、“沉沉海底”和“历历天上”。译文还原了其尾韵特点，即 grow 和 show，两句的篇幅长短与原文一致。“珊瑚”是热带海生物，骨骼相连，形如树枝，古时为名贵的饰品材料，其译文 corals 的复数后缀指珊瑚丛生。“历历”意为形象分明可数。“白榆”在古乐府中原指星星，在此诗中借星星指榆树，但其译文 poplars 为杨树。译者改变树种的原因是各树种的文化代表性不同。榆树在中国分布广泛，而西方国家分布较多的是杨树，各文化的代表树种不同，因此译者用文化对等的译法来处理“白榆”。

第二章　西赆南琛

第一节　紫毫笔

一、诗歌背景

《紫毫笔》是唐代诗人白居易创作的一首新乐府。紫毫笔是用野山兔项背的毛发制成，因色呈黑紫而得名。南北方山兔毛发的坚韧程度不同，北方的偏软，也叫淮兔毫，指安徽淮北出的山兔毛，质量较好，但现在其物种濒临灭绝。有些紫毫笔取南北毫合制而成。全诗介绍了紫毫笔的制作工艺，并最终劝诫君臣要珍惜和慎用朝中的紫毫笔，为政以德。全诗每句译文的篇幅长短与原文较为一致，其译法特色是在翻译细微行为时，译者以行为目的代替了行为本身。

二、古诗原文

紫毫笔

紫毫笔，
尖如锥兮利如刀。
江南石上有老兔，
吃竹饮泉生紫毫。
宣城之人采为笔，

千万毛中拣一毫。
毫虽轻，
功甚重。
管勒工名充岁贡，
君兮臣兮勿轻用。
勿轻用，
将何如？
愿赐东西府御史，
愿颁左右台起居。
搦管趋入黄金阙，
抽毫立在白玉除。
臣有奸邪正衙奏，
君有动言直笔书。
起居郎，
侍御史，
尔知紫毫不易致。
每岁宣城进笔时，
紫毫之价如金贵。
慎勿空将弹失仪，
慎勿空将录制词。

三、古诗译文

The Purple Hair Brush[1]

The Purple Hair Brush,
Pointed like an awl, sharp as a knife, hush;
Hares[2] hide amidst rocks in the south[3] down there,
Eating bamboo[4], drinking spring, growing purple hair.
Folks in Hsuan[5] pluck it for a writing tool;

One's picked out, out of a million by rule.
A hair is so light;
The worth is not slight.
The brushes sent as tribute to the court,
Lord and peers, treat them not as a cheap sort.
Not as a cheap sort,
Used for what purport?
Censorate, historians, use them to write;
Ministers, secretaries, use them to fight.
Holding the brush, you enter the hall grand;
Twirling the hair, on a jade step you stand.
Those evil and crafty you should chastise
His Majesty, when loose, you should advise.
Recorders, do rise,
Attendants, be wise,
You know it's hard to find a brush so nice.
When brushes are sent here from Huan each year
The price of purple hair is high, so dear.
Pray use it to admonish the Most High;
Pray use it to note what comes and goes by.

(赵彦春　译)

◎ 注释

1. Written in Long Peace in the year 809.
2. hare: a rodent (genus *Lepus*) with cleft upper lip, long ears, and long hind legs: known for its timidity and swiftness, habitating woodland, farmland or grassland. 老兔
3. the south: It literally means "South of the Yangtze River" but in fact refers to today's Jiangsu and Zhejiang Provinces. 江南
4. bamboo: a tall, tree-like or shrubby grass in tropical and semi-tropical regions. 竹
5. Hsuan: an ancient town, especially famous for its paper made of ebony wood, in present-day Hsuan, Anhui Province. 宣城

四、译文赏析

1. 江南石上有老兔，吃竹饮泉生紫毫。
宣城之人采为笔，千万毛中拣一毫。

译文：Hares hide amidst rocks in the south down there; /Eating bamboo, drinking spring, growing purple hair.

Folks in Hsuan pluck it for a writing tool; /One's picked out, out of a million by rule.

赏析：原文分为句组间押尾韵，即"毫"和"毫"，而译文为两分句组内押尾韵，如 there 和 hair、tool 和 rule。两分句组内的分句间篇幅较为对称。"老兔"指的是长有黑针尖毛的山兔。rabbit 是指一般的兔子，强调兔子的可爱，而 hare 指野兔，后肢更强健，跑得更快，因此"老兔"译为 hare。"紫毫"指山兔身上的毛发，紫毫表面有光泽，毛杆直顺，锋颖尖锐，呈黑褐色透明状，而"毫"指毫毛，其译文 purple hair 表达了原文字面义并与前句形成尾韵。"宣城"的译文 Hsuan 表达了"宣"的音但不见"城"，因该地点字义包含在了地点介词 in 里。为了形成尾韵，译者将"笔"模糊成 writing tool，并增译了 by rule。

2. 管勒工名充岁贡，君兮臣兮勿轻用。

译文：The brushes sent as tribute to the court,

Lord and peers, treat them not as a cheap sort.

赏析：原文为分句组内押尾韵，即"贡"和"用"，而译文也为分句组内押尾韵，即 court 和 sort。"管勒"中的"管"指细长圆筒形的东西，代指笔。"勒"指收住缰绳不使它前进。"管勒"在此文中引申为把紫毫收起来，具体指把笔毛与笔头粘在一起，而译者对其采用了减译法。"工名"指在笔管上工工整整地刻上"紫毫笔"的名字，而译者对其也采用减译法。"岁贡"指古代诸侯或属国每年向朝廷进献的贡品，译为 tribute to the court。由此，译者在处理刻画过于细致的行为时，采用了减译策略，以使句子篇幅不至于过长而损失诗性。

3. 搦管趋入黄金阙，抽毫立在白玉除。
臣有奸邪正衙奏，君有动言直笔书。

译文：Holding the brush, you enter the hall grand; /Twirling the hair, on a jade step you stand.

Those evil and crafty you should chastise; /His Majesty, when loose, you should advise.

赏析：原文为分句组间押尾韵，即“除”和“书”，而译文为分句组内押尾韵，即 grand 和 stand、chastise 和 advise。两分句组间的篇幅整体上具有对称性。“搦管”指执笔为文，而译者将其译成伴随状语 holding the brush。“黄金阙”比喻月宫，其译文 the hall grand 将“黄金”转化为宏伟(grand)，从而与下文形成尾韵。“抽毫”指抽笔出套，进一步引申为写作，其译文中的动词 twirling 可指用手指盘绕毛笔，译出了细致的动作。“正衙”指唐高宗时在长安城东北外侧御苑内所建设的大明宫，但在“正衙奏”的译文中，“正衙”被减译，而“奏”为一种举报的行为，译者则选择译出其行为的目的，即 chastise(严惩)。

4. 每岁宣城进笔时，紫毫之价如金贵。
慎勿空将弹失仪，慎勿空将录制词。

译文：When brushes are sent here from Huan each year, /The price of purple hair is high, so dear.

Pray use it to admonish the Most High; /Pray use it to note what comes and goes by.

赏析：原文三组分句形成尾韵，即“时”“仪”“词”，第二组分句采用重复“慎勿空将”来强调建议。译文均为分句组内押尾韵，即 year 和 dear、High 和 by。“弹失仪”中的“弹”指弹劾，“失”指失误，“仪”则指仪礼。这三个字共同指弹劾别人而不讲礼仪，其译文 admonish the Most High 译出了诗人写此句来告诫君臣的目的，而非弹劾的行为。“慎勿空将”的译文 Pray use it to 与原文的否定语义相反，译文为肯定而原文的“勿”为否定，但其劝诫的功能一致。“录制词”中的“录”指记载，“制”为动词“作”，“词”即言语。“录制词”共同指记载下来的言语，其译文 note what comes and goes by 对“词”的语义进行扩展，即言语记录中发生的事，comes and goes 也具有诗性。

第二节　红线毯

一、诗歌背景

红线毯是一种丝织地毯，是宣州(今安徽省宣城市)所管织造户织贡的。《红线毯》通过宣州进贡红线毯的事，讽刺了宣州太守等官员讨好皇帝的行为，并暴露了最高统治者荒淫享乐，而任意浪费人力物力的罪恶。全诗形式较自由，长短句协调有致，语言质朴直率、通俗易懂，感情激烈直露。此诗的译文特点是通过字面直译、音译地点特征的手法来再现地点名称给读者带来的第一印象。

二、古诗原文

红线毯

红线毯，
择茧缲丝清水煮，
拣丝练线红蓝染。
染为红线红于蓝，
织作披香殿上毯。
披香殿广十丈馀，
红线织成可殿铺。
彩丝茸茸香拂拂，
线软花虚不胜物。
美人踏上歌舞来，
罗袜绣鞋随步没。
太原毯涩毳缕硬，
蜀都褥薄锦花冷。
不如此毯温且柔，
年年十月来宣州。
宣城太守加样织，
自谓为臣能竭力。
百夫同担进宫中，
线厚丝多卷不得。
宣城太守知不知？
一丈毯，
千两丝！

地不知寒人要暖，
少夺人衣作地衣。

三、古诗译文

The Red Silk Carpet

The Red Silk Carpet,
From fine cocoons[1] and in clean water boiled,
The silk[2] dyed blue or red is reeled and coiled.
When red silk's ready, it is like flowers red;
A carpet is made and on Balm Hall spread.
Balm Hall is more than thirty meters wide;
The red carpet is spread from side to side.
The colored softer than wool is perfumed,
Its flowery patterns true to life assumed.
When palace beauties have come to the ball,
Their silk socks and 'broidered shoes please the hall.
Great Plain[3] carpets look stubby and not fine;
Silkton[4] carpets look flowery and does shine;
Lo and behold, that carpet's soft and sheer,
Sent all the way from Hsuan year after year.
Hsuan's[5] prefect did work hard for carpets rare,
Saying that he'd no more energy to spare.
A hundred bore the carpet to the hall,
Too huge that they could not roll it at all.
Does the prefect of Hsuan know this or not
For ten feet to be wrought,
A thousand ounces brought.
The earth does not feel cold but all men do;
They're robbed of silk for carpets red or blue!

（赵彦春 译）

◎ 注释

1. cocoon：the silky or fabrous case which the larvae of certain insects spin about themselves for shelter during the pupa stage. 茧

2. silk：the fine, soft, shiny fiber produced by silk worms to form their cocoons, and the thread or fabric made from this fibre is used as material for clothing. And it can be any clothing made of silk. 丝

3. Great Plain：referring to T'aiyüan if transliterated, the place where the first emperor of T'ang, Yüan Li, and the second emperor, Shimin Li, i. e. Yüan Li's son, were stationed in the Sui Dynasty. As Great Plain was once called T'ang, T'ang was adopted as the name of the T'ang Empire. 太原

4. Silkton：alias Ch'engtu, now the capital of Ssuch'uan Province, a city that has been prosperous with fine silk for thousands of years. 蜀都

5. Hsuan：an ancient town in present-day Hsuan, Anhui Province, a county instituted in the early years of the Ch'in Emperor under the Prefecture of Redshine. It became a prefecture in 281 during the Chin Dynasty. It is well-known for rich historical legacies, and best remembered for its high-quality rice paper. 宣城

四、译文赏析

1. 择茧缫丝清水煮，拣丝练线红蓝染。
染为红线红于蓝，织作披香殿上毯。

译文： From fine cocoons and in clean water boiled, /The silk dyed blue or red is reeled and coiled.

When red silk's ready, it is like flowers red; /A carpet is made and on Balm Hall spread.

赏析： 原文三个分句连续押尾韵，即“染”“蓝”“毯”，而译文均为分句组内押尾韵，即 boiled 和 coiled、red 和 spread，其中/d/尾韵在全诗中的使用频率较高。两分句组间和组内的篇幅较为对称。“缫(sāo)丝”指将蚕茧抽为丝缕，译者减译了缫丝的细致动作来控制篇幅。“拣丝练线”指挑选蚕丝并缠绕收集，其译文 reeled and coiled 采用了两个近义词来还原“拣丝练线”的画面，具有强调的作用，也形成了尾韵，具有诗性。“披香殿”是汉

代宫殿名，汉成帝的皇后赵飞燕曾轻歌曼舞于此，在此诗中借指宫廷歌舞之地；其译文 Balm Hall 中的 Balm 指香油，还原了地名“披香殿”所呈现的寓意。

2. **披香殿广十丈馀，红线织成可殿铺。**
彩丝茸茸香拂拂，线软花虚不胜物。

译文： Balm Hall is more than thirty meters wide; /The red carpet is spread from side to side.

The colored softer than wool is perfumed, /Its flowery patterns true to life assumed.

赏析： 原文三个分句连续押尾韵，即“铺”“拂”“物”，其译文均为分句组内押尾韵，即 wide 和 side、perfumed 和 assumed。可见，在翻译白居易的诗歌时，译者善于用/d/和/id/尾韵。两分句组之内的篇幅较为对称。“可殿铺”中的“可”指适合，可理解为“满殿铺”，指用红线毯铺满“披香殿”，其译文 is spread from side to side 巧妙地呈现了“铺”和“满”的画面，“满”的呈现较为委婉。“不胜(shēng)”指承受不起，在此诗中比喻红线毯的质地、图案织得柔软虚空，受不了任何物体的按压，体现其精美和帝王的奢华，其译文突出“花虚”，而减译了“线软”，以避免和前面的分句语义重复。

3. **美人踏上歌舞来，罗袜绣鞋随步没。**
太原毯涩毳缕硬，蜀都褥薄锦花冷。

译文： When palace beauties have come to the ball, /Their silk socks and ’broidered shoes please the hall.

Great Plain carpets look stubby and not fine; /Silkton carpets look flowery and does shine;

赏析： 原文无尾韵特征，而译文依然坚持以分句组内押尾韵来体现诗性，即 ball 和 hall、fine 和 shine。两分句组内的篇幅较为对称。“美人”的译文 palace beauties 增译了“宫殿”的语义。“罗袜绣鞋”指舞女的鞋袜，与“随步没”一同衬托了丝毯松软，能陷没舞鞋的质地，即所谓“不胜物”。因其译文 Their silk socks and ’broidered shoes 对“罗袜绣鞋”的描写已较为详尽，所以译者减译了“随步没”，以控制篇幅。“太原”两句意为太原出产的毛毯硬涩，四川出产的锦花褥太薄，都比不过这种红丝毯。地名“太原”的译文 Great Plain 呈现了字面义，而“蜀都”的译文 Silkton 则译出了地点盛产丝绸的特色，而“蜀”中的“虫”在甲骨文里代指野蚕。

4. **不如此毯温且柔，年年十月来宣州。**
   宣城太守加样织，自谓为臣能竭力。

译文：Lo and behold, that carpet's soft and sheer, /Sent all the way from Hsuan year after year.
Hsuan's prefect did work hard for carpets rare, /Saying that he'd no more energy to spare.

赏析：原文为分句组内押尾韵，即"柔"和"州"、"织"和"力"，其译文的尾韵位置一致，即 sheer 和 year、rare 和 spare。两分句组内的篇幅较为对称。"宣州"指安徽宣城，其译文 Hsuan 采用了音译法。译文 Lo and behold 相当于"你瞧"，其功能是表达惊讶，以翻译"不如"所体现的"此毯"的柔美程度。"十月"在译文中被删减，如果译出来，会破坏篇幅的对称，与 year after year 一起也会显得时间信息过于重复和具体。"太守"为一郡最高长官，也为郡守的尊称，其译文 prefect 为行政长官，相当于省长，与"太守"所管理的范围一致。

第三节 缭 绫

一、诗歌背景

《缭绫》是唐代诗人白居易的诗作，是《新乐府五十首》的第三十一首。此诗主题是"念女工之劳"，通过描述缭绫的生产过程、工艺特点和对比生产者与消费者的差距，表达了对纺织女工的同情，揭露了宫廷生活的穷奢极欲，反映了封建社会被剥削者与剥削者之间的矛盾。全诗运用设问、比喻、对比、夸张等手法，在艺术表现上具有独创性。全诗译文的特点是细致地选用了多种词汇来精确地翻译丝织品的不同类别，并用动作来翻译生产缭绫时用的工具。

二、古诗原文

缭 绫

缭绫缭绫何所似？

不似罗绡与纨绮。
应似天台山上明月前，
四十五尺瀑布泉。
中有文章又奇绝，
地铺白烟花簇雪。
织者何人衣者谁？
越溪寒女汉宫姬。
去年中使宣口敕，
天上取样人间织。
织为云外秋雁行，
染作江南春水色。
广裁衫袖长制裙，
金斗熨波刀剪纹。
异彩奇文相隐映，
转侧看花花不定。
昭阳舞人恩正深，
春衣一对值千金。
汗沾粉污不再着，
曳土踏泥无惜心。
缭绫织成费功绩，
莫比寻常缯与帛。
丝细缲多女手疼，
扎扎千声不盈尺。
昭阳殿里歌舞人，
若见织时应也惜。

三、古诗译文

Twine Silk[1]

Twine silk, o twine silk, what does it look like?
Not like chiffon[2], satin[3], damask[4] or gauze.

It'd be like the moon[5] o'er Mt. Sky Altar[6],
Where the forty-five high waterfall pours.
There are figures, patterns and designs bright,
Beneath them blossoms of snow and smoke white.
Who's the silk weaving? Who will the silk wear?
The Yüeh Stream[7] girl, the palace lady fair.
Last year an order came from the Most High
For maids to weave with samples from the sky.
Weaving silk with clouded wild geese in flight;
Dyed with southern spring water hue so bright.
The long is made into sleeves, the short, skirts;
Ironed will be waves and cut off will be spurts.
The colors and the lines each to each shine;
Flowers are looked at and flowers are turning fine.
The dancer in Glare Hall His eyes behold;
The twin gowns are worth a chest of gold.
If stained with sweat or dirt, it's thrown anon
Trodden or trampled, it's cared by no one.
Weaving such twine silk takes much force and pain
Don't compare it with textiles having grain
Her hands hurt dressing piles of cocoons boiled,
Tic-tacking for hours, she's no much silk coiled.
Palace dancers, if you see how it's done
You'll cherish the silk as the weaving one.

(赵彦春　译)

◎ 注释

1. silk: the fine, soft, shiny fiber produced by silk worms to form their cocoons, and the thread or fabric made from this fibre is used as material for clothing. And it can be any clothing made of silk. 绫
2. chiffon: a sheer, lightweight fabric of silk, nylon, etc. 罗

3. satin: a fabric of silk or other similar material having a smooth finish, glossy on the face and dull on the back. 绡
4. damask: a durable, lustrous, reversible fabric as of silk or linen, in figured weave, used for table linen, upholstery, etc. 纨
5. the moon: the planet of the earth, which appears at night and gives off shining silvery light, an image of purity and solitude in Chinese culture. 明月
6. Mt. Sky Altar: alias Mt. Heaven Terrace, a mountain in Chechiang Province. 天台山
7. the Yüeh Stream: the Yüeh River, probably referring to the O Ts'ao River, the largest branch of the Ch'ient'ang River. 越溪

四、译文赏析

1. 缭绫缭绫何所似？不似罗绡与纨绮。
应似天台山上明月前，四十五尺瀑布泉。

译文： Twine silk, o twine silk, what does it look like? /Not like chiffon, satin, damask or gauze.

It'd be like the moon o'er Mt. Sky Altar, /Where the forty-five high waterfall pours.

赏析： 原文为分句组内押尾韵，即"似"和"绮"、"前"和"泉"，其译文则未再现尾韵特征。原文第二分句组未在篇幅上对称，但译文较为对称。该部分的翻译难点在于细致的丝绸分类和地名。"缭绫"是唐朝时期精致的丝织贡品，其质地细致、华丽，产于越地。原文采用重复的手法，表达了女工重复生产"缭绫"的辛劳过程，其译文 Twine silk, o twine silk 也采用重复手法描绘了女工缠绕丝线的动作。"罗绡与纨绮"指罗、绡、纨、绮这四种精美的丝织品，译文 chiffon, satin, damask or gauze 精确地匹配了这四种丝织品类，分别指雪纺、缎子、锦缎、纱布。地名"天台山"的译文 Mt. Sky Altar 采用了字译法，逐字还原了天空与祭台。

2. 中有文章又奇绝，地铺白烟花簇雪。

译文： There are figures, patterns and designs bright,

Beneath them blossoms of snow and smoke white.

赏析： 原文为分句组内押尾韵，即"绝"和"雪"，与译文尾韵的位置一致，即 bright 和

white。“文章”本意为错杂的色彩，诗中指花纹图案，其译文 figures, patterns and designs 通过展开多种图案类别来表达图案的多样性，但也占用了较多篇幅，从而使“奇绝”的译文未能具体呈现出来。“地铺”是底子，“花”是花纹，诗人用“白烟”“簇雪”写出了底、花俱白的寒冷色调和轻柔的质感。其译文采用地点状语前置和形容词后置的位移，以在整体上与原文语序保持一致，并形成尾韵。

3. 织者何人衣者谁？越溪寒女汉宫姬。
去年中使宣口敕，天上取样人间织。

译文： Who's the silk weaving? Who will the silk wear? /The Yüeh Stream girl, the palace lady fair.

Last year an order came from the Most High /For maids to weave with samples from the sky.

赏析： 原文为分句组间押尾韵，即“姬”和“织”，其译文则一如既往地在分句组内押尾韵，即 wear 和 fair、High 和 sky。“汉宫姬”借指唐代宫中的妃嫔，也是皇帝之妾以及皇太子、亲王、世子、郡王妻妾的总括之称，所以其译文 palace lady 为了体现该总括性，采用了地点场景词，代指该地点出现的该类人群。“口敕”指帝王的诏书、命令，其译文 an order 直截了当。“中使”在诗中指下达皇帝命令的太监，在译文中被减译，但增译了 the Most High(皇上)，以体现“口敕”的真正来源。该分句组的句意为“太监去年来宣布皇帝的诏令，从宫中取来式样，命民间照式纺织”。

4. 广裁衫袖长制裙，金斗熨波刀剪纹。
异彩奇文相隐映，转侧看花花不定。

译文： The long is made into sleeves, the short, skirts; /Ironed will be waves and cut off will be spurts.

The colors and the lines each to each shine; /Flowers are looked at and flowers are turning fine.

赏析： 原文为分句组内押尾韵，即“裙”和“纹”、“映”和“定”，而译文尾韵位置一致，即 skirts 和 spurts、shine 和 fine。“金斗”是中国早期的熨斗，内有红炭，可直接熨烫，无需预热，所以也叫火斗，雅名为金斗。其译文 ironed 以动词被动形式来代指金斗烫过的布料。“刀剪纹”指用剪刀裁剪衣料，其译文 cut off will be spurts 将“刀剪”化为动作，和“金斗”一同体现了“工具—动作”的翻译思路。“转侧看花”指从不同的角度看花，但为控制篇幅，译文 Flowers are looked at 减译了“转侧”二字。

第三章 万物有灵

第一节 官 牛

一、诗歌背景

古往今来，大官有专车接送已不是什么新鲜事了。但在唐朝，凡是大官，不仅有“专车”接送，还有“专道”。当时若被封为丞相，府县便要以牛车载沙铺路，从丞相住宅一直铺到子城东街，此类路被称为“沙堤”。白居易认为，“沙堤”会耗费民力、财力，滋生腐败，助长为官者的特权私心，有百害而无一利。因此，白居易写下这首七言古诗，以讽刺铺设“沙堤”一事。全诗译文特点在于古代计量单位、地名、植物名的翻译，以及“整体—部分”的翻译思路。

二、古诗原文

官 牛

官牛官牛驾官车，
浐水岸边般载沙。
一石沙，几斤重？
朝载暮载将何用？
载向五门官道西，

绿槐阴下铺沙堤。
昨来新拜右丞相，
恐怕泥涂污马蹄。
右丞相，
马蹄踏沙虽净洁，
牛领牵车欲流血。
右丞相，
但能济人治国调阴阳，
官牛领穿亦无妨。

三、古诗译文

The Official Ox

Official oxen official carts draw,
Carrying the Ts'an's[1] sand, carrying more.
A picul[2] of sand, what is the weight?
What's the use, so sent, for things small or great?
Carried to Five Gates[3], west of the Broad Way,
To build the dyke where the locust trees[4] sway.
Yesterday came a new councilor curt;
He feared that his horse's hooves might get dirt.
O Right Minister[5],
Treading on sand the hooves will remain clean;
Hauling the carts the oxen bleed, so keen.
O Right Minister,
If you do well and regulate our state,
It doesn't matter if the oxen grate.

（赵彦春 译）

◎ 注释

1. the Ts'an: the Ts'an River, originating from the Ch'in Ridge southwest of Blue Field and flowing into the Pa River east of Long Peace. 浐水
2. picul: a unit of weight, a hundred catties or 50 kilograms. 石
3. Five Gates: five of the twelve gates of Long Peace. 五门
4. locust tree: a spiny tree of the pea family, having long pendulous racemes of fragrant edible white flowers. 绿槐
5. Right Minister: equivalent to Prime Minister, and Left Minister equivalent to Deputy Prime Minister. 右丞相

四、译文赏析

1. 官牛官牛驾官车，浐水岸边般载沙。
一石沙，几斤重？朝载暮载将何用？

译文：Official oxen official carts draw, /Carrying the Ts'an's sand, carrying more.
A picul of sand, what is the weight? /What's the use, so sent, for things small or great?

赏析：原文为分句组内押尾韵，即"车"和"沙"、"重"和"用"，译文与原文押韵位置一致，即 draw 和 more、weight 和 great。"官牛官牛"采用重复手法来体现牛一遍又一遍地拉着沙子，其译文 Official oxen official carts 则重复了"官"字，以控制篇幅。"浐水"即浐河，是灞河的最大一级支流，发源于秦岭北麓的蓝田县，由汤峪河、岱峪河、库峪河三源组成，其译文 Ts'an 采用音译。译文 Carrying the Ts'an's sand, carrying more 减译了"岸边"并重复了"般"字，突出了全诗官牛辛劳的主题，并具备节奏感。"一石"指计算重量的单位，约为 50 千克，其译文 picul 在《英汉科技大词典》里指百斤和担，要比 50 kilos 用词更精简。

2. 载向五门官道西，绿槐阴下铺沙堤。
昨来新拜右丞相，恐怕泥涂污马蹄。

译文：Carried to Five Gates, west of the Broad Way, /To build the dyke where the locust trees sway.
Yesterday came a new councilor curt; /He feared that his horse's hooves might get

dirt.

赏析：原文的押韵结构为ABAB，即“西”和“相”、“堤”和“蹄”，其译文仍然为分句组内押尾韵，即Way和sway、curt和dirt。“五门”指天子居处的五道门，《周礼》规定，天子五门，诸侯三门，象征遵守礼序；天子的五门分别是皋门、库门、雉门、应门、路门，其译文Five Gates照字面直译，以大写来象征地名和隐含义。“官道”指公家为了让外地官员办事顺利而修建的道路，其译文the Broad Way不直译Official Way，是因为the Broad Way与美国纽约的“百老汇大道”一致，更能提高外文读者的熟悉度。“绿槐”原产于中国，多分布于华北和黄土高原，其译文locust trees为北美刺槐，其特征与中国槐树一致，同为槐属植物。

3. 右丞相，
马蹄踏沙虽净洁，
牛领牵车欲流血。

译文：O Right Minister,
Treading on sand the hooves will remain clean;
Hauling the carts the oxen bleed, so keen.

赏析：原文为分句组内押尾韵，即“洁”和“血”，其译文尾韵位置一致，即clean和keen。右丞相为古代官职，从汉至金有尚书左丞、尚书右丞，且右丞相的官职多数大于左丞相。其译文O Right Minister照字面直译，并以语气词O来增添惋惜的情感信息。第三分句的译文增译了评价词so keen，而多义词keen除了“敏捷、热切”的字义，还有“哀号”的意思(《柯林斯词典》)。“车”本无单复数，但译者选用了复数carts，以拉多辆车来衬托牛的辛劳。

4. 右丞相，
但能济人治国调阴阳，
官牛领穿亦无妨。

译文：O Right Minister,
If you do well and regulate our state,
It doesn’t matter if the oxen grate.

赏析：原文篇幅不对称，后两分句押尾韵，即“阳”和“妨”，其译文尾韵位置一致，即state和grate。“但”在诗中不是转折词“但是”的意思，而是指“如果”。第二分句无主语，但根据其上下文的逻辑和诗人的写作意图，可推理“济人治国”的主语是“右丞相”，因此增译代词 you。“济人”“治国”“调阴阳”在译文 do well and regulate our state 中，将“人”“国”“阴阳”压缩进 state 里，而人指国人，阴阳指国运，属于整体代替部分的思路。

第二节　放　鹰

一、诗歌背景

放鹰指通过对鹰的驯养来掌控其抓捕猎物和游戏的活动。《放鹰》是白居易通过描写猎人训练放鹰的技巧，来向皇帝建言“驭臣之术”。白居易身为翰林学士，对封建君主的“驭臣之术”有着清醒的认识，并在《适意二首》之二中感慨“作客诚已难，为臣尤不易”。全诗的译文特点在于歧义句的语义选择上，译者结合全诗主旨和上下文的一致性，对歧义语义作了缜密和精确的判断，其尾韵特征也非常突出。

二、古诗原文

放　鹰

十月鹰出笼，
草枯雉兔肥。
下鞲随指顾，
百掷无一遗。
鹰翅疾如风，
鹰爪利如锥。
本为鸟所设，
今为人所资。
孰能使之然，
有术甚易知。
取其向背性，
制在饥饱时。

不可使长饱，
不可使长饥。
饥则力不足，
饱则背人飞。
乘饥纵搏击，
未饱须絷维。
所以爪翅功，
而人坐收之。
圣明驭英雄，
其术亦如斯。
鄙语不可弃，
吾闻诸猎师。

三、古诗译文

Letting Out the Falcon[1]

The tenth moon, the falcon's let out,
Pheasants[2] and hares[3] fat, grass about.
Where the hunter points, it does dart,
Leaving nothing uncaught, so smart.
Its wings as swift as a north blast;
Its claws as sharp as a hook cast;
Wings and claws are for birds, that kind,
Now used by men, as is designed.
How can a falcon be well trained?
That is easy if the knack's gained:
Look at its likes, dislikes, that lot,
And when it's hungry, when it's not.

Ne'er let it eat to its desire,
Nor let it starve lest it expire.
Ill fed, it has not strength to prey;
Well fed, from you it'll fly away.
When it's hungry, let it attack;
Ere it eats enough, have it back.
The power of its claws and its wings
Are your property, are your things.
How does a sovereign command?
The art is just like this, if scanned.
What I've said you should not despise;
It's something heard from hunters wise.

（赵彦春　译）

◎ **注释**

1. falcon: any bird of prey with long pointed wings and a short, curved, notched beak, usually trained to hunt and kill small game. In falconry, the female is called a falcon and the male a tiercel. 鹰
2. pheasant: a long-tailed gallinaceous bird noted for the gorgeous plumage of the male, often regarded as wild chicken in Chinese culture. 雉
3. hare: a rodent (genus *Lepus*) with cleft upper lip, long ears, and long hind legs: known for its timidity and swiftness, habitating woodland, farmland or grassland. 兔

四、译文赏析

1. **十月鹰出笼，草枯雉兔肥。**
下鞲随指顾，百掷无一遗。

译文： The tenth moon, the falcon's let out, /Pheasants and hares fat, grass about.
Where the hunter points, it does dart, /Leaving nothing uncaught, so smart.

赏析："十月"本为十月份(秋季)，但译文为何不直译成 October 而译为 the tenth moon？诗性的一大重要特点是委婉，如果表达过于直接，则会减少语言的诗性。"草枯"本指秋季草木枯黄，但其译文 grass about 将"枯"转译成 about("四处围绕")，译草地的广袤来代替枯黄。虽然改变了原文字义，但达到了押尾韵的目的，体现了古诗英译中尾韵的权重较大。"韝"指苍鹰落脚的臂套，在译文 it does dart 中被译成动词，并以 does 强调。"百掷"指多次放掷苍鹰，在译文中被减译，但为使篇幅对称，译者增译了评价词 so smart，以表达感叹语气。

2. 鹰翅疾如风，鹰爪利如锥。
本为鸟所设，今为人所资。

译文：Its wings as swift as a north blast; /Its claws as sharp as a hook cast;
Wings and claws are for birds, that kind, /Now used by men, as is designed.

赏析：译文押尾韵，即 blast 和 cast、kind 和 designed。原文的两个"如"均采用 as… as 结构，两个"鹰"均采用代词 its，体现了分句组之间用词的对称性。原文的"风"并未指出是哪个风向，但译者为使篇幅对称，根据语境增译了 north。"锥"本为锥子(awl)，但该字难以与上文形成尾韵，所以译者将其改译成同样尖锐的鱼钩(hook)，并增译 cast 来让读者联想钓鱼时甩出鱼钩的情景，让比喻更为生动形象。

3. 乘饥纵搏击，未饱须禁维。
所以爪翅功，而人坐收之。

译文：When it's hungry, let it attack; /Ere it eats enough, have it back.
The power of its claws and its wings /Are your property, are your things.

赏析：译文的尾韵非常明显，即 attack 和 back、wings 和 things。这四个分句以放鹰的技巧来讲述君王的驭臣之术。原文的"纵""须"表建议，其译文 let it、have it 分别再现了祈使的功能。"禁维"指拴住马的绳索，在文中比喻挽留人才，而其译文 back 剥离了绳索的字面义，但挖掘和再现了"挽留"的内涵。"功"可指功劳和成绩，也可指本领，其译文 the power 表明译者将其理解为本领。"坐收之"中的代词"之"也具有歧义性，可指收鹰，也可指收鹰的猎物。因全诗强调的主旨是驭臣之术，因此"收之"应理解为收苍鹰，而"功"应理解为能力。否则，该句会被误解为君王没收良臣的功绩，不劳而获。

第三节　秦吉了

一、诗歌背景

“秦吉了”本为鸟名，长相如同鹦鹉，脑后有肉冠，嘴、脚都为红色，善于模仿人说话。《秦吉了》以各种禽类动物来比喻封建社会中的各类人群。乳燕、母鸡比喻善良弱小的老百姓；长爪鸢、大嘴乌比喻鱼肉百姓的贪官和豪强；雕、鹗比喻执掌监察和刑狱的大员；鸾、鹤比喻供奉翰苑和郎署的近臣；秦吉了比喻能言善辩的谏官；凤凰比喻皇帝。全诗表面上是歌颂秦吉了，但实质上是间接讽刺对百姓之苦视而不见的官僚。全诗译文的特点是对多种鸟类的翻译考虑到了用词的准确度和鸟类的情感象征意义。

二、古诗原文

秦吉了

秦吉了，
出南中，
彩毛青黑花颈红。
耳聪心慧舌端巧，
鸟语人言无不通。
昨日长爪鸢，
今朝大嘴乌。
鸢捎乳燕一窠覆，
乌琢母鸡双眼枯。
鸡号堕地燕惊去，
然后拾卵攫其雏。
岂无雕与鹗？
嗉中肉饱不肯搏。

亦有鸾鹤群，
闲立扬高如不闻。
秦吉了，
人云尔是能言鸟，
岂不见鸡燕之冤苦？
吾闻凤凰百鸟主，
尔竟不为凤凰之前致一言，
安用噪噪闲言语。

三、古诗译文

The Grackle[1]

The grackle so grand
Is from Southern Land,
Plumes glossy, black, round its neck a red band.
Its ears acute, tongue clever and brain smart,
It can speak languages from every part.
Yesterday a hawk[2] with sharp claws,
Today a big-mouthed crow[3] that caws!
The hawk seized and tore a swallow's[4] nest then;
The crow pecked out the two eyes of a hen.
The hen squawked and away the swallows fled,
The eggs eaten, the chicks pecked off their head.
No vulture[5] or owl[6] there to kill?
Stuffed to their fill, they won't fight with their bill.
Also a flock of storks[7] nearby
Watch what's happening and off they fly.
O grackle so grand,
They all say you speak all tongues of the land,
Don't you see the sufferance hens and swallows stand?
They say the phoenix[8] is Lord of all birds;

Why don't you go to him and on their behalf use kind words?
Why do you sit there chattering like turds?

(赵彦春 译)

◎ 注释

1. grackle: a starlinglike bird, usually shining and sable-black with a yellow stripe around the neck, which can imitate human speech and singing. It is used as a metaphor for a remonstrant in this poem. 秦吉了
2. hawk: a diurnal bird of prey, notable for keen sight and strong flight, usually used as a metaphor for one who takes military means in contrast with a dove, one who tries to find peaceful solutions. 鸢
3. a big-mouthed crow: an omnivorous, raucous, oscine bird of the genus *Corvus*, with glossy black plumage. It is regarded as an ominous bird, a metaphor for death because it is a scavenger, feeding on carrion. It is a common image in Chinese literature, which can be found in *The Book of Songs* compiled 2,500 years ago: "Crows are all black, it's said, /So as foxes are red." 大嘴乌
4. swallow: a passerine bird, with short broad, depressed bill, long pointed wings, and forked tail, noted for fleeting flight and migratory habits. In Chinese culture, swallows are welcome to live with a family with their nest on a beam of a sitting room. 乳燕
5. vulture: a large bird of prey, related to the eagles, hawks, and falcons, having the head and neck naked or partly naked, feeding mostly on carrion. 雕
6. owl: a predatory nocturnal bird, having large eyes and head, short, sharply hooked bill, long powerful claws, and a circular facial disk of radiating feathers, regarded as ominous in Chinese culture. 鹗
7. stork: any of a family of large, long-legged wading birds having a long neck and bill. 鸾鹤
8. phoenix: In Chinese myths, phoenixes, auspicious birds, unlike ordinary ones, only perch on parasol trees. 凤凰

四、译文赏析

1. 秦吉了，出南中，彩毛青黑花颈红。
   耳聪心慧舌端巧，鸟语人言无不通。

译文：The grackle so grand Is from Southern Land, /Plumes glossy, black, round its neck a red band.

Its ears acute, tongue clever and brain smart, /It can speak languages from every part.

赏析：原文的三个分句押尾韵，即“中”“红”“通”，其译文仍为分句组内押尾韵，即 Land 和 band、smart 和 part，且篇幅较为对称。“秦吉了”为鸟名，长相如同鹦鹉，脑后有肉冠，嘴脚都为红色，善效人言，而其译文 grackle(鹩哥)的体貌特征与“秦吉了”相似，也能模仿人的声音。此外，译者还增译了 so grand 以显化“秦吉了”在朗诵时的感叹语气。“花颈红”指鸟脖子周围红色的条纹，其译文 round its neck a red band 采用了地点状语前置的翻译方法。“彩毛”本强调多种颜色的羽毛，而译文 Plumes glossy 则强调有光泽的羽毛。因为句中的“青黑”“红”已包含多种颜色，所以这种改译不会造成“彩”的丢失。

2. 昨日长爪鸢，今朝大嘴乌。
鸢捎乳燕一窠覆，乌琢母鸡双眼枯。
鸡号堕地燕惊去，然后拾卵攫其雏。

译文：Yesterday a hawk with sharp claws, /Today a big-mouthed crow that caws!

The hawk seized and tore a swallow’s nest then; /The crow pecked out the two eyes of a hen.

The hen squawked and away the swallows fled, /The eggs eaten, the chicks pecked off their head.

赏析：原文有多处为同一尾韵，即“乌”“覆”“枯”“雏”，其译文为分句组内押尾韵，即 claws 和 caws、then 和 hen、fled 和 head。“鸢”俗称老鹰，头顶及喉部白色，两翼黑褐色，腹部淡赤，四趾都有钩爪，与 hawk 种类一致。“乌”指乌鸦，在诗中“大嘴乌”与“长爪鸢”一同比喻巧取豪夺、鱼肉百姓的贪官和豪强，其译文 a big-mouthed crow 直译字面，并用 caws(呱呱叫声)和感叹号来引导读者去思考其背后的比喻内涵。“攫”指鸟用爪迅速抓取，其译文 pecked 本指啄食，但增译的 off their head 更能体现乌鸦虐杀小雏鸡的残忍。

3. 岂无雕与鹗?
嗉中肉饱不肯搏。

译文：No vulture or owl there to kill?

Stuffed to their fill, they won’t fight with their bill.

赏析：原文篇幅不对称，也无尾韵特征，但译文有明显的尾韵特征，即 kill、fill 和 bill，篇幅忠实于原文。“雕”是一种大型的鹰类猛禽，嘴呈钩状，腿部有羽毛，雌、雄都是黑褐色。“鹗”的字形本义指大嘴鸟或大嘴吞食的鸟，特指鱼鹰。“雕”与“鹗”皆为猛禽，常用于比喻奸佞或才望超群者。其译文 vulture or owl 虽然改变了原文的鸟类品种，但 vulture 和 owl 非常准确地传递了原文的贬义性。“雕”与“鹗”在西方不象征贬义，而秃鹫和猫头鹰却有贬义，因此该译法属于文化符号对等译法。

4. 亦有鸾鹤群，闲立扬高如不闻。

译文： Also a flock of storks nearby

Watch what’s happening and off they fly.

赏析： 原文以鼻音押尾韵，译文在篇幅和尾韵位置上与原文一致，即 nearby 和 fly。“鸾鹤群”指“鸾”和“鹤”聚集在一起的鸟群，这两种鸟类体形、外观、习性相似，都为大型水鸟，因此其译文 a flock of storks 将其缩减为一种鸟类，以控制篇幅，即 stork（鹳），与“鸾”和“鹤”的外观、习性相似。“闲立扬高如不闻”描写了鸾鹤趾高气昂，对周边的情况视而不见，比喻能保护百姓的封建掌权者对百姓的苦难视而不见，其译文形象地描绘了这一视而不见的行为。

第二部分　讽喻诗

第四章 心系百姓

第一节 卖炭翁

一、诗歌背景

《卖炭翁》是白居易所创作的第三十二首《新乐府》组诗。此诗写于唐宪宗元和初年(公元806年)，也是“宫市”引发社会矛盾最深的时候。他对宫市十分了解，深切地同情劳动人民，所以才能写出这首感人至深的《卖炭翁》来。中唐后，朝廷常派宦官到市场上去采购物品，一有看中的商品，就以“宫市”的名义任意掠夺而去，而白居易在长安时也亲眼目睹了这类弊政。

二、古诗原文

卖炭翁

卖炭翁，
伐薪烧炭南山中。
满面尘灰烟火色，
两鬓苍苍十指黑。
卖炭得钱何所营？
身上衣裳口中食。

可怜身上衣正单，
心忧炭贱愿天寒。
夜来城外一尺雪，
晓驾炭车辗冰辙。
牛困人饥日已高，
市南门外泥中歇。
翩翩两骑来是谁？
黄衣使者白衫儿。
手把文书口称敕，
回车叱牛牵向北。
一车炭，千余斤，
宫使驱将惜不得。
半匹红绡一丈绫，
系向牛头充炭直。

三、古诗译文

The Charcoal[1] Gray Hair

The charcoal Gray Hair,
He fells trees for charcoal in south hills there.
He's dirty with dust and smoke, front or back;
His sideburns gray and his fingers all black.
What will he do with the money he earns?
Food, clothing, and all those daily concerns.
So poor, the garment he wears is so thin;
For higher price, he hopes winter to set in.
Outside the wall at night, a foot of snow,
At dawn he drives his cart down ice to go.
So tired, the sun high, and the ox[2] so pressed,

Outside South Gate, in snow and slush he'll rest.

Lo, riders trotting up, who are they guessed?

A herald in gold and a boy white dressed.

Decree in hand, "An edict here", they shout;

To north they turn the ox and cart about.

A cart of charcoal half a ton does weigh;

What can he do now they take it away?

A foot of red silk[3], and damask[4] gauze spread,

The price for charcoal, tied to the ox's head.

（赵彦春　译）

◎ **注释**

1. charcoal：a porous amorphous form of carbon produced by destructive distillation of wood or other organic matter and used as firewood or for heating. 炭
2. ox：any of several bovid ruminants as cattle, buffaloes, bison, gaur, and yaks; especially a domesticated bull（*Bos taurus*）, used as a draft animal, a symbol of diligence in Chinese culture. 牛
3. silk：the fine, soft, shiny fiber produced by silk worms to form their cocoons, and the thread or fabric made from this fibre is used as material for clothing. And it can be any clothing made of silk. 绡
4. damask：a durable, lustrous, reversible fabric as of silk or linen, in figured weave, used for table linen, upholstery, etc. 绫

四、译文赏析

1. 卖炭翁，伐薪烧炭南山中。

译文： The charcoal Gray Hair,

He fells trees for charcoal in south hills there.

赏析： 原文尾韵明显，篇幅不对称；译文也有尾韵，即 Hair 和 there，篇幅忠实于原文。"卖炭翁"指卖木炭的老人，译文没有把"翁"直译为"老人"，而是译出了老人满头灰

发的形象(Gray Hair)，符合诗歌委婉的风格。“伐”的翻译用词精确，fells 指将树木砍倒，而 log，cut，chop 指砍树的动作且表意较为直接。“南山”指城南之山，只是某一个方向范围内的山群，而非具体某一地点，因此简译成小写 in south hills。

2. **满面尘灰烟火色，两鬓苍苍十指黑。**
卖炭得钱何所营？身上衣裳口中食。

译文： He's dirty with dust and smoke, front or back; /His sideburns gray and his fingers all black.

What will he do with the money he earns? /Food, clothing, and all those daily concerns.

赏析： 译文的尾韵特征很明显，即 back 和 black、earns 和 concerns，篇幅、句型与原文一致。“满面”本指卖炭翁满脸炭黑色，但为了押尾韵，译者将其改译成 front or back(身前身后)，对人物满身炭灰形象的描绘效果不变。“两鬓苍苍十指黑”的原文、译文均采用“名词+形容词”结构，句型与原文一致。“卖炭得钱”的译文 the money he earns 采用一般现在时，指日常所得收入，而非具体某一天。“衣裳口中食”的译文为了使篇幅对称，增译了 all those daily concerns，指日常的基本生活开支。

3. **可怜身上衣正单，心忧炭贱愿天寒。**
夜来城外一尺雪，晓驾炭车辗冰辙。

译文： So poor, the garment he wears is so thin; /For higher price, he hopes winter to set in.

Outside the wall at night, a foot of snow, /At dawn he drives his cart down ice to go.

赏析： 原文的尾韵为“单”和“寒”，头韵为“心”和“晓”，译文还原了尾韵特征，即 thin 和 in、snow 和 go。对于情感信息，如“可怜”和“心忧”，译者分别译成 So poor 和 For，分别通过程度副词 so 和反义词法来表达感叹。“身上衣”的译文 the garment 是“一件衣服”的正式用词，常用于谈及服装的制作和销售。“一尺”在中国各个朝代的长度不同，现代的三尺为一米，而一英尺约为 30 厘米。因文中的“一尺”在于体现雪的厚，而非具体厚多少，所以用外文读者熟悉的英尺(a foot of)也就足够了。

第二节　村居苦寒

一、诗歌背景

唐代中后期，内有藩镇割据，外有吐蕃入侵，唐王朝中央政府控制的领土大量减少。因此当时供养了大量军队，但是和官吏、地主、商人、僧侣、道士等不耕而食的人一起，却占了一半以上的人口。可想而知，农民当时的负担有多重。《村居苦寒》描写了寒风凛冽的冬季里农民生活的艰辛，白居易看到自己的温饱后，深感同情和自愧，觉得自己作为一个享受俸禄的基层官吏应感到惭愧不安。全诗译文特点是增译情感词、名词动词化、植物和家纺术语的处理。

二、古诗原文

村居苦寒

八年十二月，
五日雪纷纷。
竹柏皆冻死，
况彼无衣民。
回观村闾间，
十室八九贫。
北风利如剑，
布絮不蔽身。
唯烧蒿棘火，
愁坐夜待晨。
乃知大寒岁，
农者尤苦辛。
顾我当此日，

草堂深掩门。
褐裘覆絁被，
坐卧有余温。
幸免饥冻苦，
又无垄亩勤。
念彼深可愧，
自问是何人？

三、古诗译文

Bitter Winter in the Village

The twelfth moon of the eighth year,
It snowed heavily for days five;
E'en bamboos and pines[1] died, drear;
Unclad, how can folks stay alive?
To have a look I went around:
One eighth or so had not enough.
North wind cut with a rasping sound,
Their bodies in no clothes e'en rough.
They burned thistle[2] and grass, behold,
Crouched waiting for the sun to rise.
In such a bitter winter cold,
The peasant suffered many tries;
I look at myself just today;
Closed is my thatched hall, tight the door.
My fur's on the silk[3] overlay;
Where'er I am, I'm warm and more.
No hunger or cold can fret me;
No need for me to work the land.
Ashamed, I ask: who could I be,

In this dust world able to stand?

（赵彦春　译）

◎ **注释**

1. bamboos and pines：a metonymy for plants. 竹柏
2. thistle：any of various plants of the composite family，with prickly leaves and heads of white，purple，pink，or yellow flowers. 蒿棘
3. silk：the fine，soft，shiny fiber produced by silk worms to form their cocoons，and the thread or fabric made from this fibre is used as material for clothing. And it can be any clothing made of silk. 絺

四、译文赏析

1. 八年十二月，五日雪纷纷。
竹柏皆冻死，况彼无衣民。

译文： The twelfth moon of the eighth year，/It snowed heavily for days five；
E’en bamboos and pines died，drear；/Unclad，how can folks stay alive?

赏析： 译文分句组间押尾韵，即 year 和 drear、five 和 alive，且译文篇幅较为对称。“八年”非时间段，而是时间点“第八年”。“十二月”译者未直译为 December，而是委婉地译成 The twelfth moon，也使篇幅不至于过短。为实现尾韵，译者还增译了情感词 drear（“悲寂的”），将“冻死”的悲凉显性化。“况彼”指“更不用说”，起强调作用，译者通过疑问句来实现强调功能。

2. 回观村闾间，十室八九贫。
北风利如剑，布絮不蔽身。

译文： To have a look I went around：/One eighth or so had not enough.
North wind cut with a rasping sound，/Their bodies in no clothes e’en rough.

赏析： 原文两分句押尾韵，即“间”和“剑”，其译文为分句组间押尾韵，即 around 和 sound、enough 和 rough。“回观”指遍观。“村闾（lǘ）”指村落、村庄，而其中的“闾”是里巷的大门，也为里巷的代称。然而，“村闾间”在译文中被减译，译文只着重展开“回观”，但原文的标题已指明诗中的地点和语境，所以“村闾间”的语义在全诗的译文中并未消失。

“利如剑”比喻寒风凛冽，其译文 cut with a rasping sound 将名词“利剑”动词化为 cut，并增译了风的听觉信息 a rasping sound，能很好地烘托出风的凛冽。

3. 唯烧蒿棘火，愁坐夜待晨。
   乃知大寒岁，农者尤苦辛。

译文：They burned thistle and grass, behold, /Crouched waiting for the sun to rise.
In such a bitter winter cold, /The peasant suffered many tries;

赏析：译文为分句组间押尾韵，即 behold 和 cold、rise 和 tries。“蒿”为草名，如青蒿、白蒿等多种。“棘”指荆棘，即多刺的灌木。“蒿棘”一同以具体植物来泛指柴草，被分别译成 thistle(蓟)和 grass。thistle(蓟)为叶子带刺的野生植物。“愁坐”中的坐姿并非为坐在凳子上，按照唐朝人的习惯和农民的经济状况，当时应为农民“蹲伏”在火堆前取暖，因此译成 crouched。

4. 顾我当此日，草堂深掩门。
   褐裘覆絁被，坐卧有余温。

译文：I look at myself just today; /Closed is my thatched hall, tight the door.
My fur's on the silk overlay; /Where'er I am, I'm warm and more.

赏析：原文为分句组间押尾韵，即“门”和“温”，而译文分句组间押尾韵的特征更为明显，即 today 和 overlay、door 和 more。“草堂”指茅草盖的房子，也泛指山野间的住所，其译文 thatched hall 用词准确，特指用茅草铺盖的屋子。“褐(hè)裘(qiú)”指布面的皮袍子。“絁被”指绵绸被子。在处理这种细致的家纺用品时，译者将其泛译成面料 fur 和 silk。

第三节　道州民

一、诗歌背景

唐朝的“道州”为今湖南道县。《道州民》介绍了道州的百姓长得矮小，常被地方官按照土地的肥沃程度来当作贡品，即“土贡”，造成了“老翁哭孙母哭儿”和“生别离”的人间惨象。随后，记叙了阳城在任道州刺史后为民请命，打破了这一惯例。最后描写了道州人民对阳城的真诚感激，歌颂了刺史阳城为民请命的精神。全诗译文特点在于人名、书名、地名的译法上，如音译、字译、功能译法。

二、古诗原文

道州民

道州民，多侏儒，
长者不过三尺余。
市作矮奴年进送，
号为道州任土贡。
任土贡，宁若斯？
不闻使人生别离，
老翁哭孙母哭儿！
一自阳城来守郡，
不进矮奴频诏问。
城云臣按六典书：
任土贡有不贡无。
道州水土所生者，
只有矮民无矮奴。
吾君感悟玺书下，
岁贡矮奴宜悉罢。
道州民，
老者幼者何欣欣！
父兄子弟始相保，
从此得作良人身。
道州民，
民到于今受其赐，
欲说使君先下泪。
仍恐儿孙忘使君，
生男多以阳为字。

三、古诗译文

The Dwarfs of Taochow[1]

In Taochow, the seat, many dwarfs[2] you meet;
The tallest one is no more than three feet;
They're picked out as slaves and sent to court,
A local product for fun or disport.
For fun or disport? Why play of this sort?
How many families are torn apart!
Gramps' cries are so keen, and grannies' so smart!
But the intendant called Shineton[3] sends none,
Although court orders arrive one by one.
He replies he's checked law code the whole lot:
One should send what's produced, not what is not.
In Taochow here one may meet dwarfs indeed
But they are short people, not slaves you need.
Then the Emperor issues a command;
The custom of sending dwarfs is now banned.
As the order's released,
In Taochow both old and young are so pleased.
All fathers and sons can rest at ease then,
And dwarfs are regarded as common men.
The folks of Taochow
Still 'member the favor done them you know.
When they speak of him, their tears first flow.
Lo, Shineton's into their sons' name combined
Lest they forget how Shine was to them kind.

(赵彦春 译)

◎ 注释

1. Taochow：today's Tao County，Hunan Province. 道州

2. dwarf：any human being，animal or plants that is much smaller than the usual size of its species. 侏儒

3. Shineton：Shineton（753A. D. -805A. D.），from Summer County，Sha'anhsi，versed in classics and history，was appointed as Left Remonstrant. He was demoted to take the office as Prefect of Taochow in 789 A. D. 阳城

四、译文赏析

1. 道州民，多侏儒，长者不过三尺余。
市作矮奴年进送，号为道州任土贡。

译文： In Taochow，the seat，many dwarfs you meet；/The tallest one is no more than three feet；

They're picked out as slaves and sent to court，/A local product for fun or disport.

赏析： 原文尾韵特征明显，即"儒"和"余"、"送"和"贡"，译文尾韵结构一致，即 meet 和 feet、court 和 disport，且篇幅较为对称。"道州"为今湖南道县，其译文 Taochow 采用音译法，而 Tao 与道教(Taoism)词素一致。"长者"指身材高的人，原句意为"长得高的人也不过三尺多"，诗人的目的在于强调当地人的矮小，译文 The tallest one 使用的最高级，能凸显这一目的。唐朝的"三尺"与 three feet 虽逻辑上长度不等，但差异不会太大，而诗人的目的也不是为了记录具体的身高，feet 也能增加外文读者的熟悉感。"任土贡"指根据土地肥沃程度和所生产的东西制定贡赋的多少，其译文 A local product for fun or disport 体现了道州民沦为贡品玩物的悲惨遭遇。

2. 任土贡，宁若斯？
不闻使人生别离，老翁哭孙母哭儿！

译文： For fun or disport? Why play of this sort?

How many families are torn apart! /Gramps' cries are so keen，and grannies' so smart!

赏析： 原文尾韵特征较少，译文尾韵特征明显，即 disport 和 sort、apart 和 smart。"不闻"指没听说，其译文 How many 以疑问句来还原"未听说"。"生别离"指与亲人活生

生地拆散，译文 torn apart 则以“撕开”来表达分别的痛苦，而感叹号也使疑问句读出了感叹的语气。“母哭儿”指母亲与孩子分离时的痛哭，其译文 grannies' so smart！中的 so 表程度，而 smart 则指感到剧烈刺痛。

3. **一自阳城来守郡，不进矮奴频诏问。**

城云臣按六典书：任土贡有不贡无。

译文： But the intendant called Shineton sends none，/Although court orders arrive one by one.

He replies he's checked law code the whole lot：/One should send what's produced，not what is not.

赏析： 译文分句组内的尾韵特征明显，即 none 和 one、lot 和 not。“阳城”为人名，“守郡”为官名刺史，属监察之职，其译文 intendant called Shineton 采用字译法还原了“阳城来守郡”的字面义。“六典书”指《唐六典》，为唐玄宗所写，共三十卷，属于行政性法典，译文 law code 译出了书的功能，而非书名。

第五章　苛政如虎

第一节　纳　粟

一、诗歌背景

《纳粟》是一首五言古诗，被白居易编入《白氏长庆集》的讽喻诗当中。唐宪宗元和年间，白居易退居下邽去为母守丧，并作此诗。在中国古代，官员不需要缴纳税租。然而，因为白居易当时处于守丧离职期间，所以还须缴纳税租。此诗描写了白居易缴纳税租的亲身经历，表达了对自己以前身为官员无需缴纳税租的惭愧自责之情。全诗译法的特点在于词语多义性、语境推理和量词处理。

二、古诗原文

纳　粟

有吏夜叩门，
高声催纳粟。
家人不待晓，
场上张灯烛。
扬簸净如珠，
一车三十斛。
犹忧纳不中，

鞭责及僮仆。
昔余谬从事，
内愧才不足。
连授四命官，
坐尸十年禄。
常闻古人语，
损益周必复。
今日谅甘心，
还他太仓谷。

三、古诗译文

Collecting Grain Tax

At night, a loud bang on the door,
"Grain tax", a collector does roar.
Before the morning comes around;
I light up the threshing ground.
Grain's winnowed until pearls[1] there are,
Thirty qeufs[2] are good for a car.
Worrying it's not an enough load,
My boy servant now I do goad.
I was an official before;
I feel ashamed with such a sore.
I was promoted for four tiers,
And enjoyed good pay for ten years;
Old folks, as said once and again,
Can tell the moon's rise, wax and wane.
Now I wish I could give back all
To the barn in the capital.

(赵彦春　译)

◎ 注释

1. pearl：a smooth，lustrous，usually white and bluish-gray，calcareous concretion deposited in layers around a central nucleus in the shells of various mollusks or oysters，and largely used as a gem，medicine or given as a gift，representing nobility，purity and dignity in Chinese culture. 珠

2. qeuf：a measure used in ancient times for measurement of grain，about 60 kilograms. 斛

四、译文赏析

1. 有吏夜叩门，高声催纳粟。
家人不待晓，场上张灯烛。

译文： At night，a loud bang on the door，/“Grain tax”，a collector does roar.
Before the morning comes around；/I light up the threshing ground.

赏析： 原文为分句组间押尾韵，即“粟”和“烛”；译文为分句组内押尾韵，即 door 和 roar、around 和 ground。“催纳粟”本为间接引语，而其译文“Grain tax”为直接引语，增强了“催”的急促感。“家人”有多义性，可指白居易家里的人或家中仆人，而“张灯烛”无主语。白居易守丧离职，此时又是深夜，因此屋内白居易和家童点灯的可能性更大，而译者选择以第一人称“我”(白居易)为主语。

2. 扬簸净如珠，一车三十斛。
犹忧纳不中，鞭责及僮仆。

译文： Grain's winnowed until pearls there are，/Thirty qeufs are good for a car.
Worrying it's not an enough load，/My boy servant now I do goad.

赏析： 原文有三处尾韵，即“珠”“斛”“仆”；译文为分句组内押尾韵，即 are 和 car、load 和 goad。“簸”的译文 Grain's winnowed 用词精确，将“簸”动词化为 winnowed，即簸扬筛选的意思。“斛”为古量器名，也是容量单位，十斗为一斛，其译文 qeufs 为古代五谷计量单位，约 60 千克。“鞭责”字面指用鞭子责问，而其译文 I do goad 通过助词 do 来强调，goad 指用赶牛等牲畜的尖头棒来驱使、刺激别人，更贴合乡野人家的语境。

3. 昔余谬从事，内愧才不足。
连授四命官，坐尸十年禄。

译文： I was an official before；/I feel ashamed with such a sore.

I was promoted for four tiers, /And enjoyed good pay for ten years;

赏析： 原文为分句组间押尾韵，即“足”和“禄”；译文为分句组内押尾韵，即 before 和 sore、tiers 和 years。“四命官”即四次被授官职，白居易贞元十九年授秘书省校书郎，元和元年授盩厔县尉，元和三年除左拾遗充翰林学士，元和五年改京兆府户曹参军，共四次授官。其译文 four tiers 指四个层级，刚好与 ten years 形成尾韵，但其互文性需外文读者通过注释来理解。

4. **常闻古人语，损益周必复。**
今日谅甘心，还他太仓谷。

译文： Old folks, as said once and again, /Can tell the moon's rise, wax and wane.
Now I wish I could give back all, /To the barn in the capital.

赏析： 原文为分句组间押尾韵，即“复”和“谷”；译文为分句组内押尾韵，即 again 和 wane、all 和 capital。“古人语”指过去民间流传的老话，因此译文用 folks。“常”的译文 once and again 用词委婉柔和，与后文恰好形成尾韵。“损益”意为增减、兴革，“损”和“益”也为《周易》里的卦象，其译文 the moon's rise, wax and wane 增译了月亮的阴晴圆缺来作比喻以体现该抽象义，为“具体—抽象”的翻译思路。“太仓”在长安，该处储藏赋税粟米，其译文 the barn in the capital 译出了“太仓”的用途和位置，因“太仓”不特指某一地名，而是泛指首都存粮的地方。

第二节　杜陵叟

一、诗歌背景

《杜陵叟》讲述的是伤农夫之困，同情农民生活的困苦。全诗前半部分写了两个使农民生活受难的直接原因，即自然灾害和人为灾祸；后半部分揭露了官僚制度的黑暗与腐败，横征暴敛，巧取豪夺。全诗的译文特点在于跨句位移、植物名的精确、用词委婉柔和、篇幅增减有度。

二、古诗原文

杜陵叟

杜陵叟，杜陵居，

岁种薄田一顷余。
三月无雨旱风起，
麦苗不秀多黄死。
九月降霜秋早寒，
禾穗未熟皆青干。
长吏明知不申破，
急敛暴征求考课。
典桑卖地纳官租，
明年衣食将何如？
剥我身上帛，
夺我口中粟。
虐人害物即豺狼，
何必钩爪锯牙食人肉？
不知何人奏皇帝，
帝心恻隐知人弊。
白麻纸上书德音，
京畿尽放今年税。
昨日里胥方到门，
手持敕牒榜乡村。
十家租税九家毕，
虚受吾君蠲免恩。

三、古诗译文

The Old Man of Birchleaf Hill[1]

Birchleaf Man lives on Birchleaf Hill;
He's more than an acre of land to till.
Then comes a spring drought there, a season dry
Three months of hot winds blow wheat[2] shoots to die;

The ninth moon there come frosts, it getting cold;
The crops are still green, not yet turning gold.
The officials know this but don't report,
But collect all taxes and all extort.
Mulberry[3] farm sold, field pawned, taxes to pay
Where will food or clothes come from, anyway?
Clothes are from his back stripped, not stopped;
Food is from his mouth grabbed, all dropped.
They're wolves coveting people's flesh and blood;
Why tear them with teeth and claws and throw their bones, thud?
Someone does make a report to the throne
And the emperor has his goodness shown.
He sends down a rescript drawn on hemp white
To have district taxes remitted, right!
Yesterday the local official came to each door,
Rescript in hand, shouting: Tax there's no more.
Of ten households nine have paid the whole lot;
They have received imperial grace for nought.

(赵彦春　译)

◎ 注释

1. Birchleaf Hill: known as Birchleaf Pear Ridge formally; 10 kilometers from Wannien County, in today's Hsi-an, Sha'anhsi Province. 杜陵
2. wheat: a grain yielding an edible flour, the annual product of a cereal grass (genus *Triticum*), introduced to China from West Asia more than 4,000 years ago, used as a staple food in China and most of the world. In its importance to consumers, it is second only to rice. 麦苗
3. mulberry: the edible, berry-like juicy fruit of a tree (genus *Morus*) whose leaves are valued for silkworm culture, and the tree itself. 桑

四、译文赏析

1. 杜陵叟，杜陵居，岁种薄田一顷余。

译文：Birchleaf Man lives on Birchleaf Hill; /He's more than an acre of land to till.

赏析：原文为分句组内押尾韵，即“居”和“余”；译文尾韵位置一致，即 Hill 和 till。“杜陵”指地名，即汉宣帝陵，在今陕西省西安市东南的少陵原，其译文字译植物名“杜”（杜梨），与 birch 的树种相似，叶子形状一致，因此译成 Birchleaf Hill。“杜陵叟，杜陵居”的译文将两句合并成“主谓状”结构，并按照原文重复 Birchleaf 以增强节奏感。“薄田”为贫瘠的田地。关于“一顷”的翻译，在唐代，“亩百为顷”，但为了凸显农民作物收获之少，译者改译成 an acre of。

2. 三月无雨旱风起，麦苗不秀多黄死。
九月降霜秋早寒，禾穗未熟皆青干。

译文：Then comes a spring drought there, a season dry; /Three months of hot winds blow wheat shoots to die;

The ninth moon there come frosts, it getting cold; /The crops are still green, not yet turning gold.

赏析：原文分句组内尾韵明显，即“起”和“死”、“寒”和“干”；译文尾韵位置一致，即 dry 和 die、cold 和 gold。“三月”指三个月或三月份，译者通过 spring…a season 来同时还原两个语义，而下面一个分句增译 Three months 以使篇幅对称。“旱风”的译文的位移跨越了分句，以分担左分句负载的信息量。“九月”和“禾穗未熟”的译文都用词委婉，符合诗歌表意间接的风格。

3. 长吏明知不申破，急敛暴征求考课。
典桑卖地纳官租，明年衣食将何如？

译文：The officials know this but don't report, /But collect all taxes and all extort.

Mulberry farm sold, field pawned, taxes to pay /Where will food or clothes come from, anyway?

赏析：原文尾韵较少，即“租”和“如”；译文尾韵更多，即 report 和 extort、pay 和 anyway。“长吏”本泛指上级长官，但在该诗中指的是杜陵所在地的地方官，在诗中为次要信息，其译文 The officials 无需将其具体化。“急敛暴征”中“急”和“暴”的急促感在译文中通过重复 all 来强调苛税的程度，并通过 extort(“敲诈、强取”)来增强贬义。“考课”指古代考查官员政绩的好坏，以决定其官职升降，在译文中被减译。为控制篇幅，“明年”被减译，而用于支撑论点的 anyway(用于转换话题、结束谈话或回到原话题)被增译以形成尾韵。

第三节　宿紫阁山北村

一、诗歌背景

该诗约作于唐宪宗元和四年(809 年)前后，白居易当时于长安任左拾遗，诗中所描写的事件地点在鄠县(今陕西户县)的杜家庄。此诗反映了宦官掌握禁卫军军权、纵容士兵欺压百姓的历史事实，白居易通过记叙自己欣赏紫阁峰的美景后借宿村落的经历，揭露了中唐时期宦官执掌的神策军掠夺、欺压百姓的事实。全诗译文特点在于译者通过增译比喻的手法，形象地表达象征义和抽象义。

二、古诗原文

宿紫阁山北村

晨游紫阁峰，
暮宿山下村。
村老见余喜，
为余开一尊。
举杯未及饮，
暴卒来入门。
紫衣挟刀斧，
草草十余人。
夺我席上酒，

掣我盘中飧。
主人退后立，
敛手反如宾。
中庭有奇树，
种来三十春。
主人惜不得，
持斧断其根。
口称采造家，
身属神策军。
主人慎勿语，
中尉正承恩。

三、古诗译文

A Night at North Village in Mt. Purple Tower[1]

Morn and I stroll Mt. Purple Tower;
Dusk and I for the night put up
In the village, where the old man
Is pleased to offer me a cup.
Before we drink though cups are raised,
There in burst some fierce and rough men
In purple[2], carrying axes and swords.
Such grabbing wolves count more than ten.
They seize our wine and devour all;
What is in the plate they molest.
My host steps back, stands there and bows
As if he were their polite guest
In his mid-yard stands a fine tree
For thirty years cared for by him;

He does love it with all his heart
The roughs fell it and the roots trim.
"We are sent by the court for wood;
We are the Emperor's guards[3] ace."
So I tell the host not to talk
For their captain enjoys His grace.

（赵彦春　译）

◎ **注释**

1. Mt. Purple Tower: the head of the South Hills, 30 kilometers from Long Peace. 紫阁
2. Purple: the leader of the Emperor's guards dress in purple uniform. 紫衣
3. the Emperor's guards: one of the guard units to protect the Emperor of the Tang Dynasty. 神策军

四、译文赏析

1. **晨游紫阁峰，暮宿山下村。**
村老见余喜，为余开一尊。

译文： Morn and I stroll Mt. Purple Tower; /Dusk and I for the night put up
In the village, where the old man /Is pleased to offer me a cup.

赏析： 原文尾韵为"村"和"尊"，译文与其位置一致，即 up 和 cup。morn 本意是指太阳升起，后来转意为早晨，比 morning 更具有文学性。"紫阁峰"是终南山的著名山峰，在今陕西西安以南 60 余里。"紫阁"的命名源自《陕西通志》卷九引《雍胜略》："旭日射之，烂然而紫，其峰上耸，若楼阁然。"其译文 Mt. Purple Tower 采用字译法，逐字翻译。put up 意为留宿，在译文里用于扩展"暮宿"篇幅，并减译"山下村"，以避免和 In the village 语义重复。

2. **举杯未及饮，暴卒来入门。**
紫衣挟刀斧，草草十余人。

译文： Before we drink though cups are raised, /There in burst some fierce and rough men.
In purple, carrying axes and swords. /Such grabbing wolves count more than ten.

赏析：原文为分句组间押尾韵，即“门”和“人”；译文也为分句组间押尾韵，即 men 和 ten。“暴卒”为横暴的士兵，而其中的“暴”被译文 fierce and rough 扩展和强调，“卒”被模糊为 men，“入门”也被模糊为 There in burst(“突然出现”)，属于精确—模糊信息间的博弈。“紫衣”指穿三品以上紫色官服的神策军头目，译文 In purple 直译形象，而非象征义，因互文性较强的词会延长篇幅。“草草”指杂乱粗野的样子，而译文 Such grabbing wolves 用比喻手法来凸显士兵粗野的形象。

3. **口称采造家，身属神策军。**

主人慎勿语，中尉正承恩。

译文：“We are sent by the court for wood; /We are the Emperor’s guards ace.”

So I tell the host not to talk /For their captain enjoys His grace.

赏析：原文以鼻音在分句组间押尾韵，其译文尾韵位置一致，即 ace 和 grace。“采造家”指专管采伐、建筑的官府人员，其译文 the court for wood 译出了其部门的功能。“口称”被译文符号化成了双引号。“神策军”是中唐时期皇帝的禁卫军之一，但当时宦官掌握禁卫军军权，纵容士兵欺压百姓，其译文 the Emperor’s guards ace 将其泛化为“禁卫军”。“中尉”是神策军的最高长官，其译文 their captain 并未以军衔等级为翻译参照，而是以这十几个士兵的相对关系来翻译。“承恩”指得到皇帝的宠信，其译文 His grace 指皇帝的恩惠，说法不同，但都表达了和皇权的亲近。

第六章　世伪知贤

第一节　隋堤柳

一、诗歌背景

《隋堤柳》是一首七言乐府叙事长诗，隋堤之柳在诗中成为一种意象，指代亡国。隋炀帝时期开凿大运河，西起洛阳，东段从荥阳至开封，折入皖、苏，贯通邗沟，直达扬州，两岸的大堤因此被称为隋堤。然而，前朝大兴土木修凿大运河，在运河两畔广植柳树，没有成为百姓的福祉，却成为了百姓肩头沉重的负累，隋朝也在炀帝的荒淫中渐渐消耗，直到江都兵变的发生。全诗译文的特点在于古代长度单位的转换和地名的翻译上，体现了以译文读者为本的翻译思想。

二、古诗原文

隋　堤　柳

隋堤柳，
岁久年深尽衰朽。
风飘飘兮雨萧萧，
三株两株汴河口。
老枝病叶愁杀人，

曾经大业年中春。
大业年中炀天子，
种柳成行夹流水。
西自黄河东至淮，
绿影一千三百里。
大业末年春暮月，
柳色如烟絮如雪。
南幸江都恣佚游，
应将此柳系龙舟。
紫髯郎将护锦缆，
青娥御史直迷楼。
海内财力此时竭，
舟中歌笑何日休？
上荒下困势不久，
宗社之危如缀旒。
炀天子，
自言福祚长无穷，
岂知皇子封酅公。
龙舟未过彭城阁，
义旗已入长安宫。
萧墙祸生人事变，
晏驾不得归秦中。
土坟数尺何处葬？
吴公台下多悲风。
二百年来汴河路，
沙草和烟朝复暮。
后王何以鉴前王？
请看隋堤亡国树。

三、古诗译文

Sui[1] Dyke Willows[2] Gray

Sui Dyke willows gray,
So old, they have now fallen to decay.
The wind blows, o the rain does sough and sough;
Three trees or two on the Pien River[3] bow.
The old branches, the sick leaves, what sad trees!
Planted in Sui, they once enjoyed spring breeze.
In the great reign of Emperor Melt Fine[4];
On both banks willows were planted to line.
From the Yellow[5] to the Huai[6] all the way,
Green shades were cast four hundred miles to fay.
The end of the reign saw a late spring show;
The green hue was like mist, catkins[7] like snow.
The Lord went south to Yangchow[8] to tour free;
He'd have his dragon barge tied to the tree.
His generals were pulling silk hawsers there;
His censors were enjoying ladies fair.
All treasuries were exhausted, hard pressed;
When would dances and songs in the barge rest?
Squander up and poverty down won't last;
Danger will come to the empire so fast.
Emperor Melt Fine,
He thought his blessing would go without bound,
So then His prince was as Duke of Hsieh crowned.
Before his dragon barge passed P'eng[9] on route,
Rebels stormed Long Peace and did Long Peace[10] loot.
A disaster fell, all changed in the west;

He couldn't go back, and all were depressed.
Where to bury Him? There is a small tomb.
Under Lord Wu's Mound[11], a wind sighed in gloom.
For two hundred years Pien Dyke has there stayed,
Seeing sedge and smoke and all those who wade.
How could a later emperor still be?
Please look at Sui Dyke and the fallen tree.

(赵彦春　译)

◎ 注释

1. Sui: the Sui Dynasty (581A. D. -618A. D.), a transitional period between the Northern and Southern Dynasties and the Tang Dynasty. In February, Emperor Calm of Northern Chough abdicated and handed his throne over to Chien Yang, the first emperor of Sui, who reunified China. 隋
2. willow: any of a large genus of shrubs and trees related to the poplars, having generally narrow leaves, smooth branches, and often long, slender, pliant, and sometimes pendent branchlets, a symbol of farewell or nostalgia in Chinese culture. The best image is in "Vetch We Pick", a verse in *The Book of Songs*, which reads like this: When we left long ago, / The willows waved adieu. /Now back to our home town, /We meet snow falling down. 柳
3. the Pien River: an ancient river that originated from Hsingshine and flowed into the Ssu River in P'eng. 汴河
4. Emperor Melt Fine: Kuang Yang (569A. D. -618A. D.) the second emperor of Sui, one of the most famous emperors in Chinese history. 炀天子
5. the Yellow: the Yellow River, the second longest river in China, regarded as the cradle of Chinese civilization. It is 5, 464 kilometers long, with a drainage area of 752, 443 square kilometers. As legend goes, the river derived from a yellow dragon that, couchant on Midland Plain, ate yellow soil, flooded crops, devoured people and stock, and was finally tamed by Da Yu, the First King of Hsia (ca. 2070 B. C. -ca. 1600 B. C.). 黄河
6. the Huai: referring to the River Huai, one of the seven rivers in China, between the Long River and the Yellow River, 1, 000 kilometers long. 淮
7. catkin: a deciduous scaly spike of flowers, as in the willow, an image of helpless drifting or wandering in Chinese literature. 絮

8. Yangchow：an important city in today's Jiangsu Province，the greatest port in China and the centre of luxury trades in the Tang Dynasty. 江都
9. P'eng：today's Hsuchow，Chiangsu Province. 彭城
10. Long Peace：Ch'ang'an if transliterated，the metropolis of gold，the capital of the Tang Empire，with 1，000，000 inhabitants，the largest walled city ever built by man，and the capital of today's Shaanxi Province. Long Peace saw the wonder of Chinese civilization that reached the pinnacle of brilliance in Emperor Deepsire's reign. 长安
11. Lord Wu's Mound：in Yangchow，built by Sung in the Southern Dynasties，as a vantage point for arrow shooting. 吴公

四、译文赏析

1. 隋堤柳，岁久年深尽衰朽。
风飘飘兮雨萧萧，三株两株汴河口。

译文：Sui Dyke willows gray，/So old，they have now fallen to decay.
The wind blows，o the rain does sough and sough；
Three trees or two on the Pien River bow.

赏析：原文尾韵较少，即"朽"和"萧"，译文分句组内尾韵较丰富，即 gray 和 decay、sough 和 bow。隋炀帝时期开凿大运河，西起洛阳，东段从荥阳至开封，折入皖、苏，贯通邗沟，直达扬州，两岸的大堤因此被称为隋堤。其译文中 Sui 为音译，Dyke 为沟渠堤坝，而增译的 gray 起到押尾韵和渲染悲寂氛围的作用。"风飘飘"和"雨萧萧"以叠词来呈现风雨的重复与柔和，其译文中 sough and sough 指风浪的沙沙声，也采用了重复的手法。"汴河"采用音译法，而"河口"非河流的入海口，在本诗中指的是河湾，因而译成 bow。

2. 老枝病叶愁杀人，曾经大业年中春。
大业年中炀天子，种柳成行夹流水。

译文：The old branches，the sick leaves，what sad trees！/Planted in Sui，they once enjoyed spring breeze.
In the great reign of Emperor Melt Fine；/On both banks willows were planted to line.

赏析：译文尾韵特征明显，即 trees 和 breeze、Fine 和 line。"愁杀人"在本诗中指使人

极为忧愁，亦作“愁煞”，译者通过感叹句来再现情感的强烈。“曾经大业”未直接点明过去的哪个朝代，但根据背景和语境，应指唐朝前的隋朝，并增译 Planted in Sui 以表示杨柳为隋朝所种。“大业”出现过两次，但译文译法不同，分别为 Sui，In the great reign，避免了用词重复，都能通过语境指具体的朝代。“炀天子”指隋炀帝，其译文 Emperor Melt Fine 采用字译法，因“炀”本意指熔化金属，所以译成 Melt Fine。

3. **西自黄河东至淮，绿影一千三百里。**
大业末年春暮月，柳色如烟絮如雪。

译文： From the Yellow to the Huai all the way，/Green shades were cast four hundred miles to fay.

The end of the reign saw a late spring show；/The green hue was like mist，catkins like snow.

赏析： 原文尾韵为“月”和“雪”，而译文尾韵有两处，即 way 和 fay、show 和 snow。“黄河”与“淮”都为河流名词，但一个译字义，一个译字音，因为“淮”的本意是指最清的水，难以简译成一个字，而中文读者也一般不会联想该字义，因此取其音。“一千三百里”中的“里”在唐代以唐太宗李世民的双步(左右脚各迈一步)为尺寸标准，叫作“步”，三百步为一里。“一千三百里”与 four hundred miles 的长度相近。fay 指紧密连接、接合。时间“大业末年”和景色“春暮月”通过 saw 衔接。

4. **南幸江都恣佚游，应将此柳系龙舟。**
紫髯郎将护锦缆，青娥御史直迷楼。

译文： The Lord went south to Yangchow to tour free；/He'd have his dragon barge tied to the tree.

His generals were pulling silk hawsers there；/His censors were enjoying ladies fair.

赏析： 原文有三处尾韵，即“游”“舟”“楼”，而译文为分句组内押尾韵，即 free 和 tree、there 和 fair。“江都”因“江淮之水都汇于此”得名，于西汉景帝前元四年建江都县，2011 年 11 月，撤销县级江都市，设立扬州市江都区。为帮助外文读者更好地在地图上定位该位置，译者采用该处的现代地名音。文中的“龙舟”和“江都”，实际上是诗人在暗示炀帝从东都第三次乘龙舟南下江都后所遇上的“江都兵变”。“青娥”指称年轻女子。“御史”为官名，是国君亲近之职，掌文书及记事。“迷楼”是隋炀帝所建楼名。译文减译了“御史”，是为精简译文而对次要信息进行筛选，而 enjoying ladies fair 通过在“迷楼”所做之事来指代地点本身。

第二节　黑潭龙

一、诗歌背景

《黑潭龙》是新乐府诗，讽刺了“贪吏”“神龙”“巫婆”的迷信和愚昧。诗中的“传有”和“不能神”暗示了神龙只是巫婆的谣传，而贪吏进一步神化神龙，以潭上建庙为由，搜刮民脂民膏。人们也因愚昧无知，把水旱、疾病、歉收归因于所谓能呼风唤雨的神龙。诗人从“传有”到“皆言”，揭示了三人成虎的道理，一个无事实基础的传闻能变成人云亦云，可见当时人们的愚昧。全诗译文的特点在于为了押尾韵和上下文一致性，对原文的信息进行了增减和改译。

二、古诗原文

黑潭龙

黑潭水深黑如墨，
传有神龙人不识。
潭上驾屋官立祠，
龙不能神人神之。
丰凶水旱与疾疫，
乡里皆言龙所为。
家家养豚漉清酒，
朝祈暮赛依巫口。
神之来兮风飘飘，
纸钱动兮锦伞摇。
神之去兮风亦静，
香火灭兮杯盆冷。
肉堆潭岸石，

酒泼庙前草。
不知龙神享几多，
林鼠山狐长醉饱。
狐何幸？
豚何辜？
年年杀豚将喂狐。
狐假龙神食豚尽，
九重泉底龙知无？

三、古诗译文

The Black Pool Dragon[1]

The black pool is deep, black like inky clay;
There lives a dragon there as all folk say.
The pool sees an official temple stand;
The dragon's no god, made god of the land.
When floods, droughts or diseases wildly run,
All say this is what the dragon has done.
Those living nearby rear pigs and brew wine.
And as told by witches, pray to the shrine.
As wind blows, they see Dragon God[2] alight!
From paper money they burn leap flames bright.
Dragon God is gone, wind is gone, behold!
Incense dying out, bowls, basins are cold.
Meat piled up are left on the stone,
Wine spilled on grass, cups there o'er thrown.
Who knows for how long this dragon has dined?
Rats and foxes have long dined here we find.
How blessed, foxes shine!
How sad, doomed are swine[3]!

Each year swine are killed to feed foxes[4] fine.
Instead of Dragon God, foxes eat all
Does the dragon down the pool know at all?

(赵彦春 译)

◎ 注释

1. dragon: a fabulous serpent-like giant animal that can change its girth and length, a symbol of benevolence and sovereignty in Chinese culture while a black or black pool dragon has a negative image. 龙
2. Dragon God: the imaginary God ruling dragons. 神
3. swine: any of a family of omnivorous, artiodactylous mammals with a bristly coat and elongated, flexible snout, especially a domesticated pig or a hog. 豚
4. fox: a burrowing canine mammal (genus *Vulpes*) having a long pointed muzzle and a long bushy tail, commonly reddish-brown in color, known for its cunning. 狐

四、译文赏析

1. 黑潭水深黑如墨，传有神龙人不识。
潭上驾屋官立祠，龙不能神人神之。

译文：The black pool is deep, black like inky clay; /There lives a dragon there as all folk say.
The pool sees an official temple stand; /The dragon's no god, made god of the land.

赏析：原文为分句组间押尾韵，即"识"和"之"，而译文在分句组内押尾韵，即 clay 和 say、stand 和 land。"墨"在译文中被化为形容词 inky，并与增译的 clay 一同指黑色的土浆。"潭上"与"驾屋官立祠"为地点关系，译者惯用 sees 来衔接这种关系。"人不识"本为人们没有见过和不了解，但译文为肯定句，原因是译者强调了"传有"和减译了"不识"。两个"神"词义有所差异，第一个是成为神，第二个是以别人为神，分别译成主动态和被动态。

2. 丰凶水旱与疾疫，乡里皆言龙所为。
家家养豚漉清酒，朝祈暮赛依巫口。

译文：When floods, droughts or diseases wildly run, /All say this is what the dragon has done.

Those living nearby rear pigs and brew wine. /And as told by witches, pray to the shrine.

赏析：“丰凶”指收成不好，与水旱形成因果关系，水旱能与粮食歉收形成联想，因此在控制篇幅的取舍中，“丰凶”被减译。“乡里”指乡民，译文用限定词 all 作名词，借用语境来指代当地所有居民。“家家”指每家每户，其译文则指附近的人，这种译法能使 nearby 与 wine 押韵，更有诗性。朝祈暮赛中包含了时间信息，以及祈祷、赛神仪式的活动，而译文减译时间以确保篇幅对称。

3. **神之来兮风飘飘，纸钱动兮锦伞摇。**
神之去兮风亦静，香火灭兮杯盆冷。

译文： As wind blows, they see Dragon God alight! /From paper money they burn leap flames bright.

Dragon God is gone, wind is gone, behold! /Incense dying out, bowls, basins are cold.

赏析：原文有一组分句组内押尾韵，即“飘”和“摇”，而译文有两组分句组内押尾韵，即 alight 和 bright、behold 和 cold。“神之来”的译文 they see Dragon God alight 中，“来”被改译成“看”，主语“龙神”也变成了宾语，alight 为增译的形容词，意为“用火点燃和神采飞扬”，以再现语气助词“兮”的感叹。“纸钱动”和“锦伞摇”皆为“风飘飘”引起，而风进一步象征“神之来”。“纸钱”与“锦伞”的目的皆为凸显“风飘飘”，译文聚焦“纸钱”的火焰高涨来衬托风力，而“锦伞”的减译是为了控制篇幅。

4. **肉堆潭岸石，酒泼庙前草。**
不知龙神享几多，林鼠山狐长醉饱。

译文： Meat piled up are left on the stone, /Wine spilled on grass, cups there o'er thrown.

Who knows for how long this dragon has dined? /Rats and foxes have long dined here we find.

赏析：原文为分句组间押尾韵，即“草”和“饱”，而译文为分句组内押尾韵，即 stone 和 thrown、dined 和 find。“不知—几多”的未知性被译成疑问句。“几多”具有多义性，可意为多少和多久。译者考虑到了上下文的一致性，与“长醉饱”体现的时长一致，译者将“几多”译成 how long。“醉饱”的译文 dined 并未减译“醉”字，因 dine 指进餐和宴请，包含食物和酒水，此为“整体—部分”的上义词的选词思路。

第三节　天 可 度

一、诗歌背景

白居易在官场摸爬滚打后，对官场的险恶有了很深的体会。全诗第一句提出了“天可度，地可量，唯有人心不可防”的论点，再用“掩鼻”及“掇蜂”两个典故论证表面谦和但内心巧舌如簧之人会使夫妻、父子成为仇人；后半部分先提出“人心不能料”的论点，再用李义府笑里藏刀的典故来论证，揭露了专制政体下政治运作的黑暗。全诗巧用比兴、典故，使道理说得明白透彻，其译文的特色在于典故的翻译。

二、古诗原文

天 可 度

天可度，
地可量，
唯有人心不可防。
但见丹诚赤如血，
谁知伪言巧似簧。
劝君掩鼻君莫掩，
使君夫妇为参商。
劝君掇蜂君莫掇，
使君父子成豺狼。
海底鱼兮天上鸟，
高可射兮深可钓。
唯有人心相对时，
咫尺之间不能料。
君不见李义府之辈笑欣欣，

笑中有刀潜杀人。
阴阳神变皆可测，
不测人间笑是瞋。

三、古诗译文

We Can Gauge the Earth[1]

We can gauge the earth;
We can gauge the blue,
But a human heart we can never do.
We can see one's faithfulness like blood run;
But how can we distinguish a glib tongue?
Advised to "cover your nose"[2], you don't do,
Which may take your husband away from you.
Advised to stir up bees, you should not;
Which may bring father and son troubles hot.
There're fish in the sea, and birds in the sky;
You can fish for what's deep and shoot what's high.
But men, who stand eye to eye, face to face,
You can't be sure of e'en in a small space.
Don't you espy those who, like Premier Li[3], smirk and smile
Hide a knife under the cover of guile.
The law of nature one can estimate;
How can you judge a smile that covers hate?

(赵彦春 译)

◎ 注释

1. This poem contains references to various incidents of slander well-known at the time.
2. cover your nose: referring to an imperial concubine who was told by a jealous colleague that

the Emperor did not like her nose and that she should cover it with her hand when in his presence. The Emperor seeing her do this asked the jealous colleague the reason. She said that it was because the concubine found his body odour objectionable. This led to serious consequences for the concubine and to her rival gaining imperial favour. 掩鼻

3. Premier Li：referring to Yifu Li（614A. D. -666A. D. ）, a corrupt prime minister. 李义府

四、译文赏析

1. 天可度，地可量，唯有人心不可防。

译文： We can gauge the earth；/We can gauge the blue,

But a human heart we can never do.

赏析： 原文篇幅灵活，尾韵为“量”和“防”，译文尾韵一致，即 blue 和 do。“度”和“量”为同义词，其译文 gauge 也指用仪器测量。“唯有”表示强调，而前后句肯否定相反，形成转折关系，因此被译成 But。“不可防”的译文 we can never do 中不见“防”字，译者以 do 指代上文的 gauge，以人心不可度量来译不可防。

2. 但见丹诚赤如血，谁知伪言巧似簧。
劝君掩鼻君莫掩，使君夫妇为参商。
劝君掇蜂君莫掇，使君父子成豺狼。

译文： We can see one’s faithfulness like blood run；/But how can we distinguish a glib tongue?

Advised to “cover your nose”, you don’t do, /Which may take your husband away from you.

Advised to stir up bees, you should not；/Which may bring father and son troubles hot.

赏析： 原文为分句组间押尾韵，与上文一同形成四处尾韵，即“防”“簧”“商”“狼”，而译文尾韵较少和分散，即 run 和 tongue、not 和 hot。“巧似簧”指巧舌如簧，其中“簧”是乐器里用以发音的片状振动体，在诗中用于比喻善于说假话的人用动听的语言来迷惑人。其译文 glib tongue 指油嘴滑舌，具有贬义性，减译了比喻手法。“劝君掩鼻”引用了典故，据《韩非子·内储说下》，楚王的夫人郑袖性多嫉妒。郑袖对魏王送给楚王的美人说：“楚王非常喜欢你，只是讨厌你的鼻子。你见楚王应该掩鼻。”随后，郑袖又对楚王说：“美人

讨厌您身上的臭气，所以见您就掩鼻。”楚王听后勃然大怒，令士兵割掉了美人的鼻子。因此，外文读者对该译文的理解要依赖注解的引导。“参(shēn)商”指参星和商星，比喻分离不相会。“劝君掇蜂”也为离间骨肉的典故，蔡邕《琴操》载，尹吉甫娶了后妻，而后妻在尹吉甫面前造谣说尹吉甫前妻的儿子伯奇调戏她，并安排尹吉甫在暗中观察，故意放一只毒蜂在自己衣领上，让伯奇替她捉。尹吉甫真以为伯奇调戏后母，把伯奇赶出了家门。

3. **海底鱼兮天上鸟，高可射兮深可钓。**
唯有人心相对时，咫尺之间不能料。

译文： There're fish in the sea, and birds in the sky; /You can fish for what's deep and shoot what's high.

But men, who stand eye to eye, face to face, /You can't be sure of e'en in a small space.

赏析： 原文有三处形成尾韵，即“鸟”“钓”“料”，译文为两分句组内押尾韵，即 sky 和 high、face 和 space。“海底鱼”为存在事物的描述，译文用存在句 There're... 而“可”的功能为建议，译文用 You can。“唯有”的功能为强调，译文通过 But 表强调，并对“相对时”展开。然而，抽象的“人心”被改译成具象的 eye 和 face，如果其译文采用 heart to heart，“心”的“相对”容易误解为“心”的 “相应”，容易偏离原文。

4. **君不见李义府之辈笑欣欣，笑中有刀潜杀人。**
阴阳神变皆可测，不测人间笑是瞋。

译文： Don't you espy those who, like Premier Li, smirk and smile

Hide a knife under the cover of guile.

The law of nature one can estimate; /How can you judge a smile that covers hate?

赏析： 原文分句组间尾韵为“人”和“瞋”，而译文有两分句组内押尾韵，即 smile 和 guile、estimate 和 hate，译文的篇幅变化与原文一致。押头韵的 smirk and smile 强调和还原了“笑欣欣”的得意假笑。李义府是唐高宗时宰相。据《旧唐书・李义府传》载，此人表面谦和善良，但内心刻薄阴险，陷害了许多不顺其意的人。“阴阳神变”源自《周易・系辞上》：“极数知来之谓占，通变之谓事，阴阳不测之谓神。”指能够根据数的变化而预测未来就是占卜，能够变通应对就是办事，阴阳变化而不可预测就是神奇。其译文 The law of nature 指自然规律，与原文的物质世界对立面间的变化规律相对应。

第三部分　送别诗

第七章　金秋愁别

第一节　秋江送客

一、诗歌背景

贞元年间(785—805年)进士出身的白居易，曾授秘书省校书郎，再官至左拾遗，可谓春风得意。谁知几年京官生涯中，因其直谏不讳，冒犯了权贵，受朝廷排斥，被贬为江州司马。《秋江送客》一诗为诗人在江州期间送别友人之作。《旧唐书·元稹传》说："白居易诗善状风态物色。"诗人多数诗篇有景物描写，而写得最多的是秋景。该诗中，秋鸿、哀猿、孤舟、蒙蒙细雨、漠漠浮云组成一幅悲凉的画面，情调悲切，令人愁绝。诗人白居易一生结识不少友人，但由于命运坎坷、生涯飘泊，多次与亲友分离，在孤独寂寞中苦度时光。在该诗中，诗人调动浅显的词语表达了送别友人后的寂寞悲苦。

二、古诗原文

秋江送客

秋鸿次第过，
哀猿朝夕闻。
是日孤舟客，
此地亦离群。

蒙蒙润衣雨，
漠漠冒帆云。
不醉浔阳酒，
烟波愁杀人。

三、古诗译文

Seeing Off a Guest at the Autumn River

Autumn geese[1] fly off one by one;
Sad monkeys shriek there night and day.
I'm a lone guest on a lone boat,
And from the crowd I keep away.
Dim[2], dim, the rain dampens my clothes;
Thick, thick, the clouds enshroud[3] my sail.
I'm not yet drunk with Bankshine wine;
The waves and my woes[4] make me ail[5].

（赵彦春　译）

◎ **注释**

1. geese: web-footed long-necked birds, usually larger and less aquatic than ducks 鸿
2. dim: lacking in light, clarity or distinctness; offering little or no hope 蒙蒙
3. enshroud: cover as if with a shroud 冒(同帽，覆盖之意)
4. woes: intense mournfulness; misery resulting from affliction 愁
5. ail: be ill or unwell 愁杀(人)

四、译文赏析

1. **秋鸿次第过，哀猿朝夕闻。**

译文：Autumn geese fly off one by one;

Sad monkeys shriek there night and day.

赏析：原文中“秋鸿”对“哀猿”，“次第”对“朝夕”，“过”对“闻”，译文也同样用Autumn geese对Sad monkeys，one by one对night and day，fly off对shriek there，基本忠实于原诗结构和意思。其中译文中用fly off来翻译原文中的“过”，能体现出“秋鸿”在空中飞过的动态感，是以实对虚。原文中用“闻”表明诗人听到哀猿发出的声音，在译文中处理为“shriek”，一来是因为译文中的主语是Sad monkeys，是主谓搭配所需，同时也烘托了周边寂静的场景，强化了诗人在诗中表达的“孤舟客”的孤独愁苦。

2. 蒙蒙润衣雨，漠漠冒帆云。

译文：Dim，dim，the rain dampens my clothes；

Thick，thick，the clouds enshroud my sail.

赏析：原文中“蒙蒙”用来修饰“雨”，但同时雨润湿了衣服，所以“蒙”意为“细雨蒙蒙的”。译文中用了dim，指光线暗淡的、灰蒙蒙的，在表达原文意思的同时又暗指希望渺小，契合诗人的心情。原文中“漠漠”指云烟密布的样子，译文中的thick不仅能对应原文意思，又能应和前面的dim，两者都有元音/ɪ/，读起来更具韵律美。原文中“润衣雨”和“冒帆云”都是偏正结构，关键词是“雨”和“云”，译文中用了动宾结构，“雨润湿了衣服，云遮住了帆”。译文符合英文的行文习惯，同时从字数和音节上来看也很工整。

3. 不醉浔阳酒，烟波愁杀人。

译文：I'm not yet drunk with Bankshine wine；

The waves and my woes make me ail.

赏析：原文中“不醉浔阳酒”中没有提及主语是谁，但读者通读全诗能明白是指诗人，同时也能明白“烟波愁杀人”中的“人”也是指诗人。所以在译文中，译者把主语I补全，属于增译，这是为了使译文忠实地表达原始含义和风格，并使译文符合表达习惯。又把“愁杀人”的“人”译成me，指代更清晰。译文比原文中多了yet，属于增译，意指诗人还没醉酒，但已经“愁杀人”了。这是因为英语词与词、词组与词组以及句子与句子的逻辑关系一般用连词来表示，而汉语则往往通过上下文和语序来表示这种关系。此处增译保证了译文意思的明确。此外，译文中的waves和woes也形成押头韵的效果。

第二节　江楼宴别

一、诗歌背景

古往今来，文人墨客对于离别总是歌吟不绝，离情别绪是古代文人吟咏的一个永恒主题。在浓浓的感伤之外，也有其他的寄寓，或抒发友情，或寄托诗人自己的理想抱负等。古时由于交通不便、通信不发达，亲人朋友间往往一别数载，再会难期，所以离别之际，人们往往设酒饯行，吟诗话别。《江楼宴别》就是诗人白居易在江楼宴别友人之作，此中既有离别之情，又有身世命运之感。“酒”引人抒怀，是送别诗中常见之意象，如该诗中“楼中别曲催离酌”。此外，“月亮”也是经常用来展现别离之情的意象之一，如本诗中“寒流带月澄如境，夕吹和霜利似刀”，诗人白居易之所以着重展现月夜的境界，虽与唐人喜于月下听乐观舞有关，但更主要的是因为在中华民族传统的审美心理中，“月”较之其他景物更易触发人的情感，因而也更富有诗意。

二、古诗原文

江楼宴别

楼中别曲催离酌，
灯下红裙间绿袍。
缥缈楚风罗绮薄，
铮鏦越调管弦高。
寒流带月澄如镜，
夕吹和霜利似刀。
尊酒未空欢未尽，
舞腰歌袖莫辞劳。

三、古诗译文

A Farewell Party on the River Tower

The parting tune upstairs does urge our toast[1];
The lanterns light up gowns green and skirts pink.
The Ch'u songs are ethereal[2], the silks thin;
The Yueh tones are high, with some notes to clink[3].
The cold spell bears the moon that's mirror-like;
A dusk wind blows frost like a knife to cleave[4].
The cups not yet empty, cheers linger on[5];
The slender waist turns swift, whirling[6] the sleeve.

(赵彦春　译)

◎ 注释

1. toast：a drink in honor of or to the health of a person or event 酌
2. ethereal：characterized by unusual lightness and delicacy 缥缈
3. clink：make or emit a high sound 铮鏦
4. cleave：use sth. sharp and heavy to split or cut sth. in two 利
5. linger on：remain present although waning or gradually dying 未尽
6. whirling：the act of rotating in a circle or spiral 舞

四、译文赏析

1. 楼中别曲催离酌，灯下红裙间绿袍。

译文： The parting tune upstairs does urge our toast;

The lanterns light up gowns green and skirts pink.

赏析： 原诗中"别曲"和"离酌"相互对应，有诗句结构平衡和音节之考虑。译文中已用 parting tune 指明这是送别之宴，所以 toast 之前不再使用离别类的修饰词汇，转用了 our

来点出是诗人在江楼饯行朋友。原文中“灯下”是作为“红裙间绿袍”的地点状语，译文中用 The lanterns 作主语，添加了可与之搭配的动词词组 light up。把“红裙”和“绿袍”处理成 gowns green and skirts pink，是为了使 pink 和 clink 押尾韵/ɪŋk/所做的调整，正好匹配原诗中第二、第四行押韵的节律。

2. 缥缈楚风罗绮薄，铮鏦越调管弦高。

译文： The Ch'u songs are ethereal, the silks thin;

The Yueh tones are high, with some notes to clink.

赏析： 这两句是对当时江楼宴客时的乐舞之人奏乐舞蹈的情境描写，承续了首联中的红裙绿袍。诗人白居易不仅是大诗人，还是一位卓有成就的音乐家。他的生活时时处处与音乐和舞蹈相依相伴。诗中他对“楚风”和“越调”进行了评论。原句中“铮鏦”为象声词，常形容撞击声、乐器演奏声，在汉语中可以直接形容“越调”。在译文中把 with some notes to clink 放在了句末，一是因为这个短语不适合放在 The Yueh 前面，以免造成头重脚轻之感，二是因为放在句末可以与前面的 pink 押尾韵/ɪŋk/。

3. 寒流带月澄如镜，夕吹和霜利似刀。

译文： The cold spell bears the moon that's mirror-like;

A dusk wind blows frost like a knife to cleave.

赏析： 这两句是说，“月照中天，看那江上的寒流，碧澄如镜；晚风吹来，和着霜冻，其利如刀”。这两句写出秋末冬初的景象，在凄清之中，透露出诗人的悲凉心境。原诗中的“带”与“和”是“寒流”与“夕吹”发出的动作，但在英文中用了 bears 和 blows，blows 对应了“吹”，一方面是因为英文更重形的需要，所以翻译时更具象化地进行了处理。同理，A dusk wind 也是直接补充了 wind，而原句中只有“吹”，对原文的增译是为了符合英文的表达习惯。原句中“夕吹和霜利似刀”是说因为霜冻，晚风更利了。在译文中处理为 wind blows frost 就像 a knife to cleave，用刀的锋利来形容 dusk wind 的冷冽，意为离别的凄清，同时和尾联中的最后一个词 sleeve 押韵，达到诗歌形和义的双重目的。

4. 尊酒未空欢未尽，舞腰歌袖莫辞劳。

译文： The cups not yet empty, cheers linger on;

The slender waist turns swift, whirling the sleeve.

赏析： 这两句是说，“樽中之酒尚未饮空，大家还没有尽兴；乐舞之人，且莫辞劳，请继续奏乐舞蹈助兴”。这两句明白如话，朗朗上口，意韵独到。唐代宴饮之时少不了歌舞助兴，“无歌不成宴，少舞难尽欢”。虽然这是饯行友人的诗，但诗人在诗中也兼写了舞腰和歌袖。译文中用了 turns swift，whirling the sleeve 来表现原诗中腰、袖不同方向和形态的运动，同时 slender，swift 和 sleeve 又押头韵，产生了语言的音乐美和整齐美。译文中 cheers linger on 用了拟人的手法表现“欢未尽”，不但形象，而且表明了不想话别的意思。

第三节　别杨颖士、卢克柔、殷尧藩

一、诗歌背景

《旧唐书·白居易传》所提到的杨颖士，白居易在《题杨颖士西亭》《别杨颖士、卢克柔、殷尧藩》两首诗中有所提及。殷尧藩，唐代诗人。他的《忆江南》三十首，被白居易赞为“江南名郡数苏杭，写在殷家三十章”。根据白居易的叙述，殷尧藩也精通音律。他和白居易早在贞元十六年之前就已经相识。白居易在诗歌《醉中酬殷协律》中说：“泗水亭边一分散，浙江楼上重游陪。挥鞭二十年前别，命驾三千里外来。醉袖放狂相向舞，愁眉和笑一时开。留君夜住非无分，且尽青娥红烛台。”所谓的“泗水亭边一分散”大约就是《别杨颖士、卢克柔、殷尧藩》中所记载的情况。

二、古诗原文

别杨颖士、卢克柔、殷尧藩

倦鸟暮归林，
浮云晴归山。
独有行路子，
悠悠不知还。
人生苦营营，
终日群动间。
所务虽不同，
同归于不闲。

扁舟来楚乡，
匹马往秦关。
离忧绕心曲，
宛转如循环。
且持一杯酒，
聊以开愁颜。

三、古诗译文

Farewell to Yingshi Yang, K'ejou Lu and Hsiaop'an Yin

The tired bird return to the woods;
The hung clouds float back to the hill.
Lo, there goes a traveler alone;
He's on the way, he is there still.
Human life's so hard, buzz and drone[1];
They hustle and bustle[2] all day.
Although they've different things to do,
No one of them can idle[3] stay.
The horses gallop[4] to Ch'in Pass;
The boats row to the land of Ch'u.
They go, turning and turning round;
What hurts them is their parting rue[5].
Just drink your wine, do raise your cup,
So you can be soothed[6] to cheer up.

（赵彦春　译）

◎ 注释

1. buzz and drone: make a sound of rapid vibration; make a monotonous low dull sound. 营营
2. hustle and bustle: have busy and noisy activities. 群动
3. idle: not in action or at work; lacking a sense of restraint or responsibility. 闲

4. gallop：ride a horse very fast；run very quickly. 往
5. rue：sadness associated with some wrong done or some disappointment. 忧
6. soothed：cause to feel better；make the pain or discomfort less severe. 开愁颜

四、译文赏析

1. 倦鸟暮归林，浮云晴归山。

译文： The tired bird return to the woods；
The hung clouds float back to the hill.

赏析： 白居易的诗歌以明白晓畅为特点，苏轼评价“元轻白俗”，其中的“白俗”就是指白居易诗歌的特点。白居易的诗不仅语言风格，其题材和关注点也更加接地气。这两句意为“天黑后鸟儿知道飞到林子里栖息，浮云也会飘到山后等待第二天的重现”。归鸟意象经常与归人、游子一起出现。译文遵从忠实于原文的原则，文字和结构上没有太多变动。float 表现出“飘然移动的感觉”，适合原诗中的“浮云”的特质。原诗中的“暮”并未在译文中体现，因为一般 tired birds 都是飞行一天之后疲倦了飞回山林，所以这里采用了减译的方法。

2. 人生苦营营，终日群动间。

译文： Human life’s so hard, buzz and drone；
They hustle and bustle all day.

赏析： “营营”，毕生营营，追求名利，常含贬义。译文中用 buzz and drone，用蜜蜂的这种忙碌的情境来对应“营营”，从声音和意思上都完全符合。“终日”指从早到晚，用 all day 来翻译。“群动”在这里指诸种活动，译文中用 hustle and bustle。hustle 作动词时有“推挤；喧闹”的意思，作名词是“忙碌”，也可指“汲汲营营、力争上游”。hustle 还可形容工作非常认真。bustle 作动词指“匆忙”，作名词时表示“热闹的活动”。hustle 与 bustle 本身可看成意义相近的两个单词，合在一起就是固定用来形容城市的喧嚣、熙熙攘攘。这里不但显示出终日忙忙碌碌的意思，也跟诗句开头倦鸟归林，浮云归山达成了相反的效果。这里抒发了白居易自己的一些关于世界和人生的观点。

3. **扁舟来楚乡，匹马往秦关。**

离忧绕心曲，宛转如循环。

译文： The horses gallop to Ch'in Pass;

The boats row to the land of Ch'u.

They go, turning and turning round;

What hurts them is their parting rue.

赏析： 原文"扁舟"对"匹马"，译文考虑到了"舟"和"马"的数量不可能为单数，所以直接译成复数，The horses 对 The boats；原文中"来"对"往"，同时两词有相反之意，但考虑到英文中主谓搭配的需求，译文中用 gallop 对 row，没有相反之意，但是对"马"和"舟"的动作进行了具象化的描写，也很生动。具象化同时也体现在后两句译文的 they，them 和 their 中。原诗中并未说明谁"宛转如循环"，"离忧"绕谁的"心曲"，但联系前两句，译者进行了增译。这里增译是明确意思和英语句子结构的需要。原句中"关"和"环"押韵，译者在译文中调换了顺序，从而使 Ch'u 和 rue 押韵。

4. **且持一杯酒，聊以开愁颜。**

译文： Just drink your wine, do raise your cup;

So you can be soothed to cheer up.

赏析： 原诗中只说"且持一杯酒"，译文中对此进行了增译，raise your cup 之外还 drink your wine，是因为考虑到音节的需要。同时前后两句中增译了 your 和 you，后面一句中减译了"聊以"，用 so 来进行意思上的连接，同时句子译成被动，使音节数量达成了平衡。译文中 cup 和 up 押尾韵/ʌp/，不但意思上匹配，还达成了诗歌的音乐美。原诗这两句文字明白晓畅，译文也用词通俗简约，达成了风格的一致。

第八章　情深难寄

第一节　潜别离

一、诗歌背景

白居易早年有一初恋情人(湘灵)，然而唐朝注重礼法，讲究门当户对，出生世家大族的诗人碍于门第与礼法，未能冲破母亲的阻扰。虽不甘心，诗人终究没有勇气去捅开封建礼法的迷雾，而是选择了“潜离与暗别”。这首《潜别离》便表达了诗人对这段感情的无奈和喟叹。一个“潜”字，一个“暗”字，道出了分别时的无奈与悲伤。“相思”二字，可作全诗诗眼，亦奠定了全诗的感情基调。整首诗通俗易懂，接近白话，却感情真挚、动人心魄，为诀别诗中的名篇佳作。

二、古诗原文

潜别离

不得哭，潜别离。
不得语，暗相思。
两心之外无人知。
深笼夜锁独栖鸟，
利剑春断连理枝。
河水虽浊有清日，

乌头虽黑有白时。
唯有潜离与暗别，
彼此甘心无后期。

三、古诗译文

In Silence We Part

Cry no more, don't cry;
In silence we part.
Nothing can we say;
Bear our love in heart.
But you and me, none knows how our souls smart.
At night the lone bird's to the cage confined[1];
A sharp sword cuts off the branches entwined[2].
The river turbid[3] would turn clear some day;
The raven pitch-black[4] will be white some way.
But mutely[5] we leave, in silence we part;
We'll accept endless woes to gnaw our heart.

（赵彦春　译）

◎ 注释

1. confined: not free to move about; being in captivity. 锁
2. branches entwined: branches are twisted around each other and they are difficult to separate or identify. 连理枝
3. turbid: (of liquids) clouded as with sediment. 浊
4. pitch-black: extremely dark. 黑
5. mutely: without speaking. 潜

四、译文赏析

1. 深笼夜锁独栖鸟，利剑春断连理枝。

译文： At night the lone bird's to the cage confined;

A sharp sword cuts off the branches entwined.

赏析：“深笼”意为幽深的鸟笼，“夜锁”意为夜里铁链囚锁，“独栖鸟”意为孤独栖息的飞鸟，喻有情人被禁锢。译文中转换了句式，用 the lone bird 作主语，用了被动句式（be）confined to，表示被禁锢不得自由，并把 confined 放在了句尾，与后一句的 entwined 押韵。原诗中“舂断”意为在石臼或乳钵里捣碎折断，还有一种说法为“春断”，即春季里折断。译文中用 cuts off，是为了配合主语 a sharp sword，更能突出剑斩连理枝之凄然。“连理枝”，又称相思树、夫妻树、生死树，指两棵树的枝干合生在一起，常用来比喻夫妻恩爱。因英文中没有与之直接对应的意象，译文中用了 the branches entwined 实译，并把修饰词 entwined 放在了句末，达成押韵的效果。

2. 河水虽浊有清日，乌头虽黑有白时。

译文：The river turbid would turn clear some day;

The raven pitch-black will be white some way.

赏析：白居易的诗歌大多明白如话，这两句是说“河水再浑浊也有清澈的日子，乌黑的头发终究也有变白之时”，但我们别后就后会无期了。原文中用的是动词“有”，译文中译者用了 would turn 变状态为动作，清晰具象，也符合英语表达中的主谓搭配要求。原文中“日”对“时”，在译文中用 some day 对 some way，意思确切，同时也押尾韵/eɪ/。原句中“乌头”实指满头黑丝，译文中用了 the raven，这里不是指乌鸦，因为 raven 作形容词的时候，在文学作品中通常指头发乌黑光亮，所以这里 the raven 译得很巧妙。

3. 唯有潜离与暗别，彼此甘心无后期。

译文：But mutely we leave, in silence we part;

We'll accept endless woes to gnaw our heart.

赏析：原诗中“潜离”对“暗别”，都是指分离时不说话、不哭泣。译文中用了 mutely we leave, in silence we part。mutely 对 in silence，we leave 对 we part。结构正好和原文对等。相思无果默然离开，潜离也好，暗别也罢，一转身就是天各一方，也就永不再相见。所以译文中用了 endless woes to gnaw our heart 来说明“甘心无后期”后心理上被悲痛所啮咬的痛苦，而且这个痛苦永无止境。这里的“无后期”里的“无”被 endless woes 里的 endless 所体现，属于转移修辞。gnaw our heart 极具动态的描写，是对原文意思进行了具体化的处理，同时又呼应了前面的 Bear our love in heart。原诗 1、2、3、5、6、7、9 行押尾韵 i，译文采用 ABCBBDDCCBB 的韵诗，尤其是 part 和 heart 的重复使用，产生了诗歌的音乐美。

第二节　别行简

一、诗歌背景

白居易共有弟兄四人，长兄白幼文，次即白居易，再次白行简，白幼美最小，9岁时夭折。白行简虽然没有白居易名气大，但史载他敏而有辞，“文笔有兄风，辞赋尤称精密，文士皆师法之”。在白居易生活中，与弟弟白行简的联系更多。白居易的诗中，写给弟弟白行简的诗就有12首。这些诗主要写白居易对弟弟的思念、喜悦、牵挂和嘱咐等内容。唐德宗贞元末(805年)，白行简考中进士，授秘书省校书郎。元和九年(814年)夏，卢坦出任东川节度使，召白行简为掌书记。这大概是白行简第一次独自出远门，白居易牵肠挂肚，叮嘱他早点回家，写下这首《别行简》。此时白居易43岁，正患眼疾，居住在下邦(今陕西渭南县东北)金氏村，已感眼花鬓白、精力衰疲，行简又要远行，心情自然非常暗淡，唯有希望他早日归来，重相聚首。白居易笃于友于之爱，此诗为一例。

二、古诗原文

别行简

漠漠病眼花，
星星愁鬓雪。
筋骸已衰惫，
形影仍分诀。
梓州二千里，
剑门五六月。
岂是远行时？
火云烧栈热。
何言巾上泪，
乃是肠中血。

念此早归来，
莫作经年别！

三、古诗译文

Farewell to Hsingchien

Blear[1], blear, our sickly welling eyes;
Thin, thin, our sad sideburns[2] like snow.
Careworn[3], so exhausted we are!
Apart our souls and shadows go.
Tzuchow's[4] two thousand *li* away,
Mt. Swordgate's[5] in fifth or sixth moon.
Isn't it a far journey there?
The plank road seems ablaze at noon.
It's our blood that does boil inside
Rather than our sash[6]-wetting tears.
Come back as early as you can;
Don't stay apart for long long years!

（赵彦春 译）

◎ 注释

1. blear: dim or indistinct; tired to the point of exhaustion. 漠漠
2. sideburns: facial hair that has grown down the side of a man's face in front of the ears (especially when the rest of the beard is shaved off). 鬓
3. careworn: showing the wearing effects of overwork or care or suffering. 衰
4. Tzuchow: in Santai County, Sichuan Province. During the Tang Dynasty, the most influential regions in Sichuan were Xichuan, with Chengdu as the center, and Dongchuan, with Santai as the center. At that time, Santai was called Zizhou, and Chengdu was called Yizhou, and they are the two largest metropolitan cities in Southwest China at that time. 梓州
5. Mt. Swordgate: located in Jiange County, Sichuan Province. There are 70 miles of plank

roads between sword mountains, called Sword Pavilion. 剑门

6. sash: a band of material around the waist that strengthens skirt or trousers. 巾

四、译文赏析

1. 漠漠病眼花，星星愁鬓雪。

译文： Blear, blear, our sickly welling eyes;

Thin, thin, our sad sideburns like snow.

赏析： 原文中“漠漠”对“星星”，译文中也采取了叠词的形式(Blear, blear 对 Thin, thin)。其中对“星星”的翻译进行了灵活处理，突出鬓发因发愁变白，也有稀疏之感。在意思上用了明喻 like snow 对应“雪”，在韵律上和第四行的 go 押尾韵/əu/。在修辞上用 sad, sideburns 和 snow 押头韵，具有音乐美和整齐感。原诗中的“病眼花”在译文中译成了 sickly welling eyes，用 welling 一词很具象地描写了患疾的眼睛的样子，这里属于增译，一方面使意思表达更确切，另一方面也是为了平衡这两句的音节数量。

2. 筋骸已衰惫，形影仍分诀。

译文： Careworn, so exhausted we are!

Apart our souls and shadows go.

赏析： 原文中用“筋骸衰惫”表示诗人身体很累，精力衰疲；其中“筋骸”是用部分代替整体，就是指人的身体精力，如用 muscle 和 bone 不但非常刻板，还不能达意，所以译文中直接用了 we 来对应；同时用 careworn 和 exhausted 来对应“衰惫”，加以句子倒装，强调疲惫之感。此处译文和原文在结构和意思上都有灵活的处理，意在强调诗人想要表达的衰疲之感。原文中的“形影”在字形上都是同一个偏旁，在译文中，用了 souls and shadows，押头韵，也促成了字形上的相似效果，在音和形两方面巧妙处理，可谓恰到好处。把 go apart 分开，apart 提到句首，一方面是突出诗人要送别弟弟，另一方面也是为了让句尾的 go 与第二行的 snow 押韵。

3. 何言巾上泪，乃是肠中血。

译文： It's our blood that does boil inside

Rather than our sash-wetting tears.

赏析： 原文中用“何言”和“乃是”来强调不是“巾上泪”，而是“肠中血”，译文中用

It's… that… 的强调句和词组 Rather than 来对应。原句意思明白晓畅，“肠中血”用了夸张的手法，在译文中用 blood that does boil inside 来对应，增译了动词 boil，同样用了夸张的手法。同时 boil 结合原诗上句中的“泪”，对应中文中的意象“热泪”。原诗中的“巾上泪”对“肠中血”，对仗工整。“巾上泪”意为泪湿巾，所以在译文中处理成 sash-wetting tears，偏正结构不变；用动态的 wet sash 来译静态的“巾上”，用动态的 boil inside 来译静态的“肠中”，结构一致，可见译者也考虑到了译文的结构对等。在译文中把这两句话的顺序颠倒，把“肠中血”放在了“巾上泪”的前面，使得 tears 和尾联的译文最后一个词 years 押韵。

第三节 别元九后咏所怀

一、诗歌背景

元稹，字微之，年少有名。与白居易同科及第，结为终生好友，两人往来酬和长诗，动辄数十韵。在诗歌史上，像元稹、白居易二人这样大量的唱和之作并不多见，当时长安少年纷纷效仿，并将他们这种互相酬唱的诗歌称为“元和体”，当时这种诗歌也引领了一时的潮流。《别元九后咏所怀》是白居易元和元年(806 年)所作的一首五言律诗，是诗人在送别元稹之后写的，抒写了诗人对挚友的深切思念，表现了相知同心的纯真情谊。该诗可以分为三部分，前四句为第一部分，是环境烘托。中四句为第二部分，是写心情，同时也是对第一部分的深化。后四句为第三部分，也是前两部分的结论。这首诗融写景、叙事、抒情于一体，情景交融；用笔虚实相生，实处描写景物，虚处勾勒景象；全诗如行云流水，毫无生涩之感。诗人在诗中的留白更给读者留下了无数想象空间。

二、古诗原文

别元九后咏所怀

零落桐叶雨，
萧条槿花风。
悠悠早秋意，

生此幽闲中。
况与故人别，
中怀正无悰。
勿云不相送，
心到青门东。
相知岂在多，
但问同不同。
同心一人去，
坐觉长安空。

三、古诗译文

Expressing What I Feel After Yuan Nine Is Gone

In the rain, tung[1] leaves sough to fall;
Gainst the wind, hibiscus[2] flowers sigh.
Long, long, autumn comes all too soon;
I lapse into quietude[3] thereby.
Besides, from me, my friend will go;
In my chest, there's no place for glee.
Don't say I need not see you off;
My heart's flown to Green Gate[4] to be.
Need friends know each other so much?
The same heart we have, the same one.
Now Long Peace[5] is empty, it's void[6],
Because with you, my heart has gone.

（赵彦春　译）

◎ 注释

1. Tung: a Chinese tree bearing seeds that yield tung oil. 桐
2. hibiscus: a tropical plant or bush with large brightly coloured flowers. 槿

3. quietude：a state of peace and quiet. 幽闲
4. Green Gate：the southeast gate of Chang'an City in the Han Dynasty of China；the east gate of the capital in a general sense. It is called Green Gate because of its green color. 青门
5. Long Peace：the capital of China in the Han/Tang Dynasties. 长安
6. void：containing nothing. 空

四、译文赏析

1. 零落桐叶雨，萧条槿花风。

译文：In the rain, tung leaves sough to fall；

Gainst the wind, hibiscus flowers sigh.

赏析：原诗以写景起兴，既奠定了全诗伤感的感情基调，又点明了与友人分别的时间。秋季甫至，诗人看到凋零的桐叶、衰败的槿花飘落在秋风秋雨之中，目光所及皆为萧瑟之景，伤秋之情油然而生。原诗中“零落”对“萧条”，“桐叶雨”对“槿花风”，属偏正结构，更重状态。译文中采用了倒装句型，状语提前，In the rain 对 Gainst the wind；tung leaves 对 hibiscus flowers，同时根据英语句式要求添加了动词 sought to fall 和 sigh，属动宾结构，更重动作。此两行译文本身除了结构对等之外，还用了拟人的手法，用 sough to fall 和 sigh，不仅有动作，还有声音，读后有草木萧瑟、人叹息之感，可谓绝妙。此情此景又让诗人想起与友人离别时的场景，心中愈发感伤。

2. 况与故人别，中怀正无悰。
勿云不相送，心到青门东。

译文：Besides, from me, my friend will go；

In my chest, there's no place for glee.

Don't say I need not see you off；

My heart's flown to Green Gate to be.

赏析：这四句将诗人的伤秋之情与同友人分别之后的落寞之情自然地连接了起来。诗人没有写出与友人分别的具体情境，以虚笔写分别之实事。原诗用词明白直接，译文表达也清晰直接。原诗中“与故人别”的主语应该是诗人“我”，译文中用了 my friend 作主语，更重离去之感；后一句中用 there be 句型，no place for glee 对应“无悰”。Don't say 译“勿云”，体现出诗人在跟友人对话的感觉，属直译。用 has flown to 来译“到”，用了夸张的手法，比原意更形象，也更能体现不忍与知己分别之意。句末添加了 to be，属增译，是为了与前面的 glee 押尾韵/iː/。

3. **相知岂在多，但问同不同。**
同心一人去，坐觉长安空。

译文：Need friends know each other so much?
The same heart we have, the same one.
Now Long Peace is empty, it's void,
Because with you, my heart has gone.

赏析：诗歌最后一部分再次点明诗人与元稹交情之深，与中间四句遥相呼应，使得全诗浑然一体。原诗中"岂"和"但"，一问一答，表明作者对知己的理解。译文对句式进行了调整，用了设问句 Need friends know each other so much? 然后直接回答 The same heart we have，同时重复 the same one，来对应原诗中的两个"同"，来强调知心朋友的"同"，又与最后一句中的 gone 押尾韵。原诗中"同心一人去，坐觉长安空"，因为中文讲究意合，没有用"因为""所以"等连词，但在译文中考虑到英语形合的特征，把隐含的因果关系增译了出来：两句译文间用了 because 连接，并且前后句子调换了顺序，在达到押韵的效果之外，更强调了 my heart has gone with you 之意。原句中的"同心一人去"是指知心朋友离开，译文中用 my heart has gone with you 指诗人的心随朋友而去，用 my heart 替代"我"，用了提喻的修辞格，言辞感情更为强烈。此四句言简意赅，却富含哲理，引起读者共鸣：不求朋友成群，但求知己一人，外面的世界再喧嚣，知心人不在，也如空城般孤寂。

第九章　天涯沦落

第一节　夜送孟司功

一、诗歌背景

功曹是西汉时开始设置的官名。在唐朝，在府的称为功曹参军，在州的称为司功。送别诗大多写凄凄别情，但此诗略有不同。诗中诗人不说不忍离别，而说秋风江波之险恶，以行路之艰险劝说行人且慢些离去。诗歌首联开门见山，介绍了送行的主与客，并点出主题“夜送”，总领全篇；颔联承首联而下，写夜送场景，“暗”“急”“明”“高”自有一种峭拔萧飒的气息；颈联转写行路之艰险，“翻似箭”写波浪翻滚迅速，“杀如刀”写秋霜寒峭锋利；尾联顺势而下，直言“且莫开征棹”，又以秋风之阴冷凛冽作结，暗示前途的险恶，含不忍离别之情于言外。

二、古诗原文

夜送孟司功

浔阳白司马，
夜送孟功曹。
江暗管弦急，
楼明灯火高。
湖波翻似箭，

霜草杀如刀。
且莫开征棹，
阴风正怒号。

三、古诗译文

Seeing Off Personnel Chief[1] Meng at Night

I, Commander[2] Pai in Bankshine,
See off Official Meng at night.
The river's dark and the strings rash[3];
With lanterns, the tower's lit bright.
The frosty grass seems a knife keen;
The surging lake like arrows churns.
Please do not unmoor your boat[4] now;
The shady wind soughs[5] and upturns.

（赵彦春 译）

◎ 注释

1. Personnel Chief: an official name. In addition to being in charge of personnel, one can participate in the government affairs of a county. 功曹
2. Commander: a person who is in charge of sth., especially an officer in charge of a particular group of soldiers or a military operation. 司马
3. rash: imprudently incurring risk. 急
4. boat: a small vessel for travel for a long journey on water. 征棹
5. sough: make a murmuring sound. 怒号

四、译文赏析

1. **江暗管弦急，楼明灯火高。**

译文： The river's dark and the strings rash,

With lanterns, the tower's lit bright.

赏析：诗歌颔联是送别的场景描写。夜幕下的浔阳江幽渺暗淡，江畔高楼灯火通明，急促的音乐似在催促离行之人。原句中“楼明”和“灯火高”并列，但从意思上可见是因为灯才楼明，所以译文进行了结构的调整，把 with lanterns 用作伴随状态，把 the tower's lit bright 设为句子主句，逻辑清楚。把 with lanterns 提前，把 the tower's lit bright 译为被动并后置于句末，使 bright 和第二行的 night 押尾韵，采取了结构上的转译。原句中的“灯火高”，译文中省译了“高”，是因为 tower 本身有高的意思。同时在中文中“灯火”二字也是成对出现，但其实意指燃烧着的灯烛等照明物，所以译文中 lanterns 就可以表达同等意思。

2. **湖波翻似箭，霜草杀如刀。**

译文：The frosty grass seems a knife keen;

The surging lake like arrows churns.

赏析：借着江畔高楼的灯火，诗人看到江上的波浪翻滚如箭般疾速，枯草蔓延有如刀般肃杀之气。原文中这两句是并列关系，译文中进行了顺序的对调，并在句中进行了倒装，把 churns like arrows 中的 churns 后置于末尾，使得 churns 和最后一行的 upturns 押尾韵，也达成整首诗歌偶句押韵的效果。原句中“霜草杀如刀”中的“杀”并不是其字面意思，而是指其锋利，烘托肃杀之气氛，所以译文中用了 keen 来表达。原句中“湖波”是偏正结构，关键词是“波”，译文中用了 surging lake，跟 churns 搭配，意指水波剧烈翻滚，翻译灵活而巧妙。

3. **且莫开征棹，阴风正怒号。**

译文：Please do not unmoor your boat now;

The shady wind soughs and upturns.

赏析：原诗前句是诗人劝说朋友暂且不要登船启程，“且”这里相当于 the time being，所以译文中用了 now，根据一般的英文行文习惯把这个时间放在了句末。原文中“阴风正怒号”的“正”跟前面的“且”对应的是同一个时间，但因为前面已经有了 now，所以后句译文中省译了这个时间。用 soughs and upturns 来译“怒号”，更是表现出了风的动态和声音，具有画面感。

第二节 清明日送韦侍御贬虔州

一、诗歌背景

白居易生活的年代，特别是贞元以后，唐代社会饮茶之风气日益兴盛。宫廷、文武官员、文人士子、僧侣道人都以饮茶作为生活品质的象征。白居易对茶的热爱首先表现在他爱茶，尚新茶。《清明日送韦侍御贬虔州》是白居易被贬江州司马时所作，虔州即今江西赣州。该诗中韦姓官员遭贬谪，临行之前到白居易居所告别，身处贫病交迫之境的白居易以新茶待客以表达不舍之情。“留饧和冷粥，出火煮新茶”，新茶在萧条寂寞的清明日有了温暖人心的力量。诗人也表达了对韦侍御与自己被贬相同的不幸命运的喟叹，因为对于当时的人来说，上路是件凶险的事情，南行尤其如此。由于南方是贬谪之地，许多中古时段有关南方的史料出自被贬谪到南方的官员之手，官场失意带来的郁闷心情也是他们对南方充满偏见的一大因素。

二、古诗原文

清明日送韦侍御贬虔州

寂寞清明日，
萧条司马家。
留饧和冷粥，
出火煮新茶。
欲别能无酒，
相留亦有花。
南迁更何处？
此地已天涯。

三、古诗译文

Seeing Off Attendant[1] Wei Exiled to Chienchow[2] on Pure Brightness Day[3]

Lonely, on this Pure Brightness Day;
Dreary, in my house, you and me.
Dough[4] left prepared and porridge cold,
I make fire to cook some new tea.
You're going away, we must drink,
And have blooms[5] for the time we spend.
Are you exiled[6] more south than here?
This place is almost the world's end.

（赵彦春　译）

◎ **注释**

1. attendant: someone who waits on or attends to the needs of the king. 侍御
2. Chienchow: now Ganzhou, in the south of Jiangxi Province. 虔州
3. Pure Brightness Day: one of the twenty-four solar terms and the fifth solar term in spring. 清明日
4. dough: a mixture of flour, water, etc. 饧
5. blooms: flowers. 花
6. exiled: expelled from home or country by authority. 迁

四、译文赏析

1. **寂寞清明日，萧条司马家。**

译文： Lonely, on this Pure Brightness Day;
Dreary, in my house, you and me.

赏析： 原诗首联中"寂寞"对"萧条"，"清明日"对"司马家"，是偏正结构名词形式，

用了通感的修辞。译文中用了句子，增译了主语 you and me，同时因为诗人当时是江州司马，所以减译了名词“司马”，用 my house 表示“司马家”。在译文的句子中 Pure Brightness Day 作时间状语，my house 作地点状语，同时把 lonely 和 dreary 提前到句首，把转移修饰“清明日”和“司马家”的寂寞和萧条恢复到修饰 you and me 上来，强调了当时诗人贫迫的境地。

2. 留饧和冷粥，出火煮新茶。

译文： Dough left prepared and porridge cold,

I make fire to cook some new tea.

赏析： 原诗中用的是偏正结构的“留饧”和“冷粥”，译者使用了形容词后置的方法，将 left prepared 和 cold 放于 dough 和 porridge 的后面，强调了家里当时的食物情况。其中 prepared 也是根据意思增译，以表现译文中的意思完整性。原文中的“出火煮新茶”里并没有主语，译文中根据英语句子的特征增译了 I，根据搭配将“出火”译成 make fire。这两句原文文字简单、意思明确，译文用词也直接，意思明确。

3. 南迁更何处？此地已天涯。

译文： Are you exiled more south than here?

This place is almost the world’s end.

赏析： 尾联中“南迁”前并没提及主语，译文中添加了 you，此增译除了意思对应之外，也是为了符合英语句式的要求。其中“南”字灵活地在“更何处”中被翻译出来，译成 more south than here。因为南方是贬谪之地，所以后面用“此地已天涯”来表达作者对有着相同贬谪命运，同是天涯沦落人的慨叹。原文中用的是“已”，译文中灵活处理为 almost，意思确切，对诗人想要抒发的情感也表现得很强烈。这两句原诗语言比较简单，译文也用词简单，贴合原诗风格。

第三节　王夫子

一、诗歌背景

元和十三年(818 年)，诗人白居易在江州作《王夫子》送别友人。此诗一来是为了安慰朋友“委身下位无为耻”，二来表现了诗人对入仕的态度和对功名利禄的看淡，“吾观九品至一品，其间气味都相似”。古代官员之间的品秩界限非常严格，唐朝官员品级的一个明显区别就是官服的颜色。唐朝规定，三品以上的官员和亲王的官袍是紫色，五品以上是朱色，所以“大红大紫”可以表示声名显赫之意。诗人白居易在诗中咏及品服，是从担任江州司马开始的，如《琵琶行》中的“江州司马青衫湿”。该诗中的“紫绶朱绂青布衫，颜色不同而已矣”两句，不仅被后人用来研究诗人白居易对为官的态度，而且经常用来作为研究唐代俸服的资料。

二、古诗原文

王夫子

王夫子，
送君为一尉，东南三千五百里。
道途虽远位虽卑，月俸犹堪活妻子。
男儿口读古人书，束带敛手来从事。
近将徇禄给一家，远则行道佐时理。
行道佐时须待命，委身下位无为耻。
命苟未来且求食，官无高卑及远迩。
男儿上既未能济天下，下又不至饥寒死。
吾观九品至一品，其间气味都相似。
紫绶朱绂青布衫，颜色不同而已矣。
王夫子，
别有一事欲劝君，遇酒逢春且欢喜。

三、古诗译文

Reverend[1] Wang

Reverend Wang,
Good-bye, now a sheriff[2] you are,
You’ll go southeast, a thousand miles afar!

Your journey's far though you are low and plain;
With your pay[3], your wife and kids you sustain.
A young man should read the saints' books of yore[4];
A belt worn, hands drawn, he does less or more.
Near, he gives his family all his pay;
Far, he obeys the Word and aids the way.
For the Word or the way, he needs a tide;
He'd feel no shame if he does there abide.
No chance on the way, he'd pleased with his cheer;
Caring not what's high or low, far or near.
If a man could not help all those under the sky;
He himself may not starve or may not die.
I can see whether grade nine or grade one[5];
All the same they do, all the same they run.
Red ribbons, purple sash[6] or linen[7] blue,
They just have different colors, Isn't it true?
Reverend Wang,
I have one word for you to boost you up:
When having wine or glee[8], just drink your cup.

（赵彦春　译）

◎ 注释

1. Reverend: refer to scholars or teachers worthy of adoration or reverence. 夫子
2. sheriff: the principal law-enforcement officer in a county. 尉
3. pay: money got for services. 俸、禄
4. yore: (old use or literary) time long past, long ago. 古
5. grade one: the highest rank official position in ancient China. The rank of ancient officials began in the Wei and Jin Dynasties and there are nine grades from one to nine. 一品
6. ribbons, sash: The original meaning refers to ancient silk used to tie things such as jade ornaments and official seals. 绶、绂
7. linen: a fabric woven with fibers from the flax plant. 布

8. glee：great merriment，a feeling of happiness and excitement. 欢喜

四、译文赏析

1. 道途虽远位虽卑，月俸犹堪活妻子。

译文：Your journey's far though you are low and plain;

With your pay，your wife and kids you sustain.

赏析：首先，译文用了增译的手法，添加了主语 you，符合译文行文规范，同时读者也能理解这首诗是诗人对王夫子说的。原文中"位卑"是指职位、地位卑微，所以增译了 plain，用 low and plain 来译，一方面是 low 还不能完全与"卑"对等，另一方面是 plain 可以跟下一行的 sustain 押尾韵。原文中有两个"虽"，译文中用了一个 though，包含了对"途远位卑"的让步，但 though 并未放在句首，而是放于中间，前有 Your journey's far，后有 you are low and plain，这是对句子结构的考量而做的微调。因为句中已有 low and plain，如把 Your journey's far 放后面的话，会导致后半句臃肿，所以 Your journey's far 置于句首，跟原句结构相同。原句中"活妻子"是指月俸能养一家，"妻"指妻子，"子"指孩子。所以译文中用了 your wife and kids you sustain，动词 sustain 后置形成倒装与 plain 押尾韵，同时用 sustain 表示供养、抚养之意，是对"活"更具体化的翻译手法。

2. 男儿口读古人书，束带敛手来从事。
近将徇禄给一家，远则行道佐时理。
行道佐时须待命，委身下位无为耻。
命苟未来且求食，官无高卑及远迩。

译文：A young man should read the saints' books of yore;

A belt worn，hands drawn，he does less or more.

Near，he gives his family all his pay;

Far，he obeys the Word and aids the way.

For the Word or the way，he needs a tide;

He'd feel no shame if he does there abide.

No chance on the way，he'd pleased with his cheer;

Caring not what's high or low，far or near.

赏析：在这几行诗句中，诗人开始表达他对入仕的观点。男儿小时候要读圣贤书，长大入仕；推行自己的政治主张或辅佐当世之君须待时机，官级品位高低、离长安远近也没关系。所以虽然是送友人时写给对方的，但译文中还是用了 a young man 和 he 来代替任意人，目的是为了宽慰对方。用 saints' books of yore 来译"古人书"，译出了圣贤书之意，属于增译，也是具体化的手法。原句中"束带敛手"是动宾结构，表示整饰衣冠，端庄不敢妄动的样子，译文中用了 A belt worn, hands drawn，用过去分词来表示这种"从事"的状态。原文中的"从事"也是比较抽象的说法，用 does less or more 来译，是意译，同时 more 和 yore 押尾韵。原文中"行道佐时理"，译文中 用 obeys the Word 和 aids the way 来对应，一方面译文中本身结构比较对等，way 和 pay 押尾韵，另一方面，the Word 是圣言的意思，这里用这一具有文化内涵的词来对应抽象的"道"，灵活而巧妙，是"归化"的译法。同理，用 needs a tide 来译"须待命"，英文里 time and tide 表时间，这里用 tide 非常巧妙地表示出"时"的意思，是对"待命"更具体化的译法，同时 tide 和后面的 abide 押尾韵。意译还体现在用 does there abide，原句中是"委身下位"，译文用了更抽象化的手法来表示位低。原文中"官无高卑及远迩"中的"无"，译文中意译为 caring not，根据句意增译了"没关系"的意思，是诗人对友人进行劝慰。

3. **男儿上既未能济天下，下又不至饥寒死。**

译文：If a man could not help all those under the sky,

He himself may not starve or may not die.

赏析：译文中用了意译的手法，用 help all those under the sky 来译"济天下"。"天下"指所有人，但字面意思 under the sky 无法表达这层内涵，所以增补了 all those，这也算是"异化"的翻译法。原文中有"饥寒死"，因为中文中"饥寒"常在一起使用，译文中用 starve or die，使用了省译的手法。原句是用"上未能"和"下不至"的平行结构，译文中用了主从句的结构，在结构上进行了调整，属转译。

4. **吾观九品至一品，其间气味都相似。**

紫绶朱绂青布衫，颜色不同而已矣。

译文：I can see whether grade nine or grade one;

All the same they do, all the same they run.

Red ribbons, purple sash or linen blue,

They just have different colors, isn’t it true?

赏析：原文中用了“气味相似”来表明无论九品还是一品，都是差不多的景况和情形。译文中用了 All the same they do, all the same they run，是把意思具象化的手法，同时用了重复，表强调，但把 do 换成了 run，使得 run 与 one 押尾韵。文中“颜色不同而已矣”是陈述语气，译文中增译了 isn’t it true 的反问句，true 与 blue 押尾韵。

第四部分　贬谪诗

第十章 壮志难酬

第一节 题四皓庙

一、诗歌背景

四皓指的是商山四皓。秦朝末年，四位博士因不满秦始皇统治而隐居于商山，后来就用“商山四皓”泛指有名望的隐士。《题四皓庙》是诗人白居易被贬谪江州途中经过商州时游四皓驿时所写。诗人当时一路向东南，经北川驿、安山驿、麻涧、仙娥驿，至商州上洛县(今商县)。诗歌第一句中的“安刘”是四皓的代称，是他们让刘邦下定决心不废太子刘盈；第二句中提到了他们功成身退、名利与自由兼得的结局，这里诗人表示了羡慕；第三句和第四句，诗人联系自身处境，借精灵之口表达自己对未功成名就却被迫“归隐”的不甘与自嘲。这首诗虽然表达了诗人对归隐、对自由的向往，但此时的他并没有放弃政治，并为自己未作出一番事业而感到惋惜。

二、古诗原文

题四皓庙

卧逃秦乱起安刘，
舒卷如云得自由。
若有精灵应笑我，

不成一事谪江州。

三、古诗译文

A Dedication to Four Gray Pates Temple[1]

They hid there to flee Ch'in[2] and settle Liu[3];
Like clouds rolling, spreading, they were so free.
I'm exiled[4] to River Town[5], nothing done;
If there were spirits[6], they would laugh at me.

（赵彦春 译）

◎ 注释

1. Four Gray Pates Temple：There were four senior scholars hidden in Shangluo Mountain during the Qin and Han Dynasties. The temple is located in Shangluo Mountain, Shang County. 四皓庙
2. Ch'in：the name of a Chinese dynasty. 秦
3. Liu：the surname of the king of the Han Dynasty. 刘
4. exiled：expelled from home or country by authority. 谪
5. River Town：today's Jiujiang City, Jiangxi Province. 江州
6. spirits：supernatural beings that can become visible（or audible）to human beings. 精灵

四、译文赏析

1. 题四皓庙

译文： A Dedication to Four Gray Pates Temple

赏析："题"的意思是题写、书写。指就一事一物抒发感受，题写诗句于柱壁、书画、器皿等之上。英文中 dedication 用来指书、音乐或作品前部的献词，所以这里根据意思和英语文学中的习惯意译。题中"四皓"是指"商山四皓"，指秦末汉初的四位博士，他们蛰居商山，年龄都有八十多岁，须眉皓白，衣冠甚伟。如果直译会使诗句僵直且过长，不符合诗歌抽象凝练的特征。英文 pate 在古英语和口语中有"头"或"脑袋"之意，加之前面用

来指花白头发的形容词 gray，在意思和形象上正好可以匹配，如此巧译可见译者中英双语的功底深厚。

2. 卧逃秦乱起安刘，舒卷如云得自由。

译文： They hid there to flee Ch'in and settle Liu;

Like clouds rolling, spreading, they were so free.

赏析： 原句中没有主语，但从诗歌题目读者可以知晓，是"商山四皓"逃秦乱、起安刘、舒卷且得自由。但根据英语句式要求需要有发出动作的主语，所以译文中增译了 they，指题目中的 four gray pates。原句中"逃"对应"安"，译文中用 flee 和 settle 来对应，从意思、词性和结构上都能对应。原句中的"卧"译成了 hid，能形象地展现当时四位高人不满焚书坑儒、为躲避战乱而隐居商山的情景。原句中是说他们"舒卷如云得自由"，"舒卷"用作动词，译文中用转译法，将 like clouds rolling, spreading 作状语来修饰 they were so free，达到逻辑正确、通顺流畅，并突出"自由"的目的。

3. 若有精灵应笑我，不成一事谪江州。

译文： I'm exiled to River Town, nothing done;

If there were spirits, they would laugh at me.

赏析： 这部分两句采用了倒译的手法。原句中是"精灵应笑我"，因我"不成一事谪江州"，译文中先说被"谪江州"，然后再用 if 条件句"若有精灵应笑我"。这是复合句完全倒译，因为英汉词组组成和排列的顺序不同，也是为了最后一句末尾的 me 和第二句末尾的 free 押尾韵，在韵律安排上与原诗结构一致。在"不成一事谪江州"的翻译中也采用了倒译的手法，把 nothing done 放在了后面作状语，属句内成分的转译，目的是为了使逻辑更清楚、意思更清晰。白居易的诗具有"老妪能解"的特征，这两句也不例外，译文对此除了倒译之外，用词明白晓畅，特征上也能契合。

第二节　端居咏怀

一、诗歌背景

该诗写于元和十一年(816 年)诗人任江州司马之时。端居，即闲居。诗的首联和颔联用典：贾谊曾作《鵩鸟赋》，借与鵩鸟问答以抒发忧愤不平的情绪；张翰见秋风起想念吴中菰菜、莼羹、鲈鱼脍，遂辞官归隐。诗人细写贾、张二人之事并做了对比，一个“悔”字表明自己不如张翰及早归隐，最终落得像贾谊一样的贬官下场，阐发了作者的归隐之意。颈联写诗人曾怀匡时之策，有谏君之章，欲建功立业，但实际却是待罪闲居之身。“谏猎书”指汉天子迷恋游猎，司马相如劝谏狩猎的奏章。诗人在尾联笔锋一转，写自己从此之后只想放下一切因缘际会，和家人一起归隐山中，照应了前文的“悔”字。“万缘”指一切因缘，“买山居”意指退隐。

二、古诗原文

端居咏怀

贾生俟罪心相似，
张翰思归事不如。
斜日早知惊鵩鸟，
秋风悔不忆鲈鱼。
胸襟曾贮匡时策，
怀袖犹残谏猎书。
从此万缘都摆落，
欲携妻子买山居。

三、古诗译文

Singing of My Feelings When Living Free[1]

Much like Ee Chia[2] I'm exiled to the wild;
Unlike Han Chang[3] retired, I rue now.
An owl[4] surprised was seen at eve in vain;
The perch[5] I failed to have in a fall sough!
Once I did have a great time-saving plan;
Inside my sleeve a remonstrance[6] was hid.
From now all efforts would be given up;

I'd buy a mountain cot with wife and kid.

（赵彦春　译）

◎ 注释

1. living free：lead a free life；able to act at will. 端居
2. Ee Chia：（200 B. C. -168 B. C. ）born in Luoyang（now Luoyang City，Henan Province）；a famous political commentator and litterateur in the early Western Han Dynasty. 贾生
3. Han Chang：a native of Wu County in the Western Jin Dynasty who abandoned his official post in Luoyang and returned home on the pretext of wanting to eat famous dishes from his hometown. 张翰
4. owl：nocturnal bird of prey with hawk-like beak and claws and large head with front-facing eyes. 鹏鸟
5. perch：a freshwater fish that is sometimes used for food. 鲈鱼
6. remonstrance：memorial to the throne to express earnest opposition or protest. 谏猎书

四、译文赏析

1. 贾生俟罪心相似，张翰思归事不如。

译文： Much like Ee Chia I'm exiled to the wild；
Unlike Han Chang retired，I rue now.

赏析： 该诗首联用了典故，前句写贾谊在《吊屈原赋》中自述在长沙待罪的经历，后句写张翰看清形势，寻找借口成功归隐。原句中用了"心相似"和"事不如"，译文中虽然用了 much like 和 unlike，但这两个词并不能真正挑明，对于看译文来获取信息的读者而言，信息是不够明确的。所以译者用 I'm exiled to the wild 来表明自己目前的闲居处境；用 Han Chang retired，I rue now 含蓄地表达了自己的归隐之志，这是用实说对应暗语。译文中根据英语行文习惯，也增补了主语 I。

2. 斜日早知惊鹏鸟，秋风悔不忆鲈鱼。

译文： An owl surprised was seen at eve in vain，
The perch I failed to have in a fall sough!

赏析： 颔联中诗人续用典故，"鹏鸟"和"鲈鱼"两个意象分别对应了首联的前后句，

开始反思，一个“悔”字表明诗人早知有凶险但没能及时脱身，所以译文中用 in vain 和 failed to 来增补原文中暗含的意思。前一句中使用了被动语态来转译，后一句中增补主语 I，这都是英语行文的需要。

3. 胸襟曾贮匡时策，怀袖犹残谏猎书。

译文： Once I did have a great time-saving plan;

Inside my sleeve a remonstrance was hid.

赏析： 颈联借写贾谊对君主的劝谏，表明想要劝谏君王不要沉迷于射猎娱乐，要勤于国事的忠君爱国之心。原文中的“曾”用 did 来强调，目的是说明诗人自己像贾谊那般胸怀远志，怀有报国匡时之策。“胸襟”是指诗人“我”，用了提喻的手法，译文中直接用了 I 来体现，符合英文的行文习惯。后面一句用被动语态来译，用了转译的手法，hid 后置，与尾联中的最后一个词 kid 押尾韵。

第三节　江南谪居十韵

一、诗歌背景

元和十年(815 年)，宰相武元衡当街遇刺身亡，白居易上表朝廷要求缉拿凶手，却反被陷害，以无中生有之罪被贬江州司马。此时诗人感到委屈、愤怒、无奈。在经历了忠而被贬的不甘以及贬途的身心磨损后，诗人写下了这首《江南谪居十韵》。诗人很渴望建功立业，但横遭贬谪的经历使他感到自己虚度光阴，无法一展抱负，“壮心徒许国”，充满了无奈和不甘。此外，诗人在诗中感叹世事无常，勉励自己将祸福、贫富、生死看淡，“行藏与通塞，一切任陶钧”。白居易的诗一向通俗易懂又注重写实，“老妪能解，妇孺皆知”，简单却深刻，如“忧方知酒圣，贫始觉钱神。虎尾难容足，羊肠易覆轮”。

二、古诗原文

江南谪居十韵

自哂沉冥客，

曾为献纳臣。
壮心徒许国，
薄命不如人。
才展凌云翅，
俄成失水鳞。
葵枯犹向日，
蓬断即辞春。
泽畔长愁地，
天边欲老身。
萧条残活计，
冷落旧交亲。
草合门无径，
烟消甑有尘。
忧方知酒圣，
贫始觉钱神。
虎尾难容足，
羊肠易覆轮。
行藏与通塞，
一切任陶钧。

三、古诗译文

Living in Exile in the South, Twenty Lines

I'm sunken, at myself I sneer,
As I was a remonstrant[1] then.
Devoted to the land[2] in vain,
In fate I can't match other men.
No sooner had I spread my wings

Than I turned a fish, water lost.
Sunflowers[3] dried still face the sun;
Catkins leave spring once by wind tossed.
I often feel so sad ashore[4]
And will age fast at the world's end.
So lonely, I live a hard life;
Apart from drear ones, kin or friend.
Grass sprawls to cover all my path;
No cooking, the pot's[5] full of dust.
Sad, I understand a wine sage;
Poor, for Money God I do lust.
A tiger's tail won't bear your step
A small trail[6] causes wheels to slide.
Gain or loss, or else, rise or fall
Depends on God[7] who does preside.

（赵彦春　译）

◎ 注释

1. remonstrant: one of the official positions in ancient China and his duty was to directly exhort and correct the faults of the monarch. 献纳臣
2. land: a politically organized body of people under a single government; the territory occupied by a nation; the people who live in a nation or country. 国
3. sunflowers: any plant of the genus Helianthus having large flower heads with dark disk florets and showy yellow rays. 葵
4. ashore: towards the shore from the water. 泽畔
5. pot: a metal or earthenware cooking vessel that is usually round and deep. 甑
6. a small trail: a narrow and winding path that is difficult to walk. 羊肠
7. God: a man of such superior qualities that he seems like a deity to other people. 陶钧

四、译文赏析

1. 壮心徒许国，薄命不如人。

译文：Devoted to the land in vain,

In fate I can’t match other men.

赏析：原文这两句是并列关系，关键词是“壮心”和“薄命”，译文中把“薄命”这部分设为一个主句，“壮心”这部分设为状态，强调之前一直都是“济天下”，这是结构上的转译，使得句子间各部分的关系更清晰。原文中用“薄命”和“不如人”来强调命运凄惨，在中文中“薄命”是惯用搭配，译文中省译了“薄”，因为用 can’t match other men 可以满足这层意思，同时后置到句子末尾，使 men 和诗歌第二行的 then 押尾韵。此外，译文中增译了主语 I，这是英语行文的需求。

2. 才展凌云翅，俄成失水鳞。

译文：No sooner had I spread my wings

Than I turned a fish, water lost.

赏析：原文诗句中有“凌云翅”，形容志向宏伟远大、高入云霄。“凌云”两字是有文化内涵的，但是在英文中直译并不能达成这个效果，所以译文直接译成了 wings，这是“归化”的译法。同样对文中的“鳞”也是这样的处理方法，“鳞”指鱼类，所以译文中直接就用了 fish 来体现。

3. 泽畔长愁地，天边欲老身。

译文：I often feel so sad ashore,

And will age fast at the world’s end.

赏析：中文诗歌强调“言约旨远”，所以经常不见动词，如原文中“泽畔”“长愁地”“天边”“欲老身”。这些名词展现的意象展示出言尽意无穷的效果。从结构上看，是偏正结构，强调的是“长愁地”和“欲老身”。译文中根据译文的行文规则，对结构进行了转译，增译主语 I，使用与之搭配的动词 feel 和 age。“泽畔”出自《楚辞・渔父》：“屈原既放，游于江潭，行吟泽畔”，所以经常把谪官失意时所写的作品称为“泽畔吟”，但译文中很难直接对等成有这层文化内涵的对应词，所以处理成字面意思 ashore。同理可见对“天边”的处理方式。

4. 虎尾难容足，羊肠易覆轮。

译文： A tiger's tail won't bear your step

A small trail causes wheels to slide.

赏析：“虎尾”比喻危险的境地，因 tiger 在英文中本身就有凶猛之意，所以译文中按字面意思翻译为 a tiger's tail。“羊肠”意指狭窄曲折的小路，运用了比喻的修辞，译文中用 a small trail 来具象化地表达，使得意思清晰明了，同时使 tail 和 trail 达成音乐上的美感。

5. 行藏与通塞，一切任陶钧。

译文： Gain or loss, or else, rise or fall

Depends on God who does preside.

赏析：“行藏”出自《论语 · 述而》：“子谓颜渊曰：‘用之则行，舍之则藏，惟我与尔有是夫。’”意指被任用就行其道，不被任用就退隐。“通塞”出自《易 · 节》：“不出户庭，知通塞也。”意指境遇之顺逆。对于这类重隐含义的词汇，译文进行了意译，用 Gain or loss, or else, rise or fall 来涵盖诗人想要表达的得失、起落和沉浮。此外，原文中用的是“与”，但“行藏”和“通塞”其实在诗中是表示相反的两种境遇，所以在译文中用了 or else，因为 gain or loss 和 rise or fall 也是两种相反的境遇。“陶钧”原指制作陶器所用的转轮，这里指圣王，所以译文中用了 God，这符合英语文化内涵，符合目标语读者需求，用了“归化”的翻译方法。

第十一章　世事难料

第一节　闻庾七左降因咏所怀

一、诗歌背景

白居易丁忧三年，遭遇丧母失女之痛以及鹏程被阻的煎熬，当时惟宽禅师主张的“平常心是道”思想对白居易的思想起到重要的调和作用。“平常心是道”强调的是内心毫无牵绊的超脱自由，不痴恋功名利禄，不受困于逆境挫折，得与不得一切随缘。这在白居易鹏程受阻、翅膀摧折之际对其达观平和的人生观形成有重要的启迪作用。在退居下邽后，白居易与友人们的书信往来非常不便，但他们之间的诗歌唱和、文章寄赠从未断绝过。元和七年，庾玄师被贬巴东，白居易写信给对方，勉励他胸怀豁达。如其在《闻庾七左降因咏所怀》诗中强调：“人生天地之间，如鸿毛飞絮，有时可能扶摇直上，有时也可能坠落尘埃。青云直上不一定是命运通畅；一身布衣也不一定是穷途末路。外物不需要过度执著，心中却需要达成虚空自在。”

二、古诗原文

闻庾七左降因咏所怀

我病卧渭北，
君老谪巴东。

相悲一长叹，
薄命与君同。
既叹还自哂，
哂叹两未终。
后心诮前意，
所见何迷蒙。
人生大块间，
如鸿毛在风。
或飘青云上，
或落泥涂中。
衮服相天下，
倘来非我通。
布衣委草莽，
偶去非吾穷。
外物不可必，
中怀须自空。
无令快快气，
留滞在心胸。

三、古诗译文

Chanting What I Feel When Hearing Yu Seven Demoted[1]

I'm bed ridden north of the Wei[2];
You're exiled so far to East Pa[3].
Each to each, we heave a long sigh;
We are the same, the same we are.
We both sigh and sneer at ourselves;
Neither of us have a good end.
We may blame what we willed before;

What we see does in haze suspend.
A life between Heaven and earth
May be like a feather blown higher.
Or it may fly above the clouds[4],
Or it may fall down to the mire.
Those ministers before the crown
Are not our mates, sharing our tour.
We're cloth gowns that to grass retire;
We retire, not because we're poor.
Outer things we should not desire,
But we need a vacant calm chest.
Don't let the sullenness[5] stay please,
From our bosom it'd be expressed.

(赵彦春　译)

◎ **注释**

1. demoted: be moved to a lower position or rank, often as a punishment. 左降
2. north of the Wei: The name has a long history, and the regions it refers to vary from time to time. In a broad sense, it refers to the north of the Weishui River, the largest tributary of the Yellow River. 渭北
3. East Pa: In today's Zigui County, Hubei Province. In the Tang Dynasty, it was established as Guizhou and later renamed "Badong County". 巴东
4. clouds: out of touch with reality. 青云
5. sullenness: a gloomy ill-tempered feeling. 怏怏气

四、译文赏析

1. **既叹还自哂，哂叹两未终。**
后心诮前意，所见何迷蒙。

译文： We both sigh and sneer at ourselves;

Neither of us have a good end.

We may blame what we willed before;

What we see does in haze suspend.

赏析：因前面已出现过“我”和“君”，这两联中的动作可理解为是“我们”发出的，所以译文中增译了 we 和 us，这是为了符合英文行文习惯。用 sign 和 sneer 来译“叹”和“哂”，不仅意思对应，还用了押头韵的修辞，赋予了诗歌音乐美和整齐感。“哂叹两未终”中省译了“哂”和“叹”，因为前句中意思已经可以说明，同时用 neither 来否定，对应原句中的“未”，属于对否定词的转译。原句中“后心”对“前意”，译文中转换了结构，联合后面一句中的“所见”，译成 what we willed 和 what we see 达成结构上的平衡，其中用 willed 在时态上达成“前”的意思；用 does 来译原文中“何”所体现的“迷蒙”感，同时把 suspend 后置至句尾，与第六行的 end 押尾韵/end/。

2. 人生大块间，如鸿毛在风。
   或飘青云上，或落泥涂中。

译文：A life between Heaven and earth;

May be like a feather blown higher.

Or it may fly above the clouds,

Or it may fall down to the mire.

赏析：原诗中用了比喻“如鸿毛在风”，译文中也对应地用了比喻 a feather，同时用动感的 blown higher 来说明原文中“在风”的状态，并且和后面的 mire 押尾韵/aɪə(r)/。原文中“飘”对应“落”，“青云上”对应“泥涂中”，译文中用 fly 对应 fall，above the clouds 对应 down to the mire，结构和意思上完美契合。

3. 衮服相天下，倘来非我通。
   布衣委草莽，偶去非吾穷。

译文：Those ministers before the crown

Are not our mates, sharing our tour.

We're cloth gowns that to grass retire;

We retire, not because we're poor.

赏析：原文中“衮服”是指中国古代汉人朝代皇帝及上公的礼服，译文中直接用 ministers 来具体化为“王公们”；原句中是“倘来非我通”，译文中拆句成 Are not our mates, sharing our tour，用重复的手法来说明“非我通”。原句中是“委草莽”，译文中用 retire to grass，一方面顾及了“草莽”的字面翻译，另一方面又凸显了人置身于草野，过着隐居山林生活的意思。原句中的“偶去”是接着“委草莽”说的，所以译文中继续用 retire，再拆句翻译，把 poor 放在最后，与 tour 押尾韵/ʊə(r)/。

第二节　谪　居

一、诗歌背景

诗人白居易在被贬谪江州期间共创作了 288 首诗歌，这些诗歌大致可以分为讽喻诗、闲适诗、感伤诗和杂律诗四类。其中大量诗歌反映了诗人被贬期间的境遇，主要抒写诗人怀才不遇、壮志难酬的情怀，如《谪居》这首诗。元和十年(815 年)秋，白居易来到江州。面对贬谪，诗人感到困惑又苦闷，于是写下了这首谪居诗。在诗中，诗人把自己描绘成一位未老先衰、头发斑白但仍苦苦思考自己命运与际遇的人，又描写了山松被山火烧为灰烬、繁茂的花草经寒霜而凋零的景象。面对从荣华到衰落的剧变，诗人忍不住感慨，自己的衰落是一种天意，由此可以看出他内心的无奈。这首诗抒情真切，反映了诗人被贬江州、远离政治中心的现实处境，字里行间渗透了他悲苦的心绪。

二、古诗原文

谪　居

面瘦头斑四十四，
远谪江州为郡吏。
逢时弃置从不才，
未老衰羸为何事。
火烧寒涧松为烬，
霜降春林花委地。
遭时荣悴一时间，
岂是昭昭上天意。

三、古诗译文

Living in Exile

I'm forty-four, face haggard and hair white,
Exiled to be a clerk[1] in River Town[2].
In such golden days I have been deposed;
Though not so old, I'm failing, badly down!
Burned by fire, pines in the cold dale[3] turn ash[4];
Frost on the spring woods, flowers fall aground.
Does Heaven mean that? Is it Heaven's will[5]
That one's glory or decadence is bound?

（赵彦春　译）

◎ 注释

1. clerk: an employee who performs clerical work (e. g. , keeps records or accounts); a civil servant who handles documents in a local government. 吏
2. River Town: today's Jiujiang City, Jiangxi Province. 江州
3. dale: an open river valley (in a hilly area). 涧
4. ash: the residue that remains when something is burned. 烬
5. Heaven's will: will of Heaven; God's will; emperor's intention. 上天意

四、译文赏析

1. 面瘦头斑四十四，远谪江州为郡吏。

译文： I'm forty-four, face haggard and hair white,
Exiled to be a clerk in River Town.

赏析： 省略动词是中国古诗创作中的一个特点，目的是为了追求语少意足、凝练含蓄的效果，但翻译成英文时需要补足，所以原句中"面瘦头斑四十四"在译文中增译了 I'm。

用 face haggard 和 hair white 来译“面瘦头斑”，是使“瘦”和“头斑”更为具体化的翻译方法，同时把短语放在逗号后作为状态，而不是与“四十四”并列，这里用到了拆句和转译的策略。

2. 逢时弃置从不才，未老衰羸为何事。

译文： In such golden days I have been deposed;

Though not so old, I'm failing, badly down!

赏析： 原句中有“从不才”和“为何事”，但其实诗中更多地是想要表达“逢时弃置”和“未老衰羸”，所以译文中采取了省译的手法，主要强调了 have been deposed in such golden days 和 not so old 但是 badly down。第二句中用了拆句的手法，用逗号和 I'm failing 隔开 not so old 和 badly down，对句子结构进行了重构，变成了一个复杂句，并把 badly down 后置至句尾，down 与第二行的 Town 押尾韵。

3. 火烧寒涧松为烬，霜降春林花委地。

译文： Burned by fire, pines in the cold dale turn ash;

Frost on the spring woods, flowers fall aground.

赏析： 原诗中“火”对“霜”，“烧寒涧”对“降春林”，“松为烬”对“花委地”，译文中 burned 对 frost，in the cold dale 对 on the spring woods，pines 对 flowers，turn ash 对 fall aground，意思上和结构上都能与原文完美对应。原文中主语不止一个，译文选取“松”和“花”为主语，同时拆分句子，把“火烧”和“霜降”翻译为前置原因，采用拆句和转译的策略，这是为了符合英语的行文习惯。

4. 遭时荣悴一时间，岂是昭昭上天意。

译文： Does Heaven mean that? Is it Heaven's will

That one's glory or decadence is bound?

赏析： 原文中用了叠词“昭昭”，译文中用了 Heaven mean that 和 Heaven's will，用重复的手法以及强调句 Is it... that... 的句型来表达诗人的质问。对“遭时荣悴一时间”的翻译进行了灵活处理：对“遭时”和“一时间”进行了省译，同时把“荣悴”和“上天意”结合在一起翻译，将两句结构灵活调整，目的是为了使诗歌的意思表达得更确切。bound 与前面的 aground 押尾韵/aʊnd/。

第三节　彭蠡湖晚归

一、诗歌背景

彭蠡湖即今鄱阳湖，在古代有过彭蠡湖、彭蠡泽、彭泽、彭湖、扬澜、宫亭湖等多种称谓。该诗前半部分写景：首联写天色已晚，但因一"湖"字，感觉水天茫茫、境界阔大，桃花后加一"春"字，指水边的桃花让人感觉出一丝春意，这是静景。颔联写远望天边飞鸟，唯见一片白点泛动，这是远景，对应近景的落日——"半红轮"。飞鸟的白点小，对应眼前落下的"红轮"的大；飞鸟续写前句中的"春"，落日续写前句中的"晚"。两联动静结合，勾画出一幅日暮春景图。诗歌后半部分抒情：颈联诗人反问并自嘲，不必身为迁客，也不必身多疾病，接续尾联中的"愁"字，幽怨之情溢于言表。诗人对美景生悲叹，其感慨更加深沉。

二、古诗原文

彭蠡湖晚归

彭蠡湖天晚，
桃花水气春。
鸟飞千白点，
日没半红轮。
何必为迁客，
无劳是病身。
但来临此望，
少有不愁人。

三、古诗译文

Coming Back Late from P'oshine Lake[1]

Dusk[2] will fall to veil Posh'ine Lake;

Peach petals[3] on spring water run.
White, fly myriad specks[4] of the birds;
Red, sinks half the disc[5] of the sun.
Why should I have been exiled here?
No merits, but a body ill.
I've come here to have a long gaze;
Nostalgia may a wanderer kill.

(赵彦春　译)

◎ 注释

1. P'oshine Lake: today's Poyang Lake. In history, scholars have left many poems that sing about the lake. 彭蠡湖
2. dusk: the time of day when the light has almost gone, but it is not yet dark. 晚
3. petals: part of the perianth that is usually brightly colored. 花
4. specks: very small spots. 点
5. disc: something with a round shape resembling a flat circular plate. 轮

四、译文赏析

1. 彭蠡湖天晚，桃花水气春。

译文：Dusk will fall to veil Posh'ine Lake;
Peach petals on spring water run.

赏析：原诗为"湖天晚"和"水气春"，是意象，没有动词。译文中用了主谓结构，符合英语的行文习惯，用了动词 fall to veil 表现出夜幕快要降临的覆盖感，用 run on 表现了水气的动感，春意通过桃花在浩浩湖边昂然而出。动词 run 后置到句末，与第四行的 sun 押尾韵/ʌn/。

2. 鸟飞千白点，日没半红轮。

译文：White, fly myriad specks of the birds;
Red, sinks half the disc of the sun.

赏析：原诗中"鸟飞"对"日没"，"千"对"半"，"白点"对"红轮"，译文中 white 对

red，fly 对 sinks，myriad specks of the birds 对 half the disc of the sun，属于意思和结构上的完全对应，说明译者英语语言的功底深厚。原诗中的“千”是个概数，意指多，用 myriad 来译，比直译成 thousands 更具诗意。原诗中“白”和“红”是用作“鸟”和“日”的修饰，在译文中前置于句首，表状态，更具画面感。

3. 但来临此望，少有不愁人。

译文： I've come here to have a long gaze;

Nostalgia may a wanderer kill.

赏析： 原诗中用“但”和“少有”表示“都会愁”，译文中直接用了肯定句转译。用 gaze 来翻译“望”，更能表现诗人当时的心境，结合最后一行中的 kill，反映出诗人借景抒情之意。kill 后置至句子末尾，句子倒装，是为了与前面的 ill 押尾韵/ɪl/。

第十二章　与世相忘

第一节　宿西林寺，早赴东林满上人之会因寄崔二十二员外

一、诗歌背景

庐山有西林寺、东林寺、大林寺三寺。其中六朝古刹西林寺位于江西九江市濂溪区赛阳镇西林村，在东林寺之西500米处，迄今已有1700余年历史，号称“庐山北山第一寺”。“江州之贬”对白居易而言是一次巨大的人生转折，既让他重新开始对社会险恶的思考，又坚定了他“穷则独善其身，达则兼济天下”的人生格言。于是，他开始进出于庐山东林寺、西林寺等佛教寺庙，强化自己的佛教理念，并对佛教“普世关怀精神”尤为推崇。他开始“吏隐”，在庐山香炉峰北建草堂，在东林寺藏经楼读慧远大师文集，并与当地的僧人交游，学习佛法。无论是在官舍内建水池，还是在庐山草堂前建白家池，都被诗人赋予了浓厚的佛教生活色彩，尤其是能与深刻的生命伦理思考、人生际遇相结合。崔二十二指崔韶，唐朝台州刺史。

二、古诗原文

宿西林寺，早赴东林满上人之会因寄崔二十二员外

谪辞魏阙鹓鸾隔，

老入庐山麋鹿随。

薄暮萧条投寺宿，
凌晨清净与僧期。
双林我起闻钟后，
只日君趋入阁时。
鹏鹦高低分皆定，
莫劳心力远相思。

三、古诗译文

Putting Up for the Night in West Wood Temple[1], and Starting Early for Monk[2] Man's Meeting at East Wood Temple[3], Hence Sent to Stand-by[4] Ts'ui Twenty-two

Exiled, I'm away from the caps and crowns;
And old, on Mt. Lodge I join elks and deer.
Mid eve mist, at the temple I will lodge,
And attend the monks' meeting at dawn clear.
I get up at the bell tolled from Fair Wood;
On odd-numbered days, you come to the court.
Rocs[5] and wrens[6] are so ranked as high or low;
I should not work with my brains, lost in thought.

（赵彦春　译）

◎ 注释

1. West Wood Temple: located at the north foot of Lushan Mountain in Jiujiang City, Jiangxi Province; built in the second year of Taihe in the Eastern Jin Dynasty (367A. D.). 西林寺
2. Monk: a male religious living in a cloister and devoting himself to contemplation, prayer and work. 上人
3. East Wood Temple: located at the northwest foot of Lushan Mountain in Jiujiang City, Jiangxi Province. Due to its location to the east of Xilin Temple, it is named Donglin Temple. 东林(寺)

4. Stand-by：a candidate；an alternate. 员外

5. rocs：mythical birds having enormous size and strength. 鹏

6. wrens：small active brown birds with short upright tails. 鷃

四、译文赏析

1. 谪辞魏阙鹓鸾隔，老入庐山麋鹿随。

译文： Exiled, I'm away from the caps and crowns;

And old, on Mt. Lodge I join elks and deer.

赏析： 诗歌首联交代了背景：被贬江州，往庐山。原句中“魏阙”指宫门上巍然高出的观楼，其下常悬挂法令，后用作朝廷的代称；“鹓鸾”比喻朝官。直译会非常累赘且找不到完全对应的词汇，译者用了代表官员身份的官帽 caps and crowns 来代替被贬之前的身份，并且用了押头韵的修辞手法，处理得非常巧妙。译文弃用简单的 Mt. Lu 而改用 Mt. Lodge 来译“庐山”，一方面是出于句子间的音节数量的考虑，另一方面也是因为 lodge 一词有“乡间小舍”的意思，这正好和前面的“魏阙”形成对比，更能说明前面的“谪”，译者可谓深思熟虑。两句中都增译了 I，在英文中添加主语，是为了符合英语的行文需要。

2. 薄暮萧条投寺宿，凌晨清净与僧期。

译文： Mid eve mist, at the temple I will lodge,

And attend the monks' meeting at dawn clear.

赏析： 首先译文根据英语行文习惯，增译了主语 I，表明是诗人“投寺宿”和“与僧期”，对原文进行了具体化的处理。原文中“薄暮萧条”对“凌晨清净”，译文中用了 mid eve mist 和 dawn clear 来对应，减译了“萧条”，是由于 mid eve mist 本身自带萧条感；原文中的“与僧期”用译文中的 attend the monk's meeting 来对应，是把抽象词汇具体化的做法。把时间状语 at dawn clear 后置，使 clear 与第二行的 deer 押尾韵/ɪə(r)/。

3. 双林我起闻钟后，只日君趋入阁时。

译文： I get up at the bell tolled from Fair Wood；

On odd-numbered days, you come to the court.

赏析： 译文中用 get up 和 come to the court 对应原文中的“起”和“入阁”，是把意思具体化的处理方法。Fair Wood 对应“双林”，是把具体单词意思抽象化的处理方法，因为前面东林寺和西林寺里的“林”都译成了 wood，所以这里的 wood 是承接前面的译文而来；因原句中有“双”和“只”的对比，译文中分别用了 fair 和 odd 与之对应，不仅考虑到了原文意思，更考虑到了单词间的对比。

4. **鹏鷃高低分皆定，莫劳心力远相思。**

译文： Rocs and wrens are so ranked as high or low;

I should not work with my brains, lost in thought.

赏析： 译文中增译了 I，用来说明是作者自己已经明了“高低分皆定”，所以“莫劳心力”了。译文中在 lost in thought 前没有用连词连接，而是用逗号隔开，这是用了拆句法，出于译文句中音节数量的考虑。原文中的“心力”，译文中用 brains 表示，一方面是从意思上符合原文，另一方面是跟后面的 thought 对应。

第二节 自题写真

一、诗歌背景

元和三年(808 年)，白居易改授左拾遗，仍充翰林学士。在他刚担任翰林学士的时候，当时有名的画家李放(780—820 年)奉旨为他画像，白居易在像上题诗，就是这首《自题写真》。此时的白居易已经意识到，自己“多刚狷性”的性格处在朋党倾轧的朝廷，很可能会给自己带来灭顶之灾，但是“收取云泉身”绝非易事。诗人后因卷入政治斗争，一夜之间从万众瞩目的天子脚下，被贬到枫叶荻花的江州做司马。李放画画精妙传神，在开篇四句中作者意识到一个更趋向本质的自己：“合是山中人”；中间六句具体表明了“合是山中人”的因由；最后四句是作者经过这一系列的思索后而得出的结果，即及早归隐云泉，同时也呼应前四句，云泉边才是“山中人”的归宿。这首诗从题材上来说是题画诗，但全诗没有一句是用来描述画中的具体内容，而是借画超脱出去，抒发作者渴望归隐的情思。

二、古诗原文

自题写真

我貌不自识，

李放写我真。
静观神与骨，
合是山中人。
蒲柳质易朽，
麋鹿心难驯。
何事赤墀上，
五年为侍臣？
况多刚狷性，
难与世同尘。
不惟非贵相，
但恐生祸因。
宜当早罢去，
收取云泉身。

三、古诗译文

A Dedication to My Own Picture

I don't know myself, how I look;
Fang Li[1] draws a picture of me.
Spirit and form closely sized up,
A hermit in hills[2] I should be.
Cattail and sedge[3] are prone to rot,
While it's hard to tame an elk's[4] heart.
Why a courtier[5] should I have been
For five years to play a vain part?
Besides, by nature I'm upright[6];
With the world no dust I can share.
Not a privileged noble one,
I'm prone to fall into a snare.

Before it's too late, I'd resign;
By a hill spring I can recline.

（赵彦春 译）

◎ 注释

1. Fang Li：780-820，a painter in Dezong and Xianzong Periods of the Tang Dynasty. His paintings are exquisite and vivid. 李放
2. hermit in hills：one who lives in solitude；one retired from society for some reasons. 山中人
3. cattail and sedge：aquatic plant growing in wet places with solid stems. 蒲柳
4. elk：large northern deer with enormous flattened antlers in the male. 麋鹿
5. courtier：an attendant at the court of a sovereign. 侍臣
6. upright：of moral excellence. 刚狷

四、译文赏析

1. 我貌不自识，李放写我真。
静观神与骨，合是山中人。

译文： I don't know myself, how I look.
Fang Li draws a picture of me.
Spirit and form closely sized up,
A hermit in hills I should be.

赏析： 原诗中"我貌不自识"指画像中的容貌不为诗人所识，于是他"静观神与骨"，终于找到了原因，是李放画出了诗人不曾察觉出的神韵。诗人也认识了自己"合是山中人"。诗中第一句的翻译采用了倒译，把 how I look 放在了 I don't know myself 后面，这是为了符合英语行文规范。"静观神与骨"是主动句，省略了主语"我"，译文同样省略了主语，用了过去分词后置，换主动为被动。把抽象的"神"具体化为 spirit，又把个体的"骨"译成整体的 form，这属于词义的转译，目的是为了使意思更确切、更符合逻辑。翻译"合是山中人"时增加了 I，是增补主语的需要，属增译；同时对句内进行了倒装，把原句中在前面的"合是"译到了句尾(I should be)，这样使 be 和第二行的 me 押尾韵/iː/。

2. 蒲柳质易朽，麋鹿心难驯。
何事赤墀上，五年为侍臣？
况多刚狷性，难与世同尘。

译文：Cattail and sedge are prone to rot;
While it's hard to tame an elk's heart.
Why a courtier should I have been
For five years to play a vain part?
Besides, by nature I'm upright,
With the world no dust I can share.

赏析：这三联中诗人解释了“合是山中人”的因由。蒲柳的生长特性就是在早秋开始凋零，白居易在此以蒲柳自喻身体衰弱。麋鹿的本性是向往茂密森林深处的那片沼泽，所以野性难驯。这两句是作者从身体状况和自身秉性出发阐释原因。诗中用“易”和“难”正好构成对比，译文中用了 while 将两句话进行连接以产生结构上的对比，同时用 are prone to 和 is hard to 来对应原诗中的意思。“赤墀”是皇宫中用赤色丹漆涂抹的台阶，这里代指朝廷。侍臣指皇帝身边的近臣，指白居易曾担任翰林学士。原诗之意是诗人反思自己五年中(概数)在朝堂上做了什么事，译文中采用了倒装，把 a courtier 放在前面，用 a vain part 后置，表明“何事”，这是使意思更具体化的译法，使得意思更明确，同时 part 跟诗句第六行末尾的 heart 押尾韵/ɑːt/。“况多刚狷性，难与世同尘”意指作者自己也意识到狂狷的性格使他嫉恶如仇而不能随波逐流。译文中增补了主语 I，还采用了倒装的手法，将 by nature 提前，句子部分倒装，使 upright 后置，与第 5、6、8 行都押尾韵/t/；把句子 I can share no dust with the world 全部倒装，使 share 与第 12 行末尾的 snare 押尾韵/eə(r)/，此外，这一句中还用了正反移位的处理方法，把 no 放在 dust 的前面而不是 can 的后面来表示原句中的“难”，达到译文句中每个部分间的平衡。

3. 不惟非贵相，但恐生祸因。
宜当早罢去，收取云泉身。

译文：Not a privileged noble one;
I'm prone to fall into a snare.
Before it's too late, I'd resign,
By a hill spring I can recline.

赏析：这里诗人表示自己不是要李放在画中画出贵相，相反，还要感谢他传神的画技让诗人重新审视自己，并由此产生了避祸的心理，所以诗人表示自己应趁早辞官归隐，保全自己和家人。这一部分译文采取了具象化的处理。原句中的“贵相”“祸因”在译文中直接用了 a privileged noble one 和 prone to fall into a snare 来翻译，具体说明了怎样的贵和怎样的祸。并且用一个人(one)来替代“相”，是整体替成部分的做法。处理“宜当早罢去”时用了肯定译成否定的技巧，用 too late 来译“早”，然后句子倒装，使 resign 和最后一句末尾的 recline 押尾韵。“收取云泉身”用 recline by a hill spring 来具象化翻译，给读者形象地展现了一幅在葱茏苍翠的山林间，一汪清泉映着蓝天，诗人漫步其旁的闲适的画卷。

第三节　闭　关

一、诗歌背景

在《与元九书》中，诗人白居易提到“穷则独善其身，达则兼济天下”。一般认为，在被贬为江州司马后，诗人开始从“兼济天下”转向“独善其身”。“独善”这一概念最早由孟子提出，强调士人在未受重用时提升自我道德修养。后来葛洪等人从道家精神层面改变了“独善”的内涵，“独善”一词不一定与道德修养相关，而诗人白居易就继承了“独善”的这一用法。具体来说，诗人白居易的“独善”偏向一己人生的安顿，在身体层面囊括安全、闲暇、物质享乐等；在心灵上追求精神自由，摆脱官场事务带来的心理束缚，以及克服感春悲秋等情况。《闭关》这首诗中就提到了“掩关”和“且安闲”，反映出诗人白居易的“独善”思想。

二、古诗原文

闭　关

我心忘世久，
世亦不我干。
遂成一无事，
因得长掩关。
掩关来几时，
仿佛二三年。

著书已盈帙，
生子欲能言。
始悟身向老，
复悲世多艰。
回顾趋时者，
役役尘壤间。
岁暮竟何得，
不如且安闲。

三、古诗译文

The Door Closed[1]

I have forgot the world for long;
The world's concerned with me no more.
Therefore, no success have I made,
And for long, closed has been my door.
How long has my door been closed now;
It seems a few years, three or two.
I've written books to fill the bag[2];
Very soon my son can talk too.
Now I sigh how hard the world is
As my declining[3] I realize.
Lo, behold, those who serve the time
Hustle and bustle[4] while dust flies.
What can I do as the year's gone?
I'd just idle[5] while time goes on.

（赵彦春　译）

◎ 注释

1. The Door Closed: Close the door to guests and cut off communication. It means not to be disturbed by the world. 闭关

2. bag：a container used for carrying books. 帙

3. declining：the gradual and continuous process of becoming weaker. 身向老

4. hustle and bustle：move or cause to move energetically or busily. 役役

5. idle：not in action or at work；lacking a sense of restraint or responsibility. 安闲

四、译文赏析

1. 遂成一无事，因得长掩关。

译文： Therefore，no success have I made，

And for long，closed has been my door.

赏析： 这两句承接诗歌开始两行，是结果，所以用 therefore 来译"遂"，表明前后的关系。译文中添加了 I，是英文句子中的主语所需。把 I made 和 my door 后置为行尾，使 door 与第二行的 more 押尾韵。在 therefore 和 for long 后，用逗号分隔，是拆分的翻译技巧，同时也促成朗读时的音律感。

2. 始悟身向老，复悲世多艰。

译文： Now I sigh how hard the world is

As my declining I realize.

赏析： 译文中用了合句的翻译手法，把"始悟"和"复悲"两个并列动作用 as 连接合成了一个复杂句，并用了倒置法，把"始悟身向老"译在"复悲世多艰"之后，再把 I realize 倒装至句尾，以达到和 flies 押尾韵的效果。译文中添加了主语 I，符合英文句子行文需要。用 declining 来译"身向老"，是对具体概念抽象化的翻译手法。

3. 回顾趋时者，役役尘壤间。

译文： Lo，behold，those who serve the time；

Hustle and bustle while dust flies.

赏析： 译文中采用押韵的方法 hustle and bustle 来翻译"役役"的叠词效果，同时表现出劳苦不息的喟叹。"趋时者"和"尘壤间"用动词短语 serve the time 和 dust flies 来译，是转译的技巧，更能与前面的 lo，behold 这样的动词匹配，并用从句的形式，以确保句子的音节平衡。

第五部分 写景诗

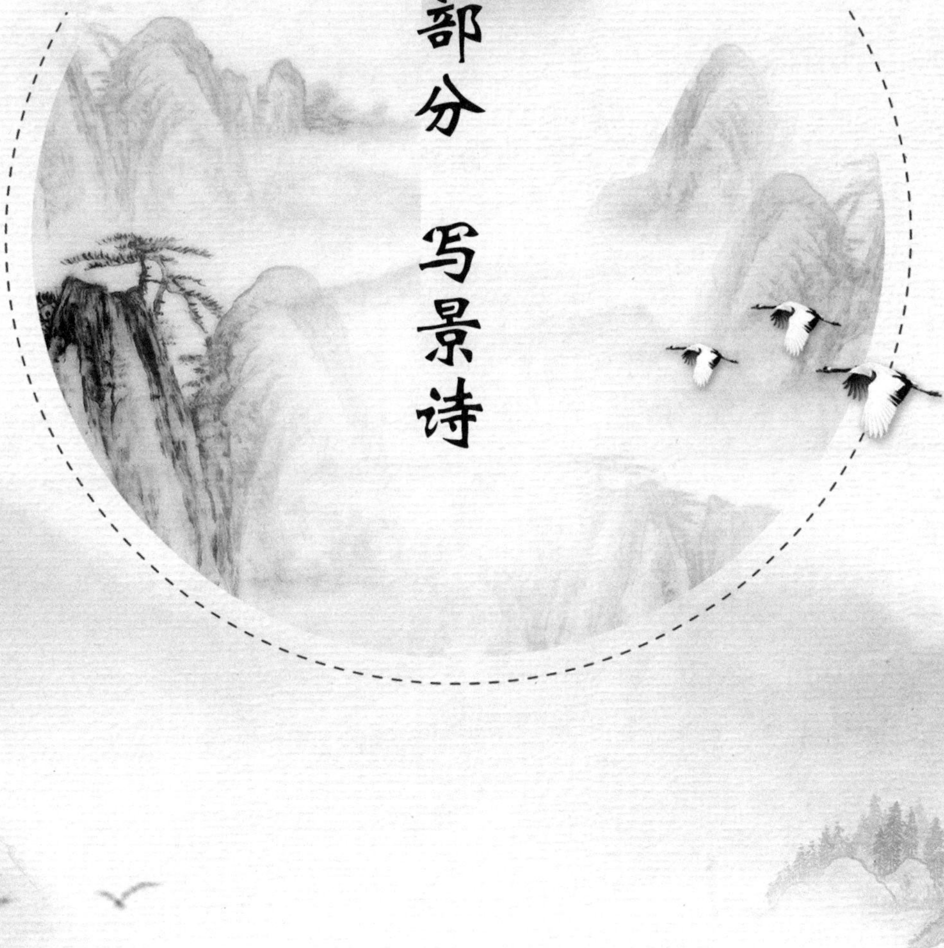

第十三章 人在旅途

第一节 江夜舟行

一、诗歌背景

元和十年(815年),白居易因上书请求缉拿刺杀宰相武元衡的凶手而得罪权势人物,被贬为江州(今江西九江)司马。白居易于八月离开京都南下,九月抵达襄阳,后经汉水、长江,到达九江,因此在诗中他自称“北客”——北方的外来客。《江夜舟行》是他在苦闷压抑的贬谪途中所写,诗中描写的也正是秋天的景象,如秋天迁徙的大雁和鸣叫的昆虫。诗歌开篇交代时间(月夜)、地点(舟途)、环境(烟淡月濛)等要素,然后从视觉(江水满涨、风舞船帆)和听觉(雁嗷嗷和虫唧唧)两个角度描写诗人夜不能寐所捕捉到的景象,最后表达了诗人愁闷又无可奈何的心情。

二、古诗原文

江夜舟行

烟淡月濛濛,
舟行夜色中。
江铺满槽水,
帆展半樯风。

叫曙嗷嗷雁，
啼秋唧唧虫。
只应催北客，
早作白须翁。

三、古诗译文

Rowing on the River at Night

My boat rows in the depth of night;
The moon does its hazy[1] light cast.
Water licks and fills out the groove[2];
The sail unfurls[3] o'er half the mast[4].
To the dawn light cry the wild geese;
Autumn insects cheep[5] and cheep on.
They hasten me, a guest from north,
To be a white-haired man anon[6].

（赵彦春　译）

◎ 注释

1. hazy: covered with haze, misty or cloudy. 濛濛
2. the groove: a long, narrow cut or depression, especially one made to guide motion or receive a corresponding ridge. Here it refers to the boat the poet is traveling by. 槽
3. unfurls: make or become spread out from a rolled or folded state, especially to be open to the wind. （帆）展
4. the mast: a tall upright post, spar, or other structure on a ship or boat, in sailing vessels generally carrying a sail or sails. 樯
5. cheep: a shrill squeaky cry made by a bird, typically a young one. 唧
6. anon: (archaic or informal) soon, shortly. 早

四、译文赏析

1. 烟淡月濛濛，舟行夜色中。

译文： My boat rows in the depth of night;

The moon does its hazy light cast.

赏析： 译者对诗歌第一句“烟淡月濛濛”的位置、结构都做了很大的调整。原文第一、二、四句末分别是“濛”“中”和“风”，押尾韵 ng，译文偶数句押尾韵，因此译者调整了原文第一句和第二句的顺序，使得成韵的 cast 和 mast 出现在偶数句中。此外，首句“烟淡月濛濛”的译文中增加了助词 does，使得该句的音节增加到 8 个，与第一句形成音节对等。“烟淡月濛濛”这一形合的汉语结构在译文中译为意合的结构(the moon's hazy light)。

2. 江铺满槽水，帆展半樯风。

译文： Water licks and fills out the groove;

The sail unfurls o'er half the mast.

赏析： 原文的“江铺”和“帆展”均为主谓结构，展现出深而阔的江水和迎风鼓起的船帆之宏伟气势。译文用 water licks 和 the sail unfurls 这两个对仗的主谓结构与原文对应，体现出江水拍打船体以及船帆翻卷的动态，意象虽有所不同但效果相似。选词上，groove 的原意是“槽”，即两边凸起中间凹下可以盛水的容器，将“槽”译为 groove 与下文的 geese 一词在词形上呼应，考虑到了译文诗句的“形美”。原文中“铺”和“展”是两个动感十足的词，传神地表达出江上风高浪急的景象，译文用 licks 的拟人色彩和 unfurls 的动感形象表现风浪造成的后果，与原诗作者的意图不谋而合。

3. 叫曙嗷嗷雁，啼秋唧唧虫。
只应催北客，早作白须翁。

译文： To the dawn light cry the wild geese;

Autumn insects cheep and cheep on.

They hasten me, a guest from north,

To be a white-haired man anon.

赏析： “嗷嗷雁”和“唧唧虫”，一个是黎明时分大雁飞过时的鸣叫，一个是夜半时分岸边草丛中昆虫的声音。江夜舟行，诗人无法看到天边的大雁和岸上的鸣虫，于是巧妙地运用听觉描写周围景物，并自然过渡到结尾的“催北客”。诗人听到两种声音说明他一夜未眠，而迁徙的大雁和秋虫最后的鸣叫都让人产生“消逝”“远去”的伤感，和贬谪的诗人长途跋涉中越来越强烈的孤单和抑郁感产生共鸣。译者通过 cheep 一词的重叠使用，保持两句在音节上的一致性。原诗的第六句和第八句结尾为“虫”和“翁”，押尾韵 ng，译文则使用 on 和 anon 作为两句的最后一词，尾韵为/ɒn/。anon 是一个较为古老的词汇，意为“很快”，使用时需放在句末作为副词。该词的选择不仅在意义上与原文契合，在风格上也极为恰当。

第二节 浦中夜泊

一、诗歌背景

《浦中夜泊》也是元和十年(815 年)白居易被贬江州司马的途中所写。首句交代诗人在夜晚独上长江大堤，第二句写江堤上看到的江水风霜等景象，最后两句转换视角，从江堤回望自己乘坐的小舟，在芦花丛中露出点点灯光。从诗歌的写作时间以及诗中的景物来看，诗歌描写的是初冬时节，芦荻花尚存枝头但满地白霜，江堤上浪高风急夜棱棱，读者自然体会到诗人低落孤寂的情绪。诗歌最后两句耐人寻味。诗人转换视角，作为旁观者回望自己一路乘坐的小船，如同旁观自己的人生，仕途的艰难险恶如同长江行舟，漫长而又艰难；小船上油灯的点点光亮似乎就是自己一生努力留下的印记，非常微弱，更增添冷峻和无奈之感。

二、古诗原文

浦中夜泊

暗上江堤还独立，
水风霜气夜棱棱。
回看深浦停舟处，
芦荻花中一点灯。

三、古诗译文

Mooring Riverside

In the dark, on the river dyke[1] I stand;
Water, wind and frost chill[2] the death of night.
I glance back at the boat moored riverside;
Amid reed[3] flowers gleams a speck[4] of light.

（赵彦春　译）

◎ 注释

1. dyke: a long wall or embankment built to prevent flooding from the sea. 堤
2. chill: make someone feel cold. 棱棱
3. reed: a tall, slender-leaved plant of the grass family, which grows in water or on marshy ground; also a general term for tall grasses of the genus Gramineae growing along rivers and lakes and in wetlands. 芦荻
4. speck: a tiny spot. 点

四、译文赏析

1. 浦中夜泊

译文：Mooring Riverside

赏析："浦"在此指与长江通流的河汊，夜间在此泊舟相对安全平稳，这是乘舟行路者的常识，但英语中并没有一个单词能够承载同样的文化意义和背景信息，因此译者将原文的"浦中"模糊地译成 riverside，交代了诗歌的背景。此外，原诗题目仅为一个四字词语，为保持译文题目同样短小精悍，译者省略了对"夜"字的翻译，使得译文也是四个音节，与原文对应。

2. 暗上江堤还独立，水风霜气夜棱棱。

译文：In the dark, on the river dyke I stand;

Water, wind and frost chill the death of night.

赏析：原诗中第二句和第四句韵脚是“棱”和“灯”，押 eng 韵，译文对应的两句也押尾韵，韵脚为 night 和 light。为保持整首诗歌每句 8 个音节的一致性，译者减译了第一句的“独”字。原诗第二句“水风霜气夜棱棱”是一个典型的汉语的意合结构，列举了诗人在江堤上感受到的萧萧江水、凛冽寒风、银霜遍野和刺骨寒夜，译者将这些意合的信息用动词谓语 chill 译为形合的结构，既符合英语的语言习惯，也突出了四个意象的核心特点，即水风霜夜传递出刺骨的凉意，亦是诗人此时的心境。原文的“棱棱”一词原本形容夜晚寒冷的样子，是一个比较模糊的形容词，而动词 chill 则更为具体。death 一词是译者的增译，形容死寂无人的夜晚，该词的增译除了使内容上生动之外，还避免了译文第二句由于主语过长造成句子头重脚轻。

3. **回看深浦停舟处，芦荻花中一点灯。**

译文：I glance back at the boat moored riverside;

Amid reed flowers gleams a speck of light.

赏析：和题目一样，由于译文无法详细解释“浦”原本的意义和背景信息，第三句中的“深浦”一词也模糊地译成了 riverside。原诗最后一句描述诗人在岸堤上回望，自己一路乘坐的小船隐没在夜色和芦荻花中，仅露出一点灯光。这句中没有动词，有一种时间停顿的静态之美。译文将意合的句子转化为形合的句子，并增加了 gleam 这一动词，该词意为“发出微弱的亮光”，很好地再现了原文的静态美。此外，译者将“一点光”译为 a speck of light，强化了 gleam 所营造的微弱的感觉。这点微光和上文描述的寒风冷夜相比是如此微不足道，凸显了诗人孤寂暗淡的心境。他虽未完全绝望，但还是对前途充满了无奈。

第三节　夜入瞿唐峡

一、诗歌背景

本诗为元和十四年(819 年)白居易自江州(今江西九江)前往忠州(今重庆)任刺史的途中经过长江三峡而作。白居易元和十年被贬任江州司马，四年后奉诏改官忠州，虽然官职上提升了，但当时的忠州是一个偏僻的山区边城。赴任途中，诗人看到路途的艰险，想到前途未卜，心情自然充满了愁苦。诗人开门见山感叹瞿塘峡的“险”和“难”，之后用屏风、匹练比喻瞿塘峡的险峻，用汹涌波涛和暗行的船只描绘瞿塘峡的难行，最后再次直抒胸臆，把自己愁绪之深比作高耸的滟滪堆，使情景融为一体。

二、古诗原文

夜入瞿唐峡

瞿唐天下险，
夜上信难哉！
岸似双屏合，
天如匹练开。
逆风惊浪起，
拔稔暗船来。
欲识愁多少，
高于滟滪堆。

三、古诗译文

Entering Big Pond Gorge[1] at Night

Big Pond Gorge is a threat to all;
It's especially hard at night.
The two banks open like twain[2] screens
The sky is a thin stretch of white[3].
Athwart[4] a wind quaking[5] waves surge;
Boats are towed with ropes[6] in the dark.
How many woes if you would know,
They're much heavier than Boulder[7] stark.

（赵彦春　译）

◎ 注释

1. Big Pond Gorge: One of the three gorges of the Changjiang River, the other two being Witch Gorge and Westridge Gorge. 瞿唐峡(今瞿塘峡)
2. twain: archaic term for two. 双
3. a thin stretch of white: a long piece of white silk cloth. 匹练
4. athwart: in opposition to; counter to. 逆
5. quake: (especially of the earth) shake or tremble. 惊
6. rope: the cables to drag sailing ships ahead. 稔
7. Boulder: called the Rippling Pile, or commonly known as the Swallow's Nest Stone, was also known as the Hesitation Stone in ancient times. It is located at the mouth of Qutang Gorge under the White Emperor City and has been a great trouble to boatmen since ancient times. 滟滪堆

四、译文赏析

1. 瞿唐天下险，夜上信难哉！

译文： Big Pond Gorge is a threat to all;

It's especially hard at night.

赏析： 白居易开篇直抒胸臆，点出瞿塘峡的“险”和“难”两大特点。译文表达出原文的直白和气势，用 threat 和 hard 两个简单明确的词表达出这两大特点。特别是用 threat to all 而非 dangerous 来翻译“天下险”，除了音节的考虑之外，更加直白地说明瞿塘峡的险在于对行船者的生命威胁。原诗为五言律诗，第二、四、六句的韵脚为“哉”“开”“来”，押尾韵 ɑi，译文每句 8 个音节，偶数句押韵，第二句和第四句的韵脚为 night 和 white，与中文的韵脚做到了一致。

2. 岸似双屏合，天如匹练开。

译文： The two banks open like twain screens,

The sky is a thin stretch of white.

赏析： 原诗颔联“岸似双屏合，天如匹练开”用两个比喻具体形象地说明瞿塘峡险峻的样子。因在夜色中只能看到峡谷和天空大致的样子，因此诗人只做了轮廓和颜色的描绘，把两岸山峰比作两扇合拢的屏风，把天空比作散开的一匹白绢，两句对仗极其工整，“岸”

对“天”，“双屏”对“匹练”，一合一开。译文保留了原文的第一个喻体 twain screens，但将“练”直接译成了“白”(white)而非 silk cloth，原因是中国文化中说到“练”自然令人想到“白”，这也是“练”最重要的特点之一。由于文化的不可译性，译者选择解释性的翻译方法。此外，出于搭配和音节的考虑，译文中的两个比喻分别译为明喻和暗喻。

3. **逆风惊浪起，拔稔暗船来。**

译文： Athwart a wind quaking waves surge;

Boats are towed with ropes in the dark.

赏析： 颔联用形象的比喻说明瞿塘峡的险，而颈联的这两句则正面描述瞿塘峡的“难”。一方面逆风惊浪、惊心动魄，另一方面船只必须“暗”中行进，也就是不能发出声音。因为根据当地迷信，船只发出声音会惹怒神灵，造成船毁人亡。这一迷信中隐含的险恶更渲染了瞿塘峡行舟之艰难。原诗颈联第一句动词在句尾，译文的结构也是将动词放在句末，surge 一词巧妙地译出原文中“起”的动态效果，而主观色彩浓重的“惊浪”则译成更为具象化的 quaking waves，即汹涌的波涛几乎要掀翻行船。颈联后一句的 dark 与尾联后一句的 stark 押尾韵，尽管原文这两句并不成韵。

4. **欲识愁多少，高于滟滪堆。**

译文： How many woes if you would know,

They're much heavier than Boulder stark.

赏析： 对“险”和“难”展开之后，诗人在尾联呼应首联的抒情，发出了“愁”的感慨。此处的“愁”不仅因为瞿塘峡舟行艰难而发愁，更是对仕途坎坷、前途未卜而发出的愁叹。译者将“愁”一词直译成 woe，意思是巨大的悲痛。而原文中形容词“高”既修饰愁的深度，也修饰滟滪堆这块江中巨石的高度，是诗人另一处巧夺天工的比喻。译者保留了句中的本体和喻体，但将“高”译成 heavy，使得其在与 woe 和 Boulder 两个词的搭配上都十分合理。原诗的无主句在翻译中增加了主语 you，符合英文的行文习惯。

第十四章　世外桃源

第一节　题杨颖士西亭

一、诗歌背景

这是一首题赠诗。古人喜欢以文会友，白居易在参观了好友杨颖士新造的西亭后，在墙上题诗赞美友人居所的美好，也表达对主人品格的赞赏。这首诗形式上虽为五言律诗，却不同于近体诗当中的五律那般四联八句，为五联古诗。诗歌首先以“静”“远”二字说明西亭的宁静清幽、远离俗世。之后，诗人描写在亭上所见的远景——“鸟灭山重重”，近景——“竹露”“杉风”，以及自身的感受——“烦襟”“病容”不再，心绪豁然旷达。最后，诗人拿西亭与蓬莱仙山对比，将对西亭的赞美推上了新高度。白居易不仅夸了西亭的美，高赞主人的品位，在自然流露的羡慕之情中更表达出自己与主人意趣相投。

二、古诗原文

题杨颖士西亭

静得亭上境，
远谐尘外踪。
凭轩东南望，
鸟灭山重重。

竹露冷烦襟，
杉风清病容。
旷然宜真趣，
道与心相逢。
即此可遗世，
何必蓬壶峰。

三、古诗译文

A Dedication[1] to Yingshi Yang's West Pavilion

This pavilion[2], what a quiet place!
Far off the world, without a trace.
If you gaze southeast in the hall,
You find no birds in the hills tall.
Dewed bamboo cools down your hot chest
A cypress[3] wind blows off all pest.
Great altitude is its real tune;
The Word and your heart do commune[4].
Up here all your life you can spend;
Why need you a high peak[5] ascend?

（赵彦春　译）

◎ 注释

1. dedication: the action of formally open or unveil (a building or memorial). 题
2. pavilion: a summerhouse or other decorative building used as a shelter in a park or large garden. 亭
3. cypress: (also cypress tree) an evergreen coniferous tree with small, rounded woody cones and flattened shoots bearing small scale-like leaves. 杉
4. commune: share one's intimate thoughts or feelings with (someone), especially on a spiritual level. 相逢

5. a high peak：referring to Penglai Immortal Island located at the eastern end of Bohai Sea. It is a legendary land of Chinese mythology and is often said to be the base for the Eight Immortal. 蓬壶峰

四、译文赏析

1. 题杨颖士西亭

译文： A Dedication to Yingshi Yang's West Pavilion

赏析： 题壁诗是古诗中常见的一种，可以是山上的石壁，也可以是亭台楼阁的墙壁。当诗人看到美景诗兴大发，或欲抒发感慨时，就会在墙上留下诗句，如著名的《题西林壁》(苏轼)、《题临安邸》(林升)等，这类诗大多以《题……》为名。本诗是白居易题在好友新居西亭的墙上赠给好友的，意在赞美友人的居所及其为人。西方没有在墙上写诗抒发情感的风俗，却有将自己的新书、新歌献给自己喜爱的人的做法，称为 dedicate。译者采用这一近似对等的措辞，并使用其名词形式 dedication 作为标题，符合英语标题的习惯。

2. 静得亭上境，远谐尘外踪。
凭轩东南望，鸟灭山重重。

译文： This pavilion, what a quiet place!
Far off the world, without a trace.
If you gaze southeast in the hall,
You find no birds in the hills tall.

赏析： 这首五联古诗开篇两句用"静"和"远"说明西亭的环境和位置，而"凭轩东南望，鸟灭山重重"则是"远谐尘外踪"的具体描述，加入了人的视角，进一步说明西亭的超乎尘世之外的绝佳环境。三、四两句是典型的汉语无主句，译者增加 you 作为人称。原诗偶数句押尾韵 ong，译诗每联的两句押尾韵，为此译者在选词上下了很大的功夫，也在翻译过程中做了一些调整。如"凭轩"原意为"站在窗边"，译者模糊地译为 in the hall；又如"山重重"原意为重峦叠嶂，译者则转译为 the hills tall。

3. 竹露冷烦襟，杉风清病容。

译文： Dewed bamboo cools down your hot chest,
A cypress wind blows off all pest.

赏析：原诗这两句描绘了亭子周边的植物——竹子和杉树，但更描绘出这两种植物对在此居住者的影响：让烦躁的心情安静下来，把疾病和烦恼一扫而光。诗人将“冷”和“清”两个形容词用作动词，颇具神韵。译者用 cools down 和 blows off 两组词组与之对应，将“烦襟”译为 chest，将“病容”译为 pest，除了出于押韵的考虑之外，和谓语动词的搭配也非常和谐。尤其是 pest 一词，表示“令人讨厌的事物”，和“病容”虽然一个是外在事物，一个是身体上的表现，但却有异曲同工之妙。

4. **旷然宜真趣，道与心相逢。**

译文：Great altitude is its real tune;

The Word and your heart do commune.

赏析：这两句描写亭中人的所感所想。诗人从亭中远眺，眼前豁然开朗，内心舒畅旷达，感受到了自然和内心的和谐一致，表达了诗人对西亭的喜爱。“旷然宜真趣”本意为“开阔的环境与率真的情趣相得益彰”，译者把“旷然”译为 altitude，将抽象模糊的概念译为具体的概念，同时将“真趣”省译，做了较大的改动。增译 tune 一词，突出西亭高的特点。后一句中的“道”在中国哲学思想中是比较复杂的概念，表达了天地万物的演化和运行机制，很难一言以译之。译者借用西方人熟悉的《圣经》中的 the Word 一词做了动态对等处理。虽然 the Word，即 the Word of God，并非汉语所谓的道，但该词在《圣经》中的重要地位和人们听到该词的反应则和我们的“道”很接近。将“相逢”译成 commune 非常精确，体现出人与神的精神沟通。

5. **即此可遗世，何必蓬壶峰。**

译文：Up here all your life you can spend;

Why need you a high peak ascend?

赏析：最后一句，诗人用反问的语气将杨颖士的西亭与蓬莱仙山相比，说“不必去蓬莱，在西亭隐居就足够好了”，将对西亭的赞美上升到一个新高度。译文与原文语气对等，用 Why need you 译出反问语气。“蓬壶峰”的文化背景具有不可译性，译者弃而不译，而是用了 peak 和 ascend 两词，并在前一句增译了 up 一词与之对应，将原诗中西亭和蓬莱之间朦胧的比较转换成具体的高度比较，也就是杨颖士若是追求更高更远，西亭绝不在蓬莱仙山之下。最后两句译者保留前面 4 组诗句的音节和尾韵规律，每句 8 个音节，韵脚为 spend 和 ascend。

第二节　遗爱寺

一、诗歌背景

遗爱寺位于江西庐山香炉峰下。元和十年(815年)白居易被贬为江州(今江西九江)司马，本诗是他上任后的第二年游览遗爱寺时而作。这首五言绝句描写了遗爱寺周边的鸟语花香、溪水山泉，虽然景色并无特别之处，但随着诗人的视线看去，跟着诗人的耳朵聆听，一切都充满了惊喜，一切都令人心旷神怡。诗人将自己代入诗中，先是临溪弄石、绕寺寻花，然后驻足聆听鸟儿啁啾和溪水汩汩。移步换景之间，诗人亦动亦静，引着读者跟随他的视线和听觉，感受到遗爱寺的盎然生机，分享他在山水间获得的惊喜和精神愉悦。

二、古诗原文

遗爱寺

弄石临溪坐，
寻花绕寺行。
时时闻鸟语，
处处是泉声。

三、古诗译文

Temple of Love[1]

To sit streamside, the stone I sweep,
And go round the fane for flowers fair.
From time to time you hear birds cheep[2],
And fountains[3] gurgle[4] everywhere.

(赵彦春　译)

◎ 注释

1. Temple of Love：Located at the foot of the Fragrant Furnace Peak on Mount Lu in Jiangxi Province, which is within the jurisdiction of Jiangzhou in the Tang Dynasty. 遗爱寺
2. cheep：a shrill squeaky cry made by a bird, typically a young one. 鸟语
3. fountain：(mainly literary) a natural spring of water. 泉
4. gurgle：make a hollow bubbling sound like that made by water running out of a bottle. 泉声

四、译文赏析

1. 弄石临溪坐，寻花绕寺行。

译文： To sit streamside, the stone I sweep,
And go round the fane for flowers fair.

赏析： 前面两句中，诗人用“弄”“坐”“寻”“行”四个动词描绘出一幅灵动活泼的画面。诗人这里不仅描述了环境特点——有石、有水、有花、有寺，更表达了自己游览的心情：理清干净石头上的杂草枯枝，本想小坐一会儿静静欣赏，但禁不住被鸟鸣花香吸引，起身又绕着寺庙一探究竟。在这份欣喜的心情衬托下，平平常常的山景也顿时生动起来。然而对译者来说，出于英语句式结构特点的考虑，并不能将这些动词一一对应译出。译者在上下两句中各挑选了一个动词——“弄”（sweep）和“（绕）行”（go round）作并列谓语，将“坐”译为不定式 to sit 充当目的状语，将“寻”译为介词 for，很大限度地保留了原诗的动词特色。原诗中一“坐”一“行”位于前面两句句末形成对仗，译文中 sit 和 go 位于每句的第二个音节，也形成对应，与原诗构成形式上的对等。译诗的尾韵结构为 ABAB，第一句和第三句的韵脚为 sweep 和 cheep，第二句和第四句的韵脚为 fair 和 everywhere，节奏明快。增译 fair 一词，增加了一个音节，并与 everywhere 押尾韵。

2. 时时闻鸟语，处处是泉声。

译文： From time to time you hear birds cheep,
And fountains gurgle everywhere.

赏析： 前面两句中诗人边行走边看景，用连动的句式使得景物随视线而变，是人动景静；后面两句诗人停下脚步侧耳倾听，“鸟语”和“泉声”让景致流出动感的诗意，是景动人静。这一联诗句的结构也随之改变，“时时”和“处处”两个叠词的使用使得诗句有工整之美，静谧的景观里顿时有了热烈的氛围。译者巧妙地使用 cheep 和 gurgle 两个拟声词将

鸟语和泉声直观地表达出来，并将前面两句的第一人称 I 转换成第二人称 you，将前面两句行为的主体与后面两句中观察者的视角剥离开来，动静结合、相得益彰。

第三节 朝回游城南

一、诗歌背景

白居易贞元十六年(800 年)中进士，先后任秘书省校书郎、盩至尉、翰林学士，元和年间曾任左拾遗、左赞善大夫。这些官职都在皇帝身边，每日接触各种尔虞我诈的官场斗争。这首五言古诗描写了诗人完成了一天的朝廷工作之后，内心如同初秋的天气那样燥热，于是驱马前往城南郊外散心游玩。山中清凉的泉水和夹道的翠竹让他身心放松，天色渐晚也不愿离开，索性“青松系我马，白石为我床”。在诗歌的后半部分，诗人从眼前闲云野鹤的心情自然过渡到自己在官场上的原则，即无论周围是“鸳鹭”还是“鸥鹤”，自己都“机心一以尽，两处不乱行”。

二、古诗原文

朝回游城南

朝退马未困，
秋初日犹长。
回辔城南去，
郊野正清凉。
水竹夹小径，
萦回绕川岗。
仰看晚山色，
俯弄秋泉光。
青松系我马，
白石为我床。

常时簪组累，
此日和身忘。
旦随鸳鹭末，
暮游鸥鹤旁。
机心一以尽，
两处不乱行。
谁辨心与迹，
非行亦非藏。

三、古诗译文

Touring South of the Town After Levee

Not tired is my horse, levee[1] o'er;
Long grow autumn days of the year.
I trot back to south of the town;
The suburbs are now cool and clear.
The dewy bamboo by the trail
Spreads to circle the mound and stream.
I look up at the hill's eve view
And bend to play with the spring's gleam.
I tie my horse to the green pine
And take the white stone as my bed.
I often try so hard at work;
Now I've forgotten all instead.
At dawn, I follow mandarin ducks[2];
At eve, I go with gulls[3] or cranes[4]
You won't go amiss either way,
If no craft of your heart remains.
Who can tell you how my mind goes?
It's neither going nor repose[5].

(赵彦春 译)

◎ **注释**

1. levee：having an audience with an emperor（a king）. 朝
2. mandarin duck：a small tree-nesting East Asian duck，the male of which has showy plumage with an orange ruff and orange sail-like feathers on each side of the body. 鸳鹭
3. gull：a long-winged web-footed seabird with a raucous call，typically having white plumage with a gray or black mantle. 鸥
4. crane：a tall，long-legged，long-necked bird，typically with white or gray plumage and often with tail plumes and patches of bare red skin on the head. 鹤
5. repose：a state of rest，sleep，or tranquility. 藏

四、译文赏析

1. **朝退马未困，秋初日犹长。**
回辔城南去，郊野正清凉。

译文： Not tired is my horse，levee o'er；
Long grow autumn days of the year.
I trot back to south of the town；
The suburbs are now cool and clear.

赏析： 开篇两联介绍了出游的时间、地点和背景。诗人忙完一天的公务之后，趁着天色尚早前往王城南郊外，享受燥热初秋的一点清凉。原文每联的第二句句尾词押 ang 韵，译文是相邻偶数句押尾韵。这里第二句和第四句的韵脚为 year 和 clear。开篇第一联的两句译文均采用倒装句式，体现形式的工整对应。

2. **水竹夹小径，萦回绕川岗。**
仰看晚山色，俯弄秋泉光。
青松系我马，白石为我床。
常时簪组累，此日和身忘。

译文： The dewy bamboo by the trail
Spreads to circle the mound and stream.
I look up at the hill's eve view

And bend to play with the spring's gleam.
I tie my horse to the green pine
And take the white stone as my bed.
I often try so hard at work;
Now I've forgotten all instead.

赏析：城南郊外的山水竹径令诗人置身世外，身心放松，天色渐晚仍不舍离去。“仰看晚山色，俯弄秋泉光。青松系我马，白石为我床”集中描写了诗人享受休闲时光的样子。这四句对仗工整，“俯”对“仰”，“泉光”对“山色”，“白石”对“青松”，译者则将这四句译为两个结构相同的句子，即重复了“I +动词+A and B”的结构，使这两组行为在形式上也构成一个有机的整体。为保持每行 8 个音节，译者省略了 evening 的第二个音节，并缩写为 eve。诗中的“簪组”原指固定发髻的簪子和带子，这里指官员，是一种借代的修辞方式。译者将“簪组累”意译为 hard at work，跨越了翻译的文化沟壑，很好地表达了诗人的意图，达到了译文的动态对等。原文的尾韵规律为每联的第二句句尾词均押 ang 韵，译文的尾韵规律是相邻偶数句押韵。这里第二句和第四句句尾押/iːm/音，第六句和第八句句尾押/ed/音。

3. 旦随鸳鹭末，暮游鸥鹤旁。
机心一以尽，两处不乱行。
谁辨心与迹，非行亦非藏。

译文：At dawn, I follow mandarin ducks;
At eve, I go with gulls or cranes.
You won't go amiss either way,
If no craft of your heart remains.
Who can tell you how my mind goes?
It's neither going nor repose.

赏析：原文的尾韵规律为每联的第二句句尾词均押 ang 韵，译文的尾韵规律是相邻偶数句押韵。这里第二句和第四句句尾押韵，韵脚分别为 cranes 和 remains。译者将“鸳鹭”(鸳鸯和白鹭)仅译成 mandarin ducks，略去了白鹭，将“鸥鹤”译为 gulls or cranes，以保持音节对等。译文中对“机心一以尽，两处不乱行”的语序进行了调整，以实现句尾押韵，并将“一以尽”这一肯定的表述方式译成否定的表述 no craft，点明诗人坦率正直的为人准则。

第十五章　四时即景

第一节　春　村

一、诗歌背景

这是一首描写乡村春天景象的五言律诗。诗人以第三者的视角，通过细致入微的观察，描绘了乡村春天欣欣向荣的自然和人文景象。从转暖的天气到桑田里的鸟儿，大自然已经散发出春天的气息。村民们为重要的赛神祭祀活动而忙碌，男人忙舂米女人忙做衣。牛马在远离村子的地方吃草，鸡和猪则在村子里走动。夕阳西下，参加赛神的人们打着鼓吹着笛回来了。人们忙碌的身影、家禽家畜悠闲的神情，加上赛神活动所寄托的美好愿望，让春日的乡村充满憧憬和希望。

二、古诗原文

春　村

二月村园暖，
桑间戴胜飞。
农夫舂旧谷，
蚕妾捣新衣。
牛马因风远，

鸡豚过社稀。

黄昏林下路，

鼓笛赛神归。

三、古诗译文

The Village in Spring

The second moon, the village's warm;

Out of mulberries[1] hoopoes[2] fly.

The farmers husk[3] grains of last year;

The silkworm maids would new clothes try.

Cattle and steeds[4] are far in wind;

Chickens and swine[5] go past the shrine[6].

Dusk falls to the road in the wood;

Drums and pipes sound as if divine[7].

（赵彦春　译）

◎ 注释

1. mulberry：（also mulberry tree or bush）a small deciduous tree with broad leaves, native to East Asia and long cultivated elsewhere. 桑
2. hoopoe：a salmon-pink Eurasian bird with a long down-curved bill, a large erectile crest, and black and white wings and tail. 戴胜
3. husk：remove the dry outer covering of some fruits or seeds. 舂
4. steed：a horse being ridden or available for riding. 马
5. swine：（farming or archaic）a pig. 豚
6. shrine：a place regarded as holy because of its associations with a divinity or a sacred person or relic, marked by a building or other construction. 社
7. divine：of, from, or like God or a god. 神

四、译文赏析

1. 二月村园暖，桑间戴胜飞。

译文： The second moon, the village's warm;

Out of mulberries hoopoes fly.

赏析： 原诗首联两句动词置于句尾，译文的第二句也采用倒装语序，与原文构成形式对等，正常语序应为 hoopoes fly out of mulberries。原诗首联和颈联的首句押尾韵 uɑn，韵脚为“暖”和“远”，颔联和尾联首句押尾韵 u，韵脚为“谷”和“路”，颔联和颈联的第二句押尾韵 i，韵脚为“衣”和“稀”。译文首联、颔联的第二句押尾韵/ɑɪ/，韵脚分别是 fly 和 try；颈联、尾联的第二句押尾韵/ɑɪn/，韵脚分别是 shrine 和 divine。

2. 农夫舂旧谷，蚕妾捣新衣。

译文： The farmers husk grains of last year;

The silkworm maids would new clothes try.

赏析： 本联两句对仗非常工整，“农夫”对“蚕妾”，“舂旧谷”对“捣新衣”。青黄不接的二月，所谓“旧谷”就是去年秋收的稻谷，而非多年的陈谷子，译为 grains of last year 而不是 old grains，不仅有音节上的考虑，而且内容更加明确。“捣新衣”一句，唐诗中的“捣衣”是制作衣物的一个程序，用杵捶打葛麻衣料，使之柔软熨帖，易于缝制。但如果直译成 beat the new clothes 会令人非常费解，因此译者转换成 try 一词，既有押韵的考虑，也避免了因时代和文化背景差异造成读者的理解障碍。

3. 牛马因风远，鸡豚过社稀。

译文： Cattle and steeds are far in wind;

Chickens and swine go past the shrine.

赏析： 原诗“牛马”对“鸡豚”，描绘家禽家畜在村庄内外的活动：牛马在村外活动，而鸡豚则在村里踱步，乡村祠堂之外的地方就看不到了。“社”即神庙或祠堂，译者用的 shrine（神社）一词与后文的 divine（神灵）不仅尾韵一致，意义上也相互照应。此外，译者将“马”译为 steeds，“豚”译为 swine 主要是出于音韵考虑，使 cattle 与 chickens 互押头韵，steeds 和 swine 也互押头韵，不仅内容对仗，形式和声音上也对仗。

4. **黄昏林下路，鼓笛赛神归。**

译文：Dusk falls to the road in the wood;

Drums and pipes sound as if divine.

赏析：译者将“黄昏”译为 dusk，使尾联两句的第一个词 dusk 与 drums 互押头韵，与颈联形成巧妙呼应。“赛神”是一种神祇崇拜活动，形式多样，目的是感谢神恩，本诗的赛神活动显然包含打鼓和吹笛等演奏形式。译者将最后一句做了减译，并将“赛神”这一名词译为形容 divine，并减译了“归”一词，使得内容更易理解。

第二节　禁中月

一、诗歌背景

唐贞元十九年(803 年)春，白居易以书判拔萃科登第，被授秘书省校书郎一职，此诗很可能作于他任校书郎期间。“禁中月”的意思是在皇帝居所赏月有感而作。本诗描绘了从明月升起到“稍上宫墙”，再到照射水塘的过程，语调轻快自然。对月光下亭台楼阁的描写，更衬托出月亮的清冷和明亮。诗中既流露出诗人孤单寂寞的心情，也表达了诗人如同明月一样清朗的胸怀。

二、古诗原文

禁　中　月

海水明月出，
禁中清夜长。
东南楼殿白，
稍稍上宫墙。
净落金塘水，
明浮玉砌霜。

不比人间见，
尘土污清光。

三、古诗译文

The Moon o'er the Palace[1]

The moon does rise above the sea;
In the palace long is the night.
A bit high o'er the palace wall,
It washes Southeast Tower with white.
Purity's poured onto Gold Pond[2];
The marble[3] steps like hoarfrost[4] sheen.
It's not seen in the human world,
Where dust or dirt may soil[5] the clean.

（赵彦春　译）

◎ **注释**

1. Palace: the official residence of a sovereign or other exalted person. 禁
2. Gold Pond: the royal pond in the Palace, also means the golden color of the water in the moonlight. 金塘
3. marble: a hard-crystalline metamorphic form of limestone, typically white with mottling or streaks of color, that could be polished and is often used in sculpture and architecture. 玉
4. hoarfrost: a grayish-white crystalline deposit of frozen water vapor formed in clear still weather on vegetation, fences, etc. 霜
5. soil: make dirty. 污

四、译文赏析

1. 海水明月出，禁中清夜长。

译文：The moon does rise above the sea;

In the palace long is the night.

赏析：这首五言律诗每联的对句(偶数句)押尾韵 ɑng，韵脚分别为“长”“墙”“霜”和“光”。译文的尾韵结构为一、二联和三、四联的对句分别押尾韵/aɪt/和/iːn/，韵脚分别为 night 和 white，sheen 和 clean。译者在首联第一句中增加助词 does 以保持每行 8 个音节。此外，译者减译了原诗中“明”和“清”两个形容词，使译文更加洗练，也符合英语的表达习惯。

2. 东南楼殿白，稍稍上宫墙。

译文：A bit high o'er the palace wall,

It washes Southeast Tower with white.

赏析：出于押韵的考虑，译者改变了颔联两句的顺序，并将“白”一词译成动词谓语 washes，用拟人的修辞手法表现出明亮的月光给宫殿带来的奇妙变化，同时使译文的句子更符合英语形合的特点。“稍稍”一词表明月亮较之前所起的变化，译者用 a bit 表达出这种变化。

3. 净落金塘水，明浮玉砌霜。

译文：Purity's poured onto Gold Pond;

The marble steps like hoarfrost sheen.

赏析：颈联两句是颔联的延续，描写了月光落在池水和汉白玉台阶上的效果。“净”本是一个副词，形容月亮发出清冷光芒的样子，译者转译为名词，突出了月光皎洁的特点。译者用 poured 一词表现月色如水、洒落池中的效果，十分传神；sheen 的意义为 shine brightly，该词的选用确切地表达出月光“明浮”在汉白玉台阶上的效果。在音律上，上句中 purity，poured 和 Pond 三个押头韵的词赋予句子明快的节奏感，如同明月洒在水上的闪闪金光。出于音节数考虑，译者使用双音节的 hoarfrost 而非单音节的 frost。

4. 不比人间见，尘土污清光。

译文：It's not seen in the human world,

Where dust or dirt may soil the clean.

赏析：尾联中诗人表达自己的心境也如同月光一样清清亮亮，希望能够远离尘世间的污浊，不受污染。译者用关系副词 where 使上下句构成主从复合句，将中文的意合转换为英语的形合。dust or dirt 这一词组既押头韵也押尾韵，与原文的“尘土”在形式和内容上都形成对等。

第三节　江州雪

一、诗歌背景

元和十年(815年)白居易被贬谪江州司马，这首诗是他在江州司马任上所作，时年43岁。白居易曾在京城长安担任诸职，贬谪生活中他既有伤感，也有豁达和恬淡。这首五言古诗描写了江州雪后初晴的一日，他策马出城看到庐山白雪覆盖，不觉想起京城长安，有着一丝忧伤的情绪。然而江州与长安雪后的景象并不相同：这里的冰凌像细长的谷穗，沾了积雪的柳条如同柳花盛开；暖风吹拂，冰雪都已开始融化。诗人虽然有些遗憾，但与岭南相比，江州能看到雪还是幸运的。诗人虽然没有直抒胸臆，但读者不难读出诗人努力与当时的自己以及处境达成和解。

二、古诗原文

江州雪

新雪满前山，
初晴好天气。
日西骑马出，
忽有京都意。
城柳方缀花，
檐冰才结穗。
须臾风日暖，
处处皆飘坠。
行吟赏未足，
坐叹销何易。
犹胜岭南看，
雰雰不到地。

三、古诗译文

The River Bank[1] Snow

It's good weather, now it's just fine.
New snow fills out the hills ahead[2].
At twilight I ride my horse out,
It's much like Capital[3] instead.
Icicles[4] like ears neath the eaves;
Willows[5] show their flowers by the wall.
All at once, the zephyr[6] turns warm;
Here and there catkins[7] drift and fall.
I sit there and sigh without end,
Not just going, chanting around
It's a better than the Five Ridges[8],
As the catkins don't reach the ground.

(赵彦春　译)

◎ 注释

1. River Bank: the name of a state in the Tang Dynasty, with its capital at today's Jiujiang, Jiangxi Province. 江州
2. the hills ahead: referring to Lushan, also known as Kuanglu (匡庐) in ancient times. It is situated in Jiujiang, which was known as River Bank in the Tang Dynasty, and is one of the most renowned mountains in the country. 前山(即庐山)
3. Capital: referring to Long Peace, the capital of the Tang Dynasty, with a population of about one million at that time. 京都
4. icicle: a hanging, tapering piece of ice formed by the freezing of dripping water. 冰
5. willow: (also willow tree) a tree or shrub of temperate climates that typically has narrow leaves, bears catkins, and grows near water. Its pliant branches yield osiers for basketry, and its wood has various uses. 柳

6. zephyr：(literary) a soft gentle breeze. (暖)风
7. catkin：a flowering spike of trees such as willow and hazel. Catkins are typically downy, pendulous, composed of flowers of a single sex, and wind pollinated. 柳花
8. the Five Ridges：the five mountains in the south of China consisting of Yue Cheng Ling, Du Pang Ling, Meng Zhu Ling, Ji Tian Ling and Da Yu Ling, which are roughly distributed from eastern Guangxi to eastern Guangdong and the borders of four provinces including Hunan, Jiangxi as well as Guangxi, Guangdong. Historically, it roughly included parts of Guangdong (including Hainan, Hong Kong and Macau), Guangxi and eastern Yunnan Provinces, and south-western Fujian Province. 岭南

四、译文赏析

1. **新雪满前山，初晴好天气。**
   日西骑马出，忽有京都意。

译文： It's good weather, now it's just fine.
New snow fills out the hills ahead.
At twilight I ride my horse out,
It's much like Capital instead.

赏析： 开篇两联，诗人交代了天气、背景、时间和地点。雪后初晴的傍晚，诗人远望庐山积雪，欣喜地骑马出城赏雪，一下子回想起自己身在长安时所见的景象，不免有一丝惆怅。两联的对句(偶数句)押尾韵，韵脚为“气”和“意”，译文也是对句押尾韵/ed/。译者调整了第一联中第一句和第二句的顺序，既出于押韵的考量，也使得译文逻辑上更清晰合理。第一联第二句中，fills 和 hills 两词形成句中押韵。译者将“忽”一词译为 instead 而非 suddenly，表达出诗人感受的变化，而非环境的改变。

2. **城柳方缀花，檐冰才结穗。**
   须臾风日暖，处处皆飘坠。

译文： Icicles like ears neath the eaves;
Willows show their flowers by the wall.
All at once, the zephyr turns warm;
Here and there catkins drift and fall.

赏析：两联的对句(偶数句)押尾韵，韵脚为“穗”和“坠”，译文也是对句押尾韵/ɔːl/。出于押韵的考量，译者调整了第三联第一句和第二句的顺序。诗人用“结穗”形容檐下冰凌，非常巧妙新颖，译者保留了这个比喻的意象，用 icicles like ears 比喻冰凌像谷穗(ears of grain)，出于音节的考虑，将暗喻转化为明瑜。这里的柳花其实是柳条上积了雪，垂下的样子如同柳树开了花。catkins 本意是柔荑花，即杨树、柳树等植物开花时下垂的穗状花序。冰凌和柳花都是向下垂挂的样子，只是一个坚硬，一个轻柔。译者用 catkins 同时指代冰凌和柳花，点明两者的共同之处，措辞巧妙。Zephyr 原指希腊神话中的西风神。西风神是春的使者，他吹来温暖湿润的空气滋润万物生长。诗人使用这一富有文化内涵的词，是“归化”的译法。

3. **行吟赏未足，坐叹销何易。**
犹胜岭南看，雰雰不到地。

译文：I sit there and sigh without end,
Not just going, chanting around.
It’s a better than the Five Ridges,
As the catkins don’t reach the ground.

赏析：两联的对句(偶数句)押尾韵，韵脚为“易”和“地”，译文也是对句押尾韵/raʊnd/。出于押韵及逻辑关系的考量，译者调整了第五联第一句和第二句的顺序。第五联的两句中各有三个动词“行”“吟”“赏”和“坐”“叹”“销”，译者减译了“赏”和“销”两词以符合英语的表达习惯。诗人赏雪赏到一半雪就开始融化，不免感到遗憾叹息。不过，江州的雪上比长安不足，下比岭南有余。“雰雰”原意是“飘落的样子”，诗人意指岭南没有积雪，雪花没来得及飘下来就融化了。这里译者继续使用 catkins 一词来指代柳树上的雪花，并增加 as 一词表示因果关系，将汉语的意合关系转换为英语的形合关系。

第六部分 悼亡诗

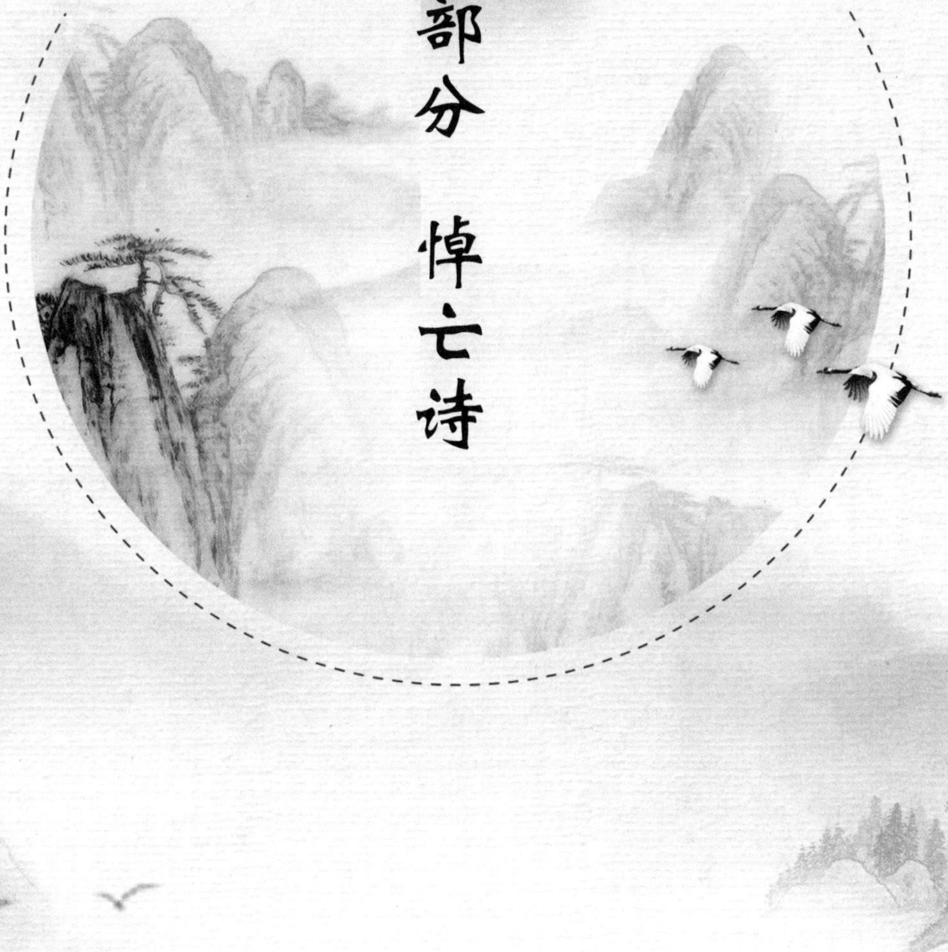

第十六章　天妒英才

第一节　哭刘敦质

一、诗歌背景

刘敦质，字太白，是唐朝著名史官刘知几的曾孙。他曾是白居易的同学，也是白居易在京城为官时结识的挚友，经常一起出游并题诗留念。白居易称刘敦质为风流儒雅的人（“儒风爱敦质”）。刘敦质英年早逝，白居易在多首诗中曾提及他。这首悼亡诗应是刘敦质刚刚去世时所作，白居易从墓地的环境描写开始，重在突出亡友高贵的品质和所受到的不公正待遇，感情上沉重而悲壮。虽然诗人似在责问苍天，但是不难理解他实际上表达是对时代和官场的强烈谴责。

二、古诗原文

哭刘敦质

小树两株柏，
新土三尺坟。
苍苍白露草，
此地哭刘君。
哭君岂无辞，

辞云君子人。
如何天不吊，
穷悴至终身。
愚者多贵寿，
贤者独贱迍。
龙亢彼无悔，
蠖屈此不伸。
哭罢持此辞，
吾将诘羲文。

三、古诗译文

Mourning Tunchih Liu

There grow young trees, cypresses[1] two;
A new tomb of new earth does appear.
The grass is wet with crystal dew;
I've come to mourn Mister Liu here.
How can I not chant now I cry;
I chant: you are a man so good.
Why no mourning comes from the sky?
All life you've been haggard[2], no food.
The stupid enjoy a long life;
The sage[3] are so stringent[4] instead.
A dragon regrets not its strife;
An inchworm[5] extends not its head.
I'll keep this verse now I have cried
And the great kings and lords I'll chide[6].

（赵彦春 译）

◎ 注释

1. cypress：（also cypress tree）an evergreen coniferous tree with small，rounded woody cones and flattened shoots bearing small scale-like leaves. 柏
2. haggard：looking exhausted and unwell，especially from fatigue，worry，or suffering. 穷悴
3. sage：a profoundly wise man，especially one who features in ancient history or legend. 贤者
4. stringent：（of financial conditions）difficult and very strictly controlled because there is not much money 贱迍
5. inchworm：a caterpillar of a geometrid moth，which moves forward by arching and straightening its body. 蠖
6. chide：scold or rebuke. 诘

四、译文赏析

1. **小树两株柏，新土三尺坟。**
   苍苍白露草，此地哭刘君。

译文：There grow young trees，cypresses two；
A new tomb of new earth does appear.
The grass is wet with crystal dew；
I've come to mourn Mister Liu here.

赏析：诗人从环境描写入手，描写了刘君简陋的新坟，直入“哭刘君”的主题。译文的尾韵结构为 ABAB，这里的 two 和 dew 押韵，appear 和 here 押韵，朗朗上口。第一句译者采用了 young trees，cypresses two 同位语加倒装的结构，第二句则增加助动词 does，不仅出于音节和押韵的考量，也使得句式结构富于变化、有韵律感。将“小树”译为 young trees 而非 small trees，与第二句的 new 对应，新坟上的一草一木都让诗人感到陌生，表现诗人对朋友离去这个事实还感到非常陌生、难以接受。

2. **哭君岂无辞，辞云君子人。**
   如何天不吊，穷悴至终身。

译文：How can I not chant now I cry；
I chant：you are a man so good.
Why no mourning comes from the sky?

All life you've been haggard, no food.

赏析：译文的尾韵结构为ABAB，这里的cry和sky押韵，good和food押韵。诗人先垫定“哭”的基调：赞誉刘君品性高洁，谴责上天不公。译者用so good和no food这两个非常直白的措辞翻译“君子”和“穷”两词，不仅出于押韵的考虑，更和原诗直截了当以及白居易诗歌接地气的风格极为接近。

3. 愚者多贵寿，贤者独贱迍。
　龙亢彼无悔，蠖屈此不伸。

译文：The stupid enjoy a long life;
The sage are so stringent instead.
A dragon regrets not its strife;
An inchworm extends not its head.

赏析：译文的尾韵结构为ABAB，这里的life和strife押韵，instead和head押韵。诗人一改前面日常对话的风格，用颇具修辞色彩的语言和对比的方式彰显刘君的高贵品德和悲惨遭遇。居高位者本应“龙亢有悔”，也就是身居高位应戒骄戒躁，否则会因失败而后悔，然而老天不公，愚笨的人享受富贵长寿，居高位者安安稳稳，反倒是刘君这种贤才一贫如洗，有雄才大略却不得志。译者保留了原文“龙”(dragon)和“蠖”(inchworm)的意象，是一种“异化”的翻译，因为这四句的并列结构有助于读者准确理解这两个比喻的确切含义，不会因为异化的翻译而造成理解障碍。

4. 哭罢持此辞，吾将诘羲文。

译文：I'll keep this verse now I have cried,
And the great kings and lords I'll chide.

赏析：译者改变了之前ABAB的韵律结构，使尾联两句互押尾韵。末句采用倒装结构，将动词chide置于句末，既出于押韵的考虑，又使得两句句式对应，突出悲伤和不平的语气。“羲文”原为伏羲氏和周文王的合称，伏羲氏是华夏民族的人文始祖，三皇之一；周文王是周朝的奠基者，是中国历史上著名的明君。译者用意译的方式译为great kings and lords，避免文化差异带来的理解障碍。诗人似在责问远古的贤君伏羲氏和周文王，但实际上表达了对人世间的不平之事以及官场黑暗的强烈谴责，与前面责问“如何天不吊”表达类似。

第二节　哭李三

一、诗歌背景

李三，即李顾言，字仲远，排行第三，曾任监察御史，居长安常乐里，与元稹、白居易是挚友，于元和十年(815年)春卒。元和六年(811年)时，白居易的母亲病逝于长安宣平里邸，白居易辞去官职，率领全家人扶柩回到渭上故里，遵礼丁忧(中国封建社会传统的道德礼仪制度，朝廷官员在位期间，父母去世必须辞官回到祖籍，为父母守制二十七个月)。三年后，白居易仍在故乡渭上务农，欲仕不得，心情十分苦闷。这年暮秋时节，李顾言来渭上看望白居易，令他非常感动，因此有"去年渭水曲，秋时访我来"之说。白居易在《村中留李三顾言宿》中也记录了这次拜访。本诗中诗人以回忆开场，感叹半年之间与李三阴阳两隔，感慨万分。

二、古诗原文

哭李三

去年渭水曲，
秋时访我来。
今年常乐里，
春日哭君回。
哭君仰问天，
天意安在哉？
若必夺其寿，
何如不与才？
落然身后事，
妻病女婴孩。

三、古诗译文

Mourning Li Three

On the bent of the Wei[1] last year,
You called on me an autumn day.
In Constant Glee Lane[2] here this spring,
I mourn that you have gone away.
While mourning you, I ask the sky:
What is your will, what is your plan?
If you must take away his life,
Why you gave talent[3] to this man?
Now he's gone, he's left all in life,
His little daughter and sick wife.

(赵彦春 译)

◎ **注释**

1. the Wei: The Wei River, known as Weishui in ancient times, is the largest tributary of the Yellow River. It originates in the Bird Rat Mountain in Weiyuan County, Dingxi City, Gansu Province, and flows across eastern Gansu and central Shaanxi, mainly through present-day Tianshui in Gansu Province and the Guanzhong Plain in Shaanxi Province, including Baoji, Xianyang, Xi'an and Weinan, before merging into the Yellow River in Tongguan County, Weinan City. The mainstream is 818km long, with a total basin area of 134,766 square kilometers. 渭水
2. Constant Glee Lane: an old neighborhood in Chang'an, located in the eastern part of the city. 常乐里
3. talent: natural aptitude or skill. 才

四、译文赏析

1. 哭李三

译文: Mourning Li Three

赏析：这是一首悼亡诗。“哭”意为“吊唁”，意思是祭奠死者并慰问家属，也是悼亡诗题目中常用的表达方式。mourn 一词符合该场合的意义，且措辞正式，用其动名词形式符合英语标题的表达习惯。

2. 去年渭水曲，秋时访我来。
今年常乐里，春日哭君回。

译文：On the bent of the Wei last year,
You called on me an autumn day.
In Constant Glee Lane here this spring,
I mourn that you have gone away.

赏析：开篇两联诗人对比半年间两次见面的巨大反差，悲伤之情跃然纸上，为后面“哭”的内容做了气氛上的铺垫。这两联对仗十分工整，译文也力求句子结构和措辞工整对应，如 On 对 In，You called 对 I mourn。但基于音节和押韵的考虑，译者对诸如“去年”“今年”以及“秋时”“春日”这几个时间状语做了相应的调整。原文为五言古诗，尾韵结构为除第二联外，每联对句句尾押韵。译文的尾韵结构为第一联和第二联、第三联和第四联的对句分别押尾韵/eɪ/和/æn/，最后一联两句押尾韵/aɪf/。

3. 哭君仰问天，天意安在哉？
若必夺其寿，何如不与才？

译文：While mourning you, I ask the sky:
What is your will, what is your plan?
If you must take away his life,
Why you gave talent to this man?

赏析：原文这二联的两个对句句尾押韵，韵脚为“哉”和“才”。译文两句句尾 plan 和 man 押尾韵/æn/。诗人与苍天对话，责问苍天为何赋予李君才华却又过早剥夺他的生命。诗人巧妙地设计了反问语气，惋惜之情彰显无遗。译文保留了反问的语气，并将原文否定形式的“不与才”译为肯定的“you gave talent”，属于反说正译，更符合英语表达习惯，便于读者理解。出于音节数考虑，Why you gave talent to this man 一句省略了助动词 do，这种省略在诗歌中很常见。

4. 落然身后事，妻病女婴孩。

译文：Now he’s gone, he’s left all in life,
His little daughter and sick wife.

赏析：原文尾联两句本无韵，译文则按照英语诗歌的习惯增加了尾韵/aɪf/。“落然”表示凄凉的样子，“身后事”指去世后留下的事情。译者增译了 Now he’s gone，并将“身后事”具体化为所有的亲人——all in life，使译文前后逻辑连贯，意义更为明确。出于押韵的考虑，译者调整了“妻病”和“女婴孩”的前后位置，使 life 与 wife 押尾韵。

第三节 伤杨弘贞

一、诗歌背景

杨弘贞排行第九，生平不详。元和四年(809 年)中进士，在《文苑英华》中为“杨宏真”或“杨真宏”，或为后人避讳而改动。杨弘贞才学无量，擅长诗赋，《全唐文》共收录了他的七篇赋作。但他英年早逝，离世时未满三十岁，白居易对此无比惋惜，同时也以杨弘贞自喻，觉得自己像他一样，空有才情、命运多舛。白居易在不少诗作中都曾提及杨弘贞，如《重过寿泉忆与杨九别时因题店壁》《酬杨九弘贞长安病中见寄》等。

二、古诗原文

伤杨弘贞

颜子昔短命，
仲尼惜其贤。
杨生亦好学，
不幸复徒然。
谁识天地意，
独与龟鹤年。

三、古诗译文

Mourning Hungchen Yang

Hui Yan[1] died young, so short his life;

For his worth Confucius[2] felt pain.
Mister Yang was a sage[3] one too,
So sad, his life could not remain.
Who knows the will of Sky and Earth?
But macrobians[4], turtle[5] or crane[6].

（赵彦春　译）

◎ 注释

1. Hui Yan：（c. 521 B. C. -481 B. C. ）a Chinese philosopher. He was the favourite disciple of Confucius and one of the most revered figures of Confucianism. He is venerated in Confucian temples as one of the Four Sages. 颜子
2. Confucius：or Kongzi，（c. 551 B. C. -c. 479 B. C. ），a Chinese philosopher and politician of the Spring and Autumn Period who is traditionally considered the paragon of Chinese sages. Confucius's teachings and philosophy underpin East Asian culture and society，remaining influential across East Asia to this day. He is venerated in Confucian temples as one of the Four Sages. 仲尼
3. sage：a profoundly wise man，especially one who features in ancient history or legend. 好学
4. macrobian：having an exceptionally long life span. 年
5. turtle：a slow-moving reptile，enclosed in a scaly or leathery domed shell into which it can retract its head and thick legs，known for its long lifespan in Chinese culture. 龟
6. crane：a tall，long-legged，long-necked bird，typically with white or gray plumage and often with tail plumes and patches of bare red skin on the head，known for its long lifespan in Chinese culture. 鹤

四、译文赏析

1. 伤杨弘贞

译文： Mourning Hungchen Yang

赏析：“伤”是“哀伤、叹息”的意思，这里是对杨弘贞的死表示哀悼，也是悼亡诗题目中常用的表达方式。mourn 一词措辞正式，符合该场合的意义，用其动名词形式符合英语标题的表达习惯。

2. 颜子昔短命，仲尼惜其贤。

译文：Hui Yan died young, so short his life;

For his worth Confucius felt pain.

赏析：颜回死时仅四十岁（也有说三十几岁），孔子对他的死“哭之恸”，并对鲁哀公说：“有颜回者好学，不迁怒，不贰过。不幸短命死矣，今也则亡。”诗人开篇用颜子的典故，将亡友杨弘贞与孔子最中意的学生相比，为悼文奠定了很高的基调，表达了对贤才英年早逝的深深惋惜。译者将原文中的“惜”译为语气更为强烈的 felt pain，较符合西方文化中外露的情感表达方式。原诗为每联对句（偶数句）押尾韵，韵脚为“贤”“然”“年”，译文也遵循这一尾韵规律，每联对句押尾韵/eɪn/。

3. 杨生亦好学，不幸复徒然。

译文：Mister Yang was a sage one too,

So sad, his life could not remain.

赏析：诗人从颜回的典故回到亡友身上，用“亦”一词表明两者的共同之处，即“好学”。由上下文可见“好学”并非“喜欢学习”的意思，而是与“贤”同义。sage 一词意为“贤明、睿智之人”，孔子和弟子颜回都被誉为儒家“四圣”（the Four Sages）（另两位是曾子和孟子）；西方文化中也有“七贤人”之称（the Seven Sages），指的是古代希腊七位名人，他们大多是著名的哲学家，如泰勒斯以及立法者梭伦等。虽然两种文化中 sage 的具体所指并不相同，但在读者心目中产生的敬畏效果类似，属于功能对等的译法。

4. 谁识天地意，独与龟鹤年。

译文：Who knows the will of Sky and Earth?

But macrobians, turtle or crane.

赏析：尾联中诗人采用疑问语气，质疑苍天，表达对友人英年早逝的惋惜，译者也采用了疑问句，与原文的形式和语气形成对等。will 为名词，表示“意愿”；而“天地”译者则直译为 Sky and Earth 而非西方习惯使用的 God 一词，与“天地”形成形式和内容上的对等，这一异化的翻译方式对译文读者并不会造成理解障碍。此外，译者还直译了“龟”“鹤”这两种中国文化中代表长寿的动物，也属于异化的翻译方式，但增译了 macrobians（“长寿的生物”）一词，以弥补西方读者的文化空白，避免理解障碍。末句的翻译十分巧妙，原文是“动词+名词”的结构，直译就是 only give turtles and cranes long life，译者仅译为“But+名词”的结构，既符合英语形合的表达习惯，也十分简洁和明确。

第十七章　魂牵梦萦

第一节　梦微之

一、诗歌背景

元稹(779—831 年)，字微之，别字威明，河南洛阳人。唐朝大臣、文学家。唐贞元十九年(803 年)，24 岁的元稹和长他七岁的白居易同科及第并成为校书郎。两人倾慕对方的文采，政治抱负相似，从此成为一生的挚友。他们一起倡导新乐府运动，共创“元和体”，世称“元白”。元和十年(815 年)元稹被贬为通州司马，同年白居易被贬江州司马。此后，二人只能互通书信、倾诉衷肠。太和五年(831 年)，元稹病逝于武昌。此诗作于开成五年(840 年)，白居易这年六十八岁，距元稹去世已八年有余，但诗人对老友的思念如故。某夜梦到元稹后，诗人创作了这首诗。

二、古诗原文

梦微之

夜来携手梦同游，

晨起盈巾泪莫收。

漳浦老身三度病，

咸阳宿草八回秋。

君埋泉下泥销骨，
我寄人间雪满头。
阿卫韩郎相次去，
夜台茫昧得知不？

三、古诗译文

Dreaming of Yuan Nine

We toured hand in hand in my dream at night;
Wakened up in the morn, I keep my tears.
I've fallen ill riverside[1] for three times;
In Long Peace grass has grown mild for eight years.
Down in Hades[2], your bones in soil decay;
In this world, my hair is o'er grown with snow.
Ah Wei[3] and Lang Han[4] have also died now;
The dark inside the tomb can they e'er know?

（赵彦春　译）

◎ **注释**

1. riverside: referring to Zhangpu, a place in the south of Zhangzhou, Fujian Province. 漳浦
2. Hades: the underworld; the abode of the spirits of the dead. 泉下
3. Ah Wei: the youngest son of Yuan Nine. 阿卫
4. Lang Han: the son in law of Yuan Nine. 韩郎

四、译文赏析

1. **夜来携手梦同游，晨起盈巾泪莫收。**

译文： We toured hand in hand in my dream at night;
Wakened up in the morn, I keep my tears.

赏析：原诗为七言律诗，首联两句押尾韵 ou，颈联的偶数句也押同样的尾韵。译文每行 10 个音节。首联中译者巧妙地使用 we 和 wakened 两词作为句首词，使两句押头韵。因音节限制，morning 采用了缩写形式 morn。

2. **漳浦老身三度病，咸阳宿草八回秋。**

译文：I've fallen ill riverside for three times;

In Long Peace grass has grown mild for eight years.

赏析：漳浦在福建，但白居易并不在漳浦，而是用建安七子之一的刘桢病卧漳浦的典故自喻，而元稹安葬在陕西省咸阳县，因此该联分别是说自己疾病缠身而元稹已离世八年有余。漳浦的典故因过于复杂，译者简单地译为 riverside 并不影响译文的整体意义，而"三度""八回"对仗工整，译者也将其译为十分对应的 for three times 和 for eight years。

3. **君埋泉下泥销骨，我寄人间雪满头。**

译文：Down in Hades, your bones in soil decay;

In this world, my hair is o'er grown with snow.

赏析：译文三、四联对句押尾韵/əʊ/，韵脚为 snow 和 know。译者将"泉下"译为 Hades，即希腊神话中的地下世界，也是人死后所去的地方，为西方读者所熟悉，属于归化的译法。颈联两句诗人感叹与朋友天人永隔，"我"的"雪满头"不仅是岁月，更是思念。诗人悲切之情深切，译者也译得铿锵顿挫，尤其是将"泥销骨"译为 your bones in soil decay，将动词 decay 倒装到状语 in soil 之后，使得整句的音节轻重相间，极富韵律感。

4. **阿卫韩郎相次去，夜台茫昧得知不？**

译文：Ah Wei and Lang Han have also died now;

The dark inside the tomb can they e'er know?

赏析：阿卫、韩郎分别是元稹的儿子和女婿，元稹死后的八年内两人接连去世，风烛残年的白居易向梦中的友人告知他家的近况，如同与老朋友见面拉家常，平淡之中透着凄凉。译者保留了原文的疑问语气，营造出魂牵梦绕、余音未绝之感。

第二节　梦裴相公

一、诗歌背景

裴垍(jì)(？—811)，字弘中，绛州闻喜(今山西闻喜县)人，唐宪宗元和初年曾经在学士院担任翰林学士，后来担任宰相。裴垍为人正直、知人善任。裴垍欣赏白居易的才学，白居易在贞元十九年吏部试拔萃科、元和元年的制举“才识兼茂明于体用科”的考试中，都得到主考官裴垍的赏识，后来在裴垍的举荐下进入翰林院，曾与裴垍共事。白居易对裴垍不仅怀有知遇之恩，也充满了钦佩。本诗作于816年，裴垍去世已有五年。白居易梦见自己和裴相公如往日那样在金銮殿一起工作，对方的音容笑貌清清楚楚地呈现在眼前，醒来回味如此真实的梦境，想起两人昔日的感情，不禁泪流满面。

二、古诗原文

梦裴相公

五年生死隔，
一夕魂梦通。
梦中如往日，
同直金銮宫。
仿佛金紫色，
分明冰玉容。
勤勤相眷意，
亦与平生同。
既寤知是梦，
悯然情未终。
追想当时事，
何殊昨夜中？

自我学心法，
万缘成一空。
今朝为君子，
流涕一沾胸。

三、古诗译文

Dreaming of Minister[1] Pei

It's been five years since you left me;
At night your soul did to me fall.
In my dream, the same as before,
We were on shift in Golden Hall[2].
It seems all were purple and gold;
There beamed your fair crystalline[3] face.
Isn't it just like our normal life
That we cherish our love and grace?
Awake, I knew it was a dream;
Altho our feelings still clung tight.
What happened then in our past life
Is just like what happened last night.
As I have now learned Dhata-mind[4],
Everything has turned into none[5].
But still, my friend, for you today
My tears, wetting my clothes, drip on.

（赵彦春　译）

◎ 注释

1. Minister: the title for the high ranking officials. 相公
2. Golden Hall: a palace complex within the Daming Palace in Chang'an, the capital of the Tang Dynasty located on a high platform to the west of the Penglai Hall in the rear court. It

was the place where the emperor summoned his ministers to the inner court and discussed important matters. 金銮宫

3. crystalline: having the structure and form of a crystal; composed of crystals. 冰玉

4. Dhata-mind: Dharma(法) is a Buddhist terminology, referring to the nature of reality regarded as a universal truth taught by the Buddha. In context, it also means "right way of living" and "path of rightness". Dhata-mind is an austerity practice practiced by monks. A monk who practices austerities is able to remove his greed for food, clothing and shelter, just as he removes the dust from his clothes. 心法

5. none: opposite of "there", meaning emptiness, purity, non-being. The idea that there is no self, no entity, no I, etc., in all things that exist is called "none". It is also referred to as the illusion of things, or the emptiness and purity of the rational body. 空

四、译文赏析

1. 梦裴相公

译文： Dreaming of Minister Pei

赏析： 在唐代，"相公"是宰相的专属称谓。宰相是辅助帝王掌管国事的最高官员的通称，是除皇帝外的国家最高领导层。宰相不是一个具体的官名，唐朝的中书令、侍中、尚书令，及参议政事的中书侍郎、门下侍郎都是宰相。裴垍在唐宪宗时任中书侍郎、同平章事，因此译为 Minister。

2. 五年生死隔，一夕魂梦通。
梦中如往日，同直金銮宫。

译文： It's been five years since you left me;
At night your soul did to me fall.
In my dream, the same as before,
We were on shift in Golden Hall.

赏析： 这首五言古诗的每联对句均押尾韵 ong，第一、二联的韵脚为"通"和"宫"。译文每行 8 个音节，尾韵规律为相邻两联对句押尾韵/ɔːl/。出于押韵考虑，译者将首联对句动词放句末，并增加助动词 did。诗人开门见山，梦见与裴相公昔日在一起工作的情形。"直"即"值"，也就是两人在金銮宫一同值班，译者将此直译为 on shift。

3. 仿佛金紫色，分明冰玉容。
   勤勤相眷意，亦与平生同。

译文：It seems all were purple and gold;
There beamed your fair crystalline face.
Isn't it just like our normal life
That we cherish our love and grace?

赏析："勤勤"表示不间断，"相眷"意为互相眷恋。诗人在梦中看到裴相公在金銮殿金紫色光芒中的身影，也看到了裴相公刚正不阿的容貌，更回想起两人共事时的心心相通、互相关爱。译者以 It seems 和 There beamed 作为第三联两句的开始，结构和措辞上都非常工整，与原文的"仿佛"和"分明"对应，又将"容"的意义表现其中，非常传神。译者将第四联的陈述句译为反问句，使得语气较第二联的 the same as before 更为强烈，也避免了重复。

4. 既寤知是梦，悯然情未终。
   追想当时事，何殊昨夜中？

译文：Awake, I knew it was a dream;
Altho our feelings still clung tight.
What happened then in our past life
Is just like what happened last night.

赏析：诗人从梦中醒来惆怅万分，惊诧于梦中所见竟然与旧时一模一样，说明诗人经常想念裴相公，以至于若干年后还能清楚地回忆他的音容笑貌。"既寤知是梦，悯然情未终"一联译者将意合的句子译成"形容词状语+主句+宾语从句+让步状语从句"的形合结构，并反说正译，用 clung tight 一词精准地表达出"情未终"。

5. 自我学心法，万缘成一空。
   今朝为君子，流涕一沾胸。

译文：As I have now learned Dhata-mind,
Everything has turned into none.
But still, my friend, for you today
My tears, wetting my clothes, drip on.

赏析：白居易晚年为居士，自称皈依佛门，经历过人生的起起落落，感悟到"馀物净浮云”，认为万事皆空。然而“今天”的梦中相见却令诗人不能保持内心的平静、将思念和友情置之身外，不禁泪流满面。Dhata（法）是佛教术语。《俱舍论》称“能持自相故名为法”，意思是凡具有质的规定性并为人们所认识的一切事物和现象称为法。五位七十五法中的“心法”即精神现象，佛教弟子通过修行练心法以排除杂念和欲望，因此译者用 mind 一词表示“心”。

第三节　感旧纱帽（帽即故李侍郎所赠）

一、诗歌背景

李侍郎指中大夫尚书刑部侍郎、工部尚书李建（764—821 年），字杓直，荆州石首县（今湖北石首市）人，祖籍陇西成纪（今甘肃省秦安县）。出身清贫，努力学习。贞元年间，考中进士第二名，起家校书郎，任右拾遗、翰林学士。唐宪宗时期历任京兆尹、澧州刺史，拜太常少卿、检校礼部侍郎，知贡举。唐穆宗即位，授刑部侍郎。长庆元年（821 年）去世，享年 57 岁，获赠工部尚书。李建和当时的白居易、元稹等人是生死之交。白居易曾有多篇诗文提及他，如《同李十一醉忆元九》《春早秋初因时即事兼寄浙东李侍郎》《祭李侍郎文》等。诗人睹物思人，语气悲凉，情感真切。

二、古诗原文

感旧纱帽（帽即故李侍郎所赠）

昔君乌纱帽，
赠我白头翁。
帽今在顶上，
君已归泉中。
物故犹堪用，
人亡不可逢。

岐山今夜月，
坟树正秋风。

三、古诗译文

Thought at the Old Gauze Hat[1], a Gift from the Late[2] Attendant Li

I cherish the gauze hat, a gift
From you for my gray pate[3], white hair.
Now the hat is still on my top,
But you are down in Hades[4] there.
A thing can be used though it's old;
A man can't be met once he's gone.
To Mt. Offset[5] snow falls tonight;
To the tomb trees a wind blows on.

（赵彦春 译）

◎ 注释

1. gauze hat：one of the most important forms of Chinese headwear as an integral part of the official uniform in ancient China with a history of more than one-thousand years. It first appeared in the Eastern Jin Dynasty. This kind of hat became a part of clothing for government officers in the Sui Dynasty, and was popularized in the Tang Dynasty. During the Song Dynasty, the "double wing" was added, and since the Ming Dynasty, the black hat officially has become synonymous with being an official for the eunuch. 乌纱帽
2. late：（of a specified person）no longer alive. 故
3. pate：a person's head. 头
4. Hades：the underworld；the abode of the spirits of the dead. 泉中
5. Mt. Offset：or Qishan County, part of Baoji City, Shaanxi Province, located in the western part of Guanzhong, in the northeastern part of Baoji City. 岐山

四、译文赏析

1. 感旧纱帽(帽即故李侍郎所赠)

译文：Thought at the Old Gauze Hat，a Gift from the Late Attendant Li

赏析：原诗题为动词短语“感旧纱帽”，并用括号方式对旧纱帽进行补充说明。译者按照英语习惯，将诗题译为名词 Thought 短语，并以同位语短语 a Gift from the Late Attendant Li 补充说明。Late 表示“已故的”，乌纱帽(black gauze cap)是古代官吏戴的一种帽子，这原是民间常见的一种便帽，官员头戴乌纱帽起源于东晋，但作为正式官服的一个组成部分始于隋朝，兴盛于唐朝。

2. 昔君乌纱帽，赠我白头翁。
帽今在顶上，君已归泉中。

译文：I cherish the gauze hat，a gift

From you for my gray pate，white hair.

Now the hat is still on my top，

But you are down in Hades there.

赏析：原诗四联每联对句押尾韵 ng，这两联的韵脚为“翁”和“中”。译文相邻两联互押尾韵，首联和颔联押尾韵/eə(r)/。原文首联主语为“乌纱帽”，因此动词“赠”本是被动，译者用 cherish 作为谓语将句子巧妙地转化为主动结构，表达上情真意切，而用“同位语+介词短语”的结构 a gift for 译出原文的动词，符合英语表达习惯，也译出了原诗“赠”一词的意义。译者将“归泉中”译为 down in Hades，Hades 即希腊神话中的地下世界，也是人死后所去的地方，为西方读者所熟悉，属于归化的翻译方式。

3. 物故犹堪用，人亡不可逢。
岐山今夜月，坟树正秋风。

译文：A thing can be used though it’s old；

A man can’t be met once he’s gone.

To Mt. Offset snow falls tonight；

To the tomb trees a wind blows on.

赏析：译文这两联互押尾韵/ɔn/，韵脚为 gone 和 on。译者巧妙构思，在句子结构和措辞上与原文一样对仗工整，原文的“物故”对“人亡”，“岐山”对“坟树”，“夜月”对“秋风”，而译文的 A thing can be 和 A man can’t be 相对，To Mt Offset 与 To the tomb trees 相对，snow falls 与 wind blows 相对，营造出阴阳两隔的凄凉之感。

第十八章　彩云易散

第一节　重伤小女子

一、诗歌背景

本诗为白居易于唐宪宗元和十年(815年)为悼念亡女金銮子所作，“小女子”即白居易的爱女金銮子。白居易36岁时才得此女儿，将其视为掌上明珠。不幸的是，元和六年(811年)金銮子刚满三岁就生病夭折了。此时白居易的母亲刚刚去世，自己又久病不愈，女儿的死对他的打击非常大，女儿死时他因为正为母亲守孝，没有俸禄，甚至无法厚葬爱女，只好让妻子杨氏当了手上的玉镯，才将爱女裹尸薄葬。白居易曾作《病中哭金銮子》《念金銮子二首》等诗歌悼念女儿。此诗为女儿死后四年所作，因此题目为“重伤”。虽隔数年，女儿的一颦一笑依旧在眼前，诗人的伤感之情丝毫不减，整首诗中弥漫着诗人对女儿的无限思念。

二、古诗原文

重伤小女子

学人言语凭床行，
嫩似花房脆似琼。
才知恩爱迎三岁，
未辨东西过一生。

汝异下殇应杀礼，
吾非上圣讵忘情。
伤心自叹鸠巢拙，
长堕春雏养不成。

三、古诗译文

Mourning My Little Daughter Again

Babbling human speech, walking by the bed;
Tender like a bud, fragile like a gem[1].
You knew what love was, going on three,
And died, when able to tell "us" from "them".
You not of Lower Death[2], no rite[3] was held;
As I'm no saint[4], how could I have no love?
How sad, I sigh how crude the bird nest was!
There I could not bring up my turtledove[5].

(赵彦春 译)

◎ 注释

1. gem: a precious or semiprecious stone, especially when cut and polished or engraved. 琼
2. Lower Death: the death between the age of eight and eleven. 下殇
3. rite: a religious or other solemn ceremony or act. 礼
4. saint: a person acknowledged as holy or virtuous and typically regarded as being in heaven after death. 上圣
5. turtledove: a small bird with a soft purring call like dove, noted for the apparent affection shown for its mate. 春雏(鸠)

四、译文赏析

1. 学人言语凭床行，嫩似花房脆似琼。

译文： Babbling human speech, walking by the bed;

Tender like a bud, fragile like a gem.

赏析：首联两句诗人用两组动词和两组比喻描述了女儿的可爱，译者并没有将意合的中文句子转化为形合的英文结构，而是译为两个并列的分词短语 babbling human speech, walking by the bed 和两个并列的形容词短语 tender like a bud, fragile like a gem，保留了原文的明喻结构，与原文在内容上和形式上几乎完全对等，如同一幅画卷，将小女儿可爱的模样呈现在读者眼前。

2. **才知恩爱迎三岁，未辨东西过一生。**

译文：You knew what love was, going on three,

And died, when able to tell "us" from "them".

赏析：原文偶数句押尾韵 ng，译文第一、二联偶数句押尾韵/em/。原诗首联和颔联所有句子均为无主句，根据颈联的"汝"字，诗人在整首诗中都使用第二人称 you，也让感情流露更为直接和强烈。"未辨东西过一生"表示女儿早夭，死时尚懵懂不懂世间事物，译者译为 died, when able to tell... 采用反说正译的方式，符合英语表达习惯；出于押韵的考虑，译者将"辨东西"译为 tell "us" from "them"，虽然内容不同但功能对等。

3. **汝异下殇应杀礼，吾非上圣讵忘情。**

译文：You not of Lower Death, no rite was held;

As I'm no saint, how could I have no love?

赏析："下殇"出自《仪礼·丧服》："年十九至十六为长殇，十五至十二为中殇，十一至八岁为下殇，不满八岁以下皆为无服之殇。"也就是说，孩子三岁死去按照习俗不应该举行隆重的葬礼，译者将"下殇"按字面译为 Lower Death，将"上圣"译为 saint，还将原文的否定句"讵忘情"改译为反问句 how could I，语气十分强烈，将父亲的丧女之痛表达得淋漓尽致。

4. **伤心自叹鸠巢拙，长堕春雏养不成。**

译文：How sad, I sigh how crude the bird nest was!

There I could not bring up my turtledove.

赏析：原文偶数句押尾韵 ng，译文第三、四联偶数句押尾韵/ʌv/。原诗尾联为无主句，根据颈联的"吾"字，诗人在此使用第一人称 I。诗人对女儿的夭折不仅伤心，更是自责未尽到父亲的责任。尾联有两处暗喻："鸠巢"喻指诗人家里条件不好，因为斑鸠以不会筑巢闻名；"春雏"喻指诗人三岁的女儿，如同春天里刚刚出生还没有生存能力的小鸟。译者保留了两处暗喻，翻译时对前后顺序进行了一些调整，将“鸠巢拙”译为 crude the bird nest was，而将“春雏”译为 turtledove，即斑鸠，从而使译文的上下两句相互对应、浑然一体。

第二节　简简吟

一、诗歌背景

这一首新乐府诗，约作于长庆三年(823 年)前。“新乐府”即“新题乐府”，是相对于古乐府而言。唐朝时白居易、元稹大力倡导了以创作新题乐府诗为中心的诗歌革新运动。新乐府诗题材比较广泛，内容比较深入，同时更注重体现现实生活，多用浅显的语言。即“文章合为时而著，歌诗合为事而作”。诗歌的前半部分描绘了少女苏简简的美貌和才情，诗人用“芙蓉”“柳叶”“玲珑”“飘飖”“蔷薇”“有光”等诸多美好的事物描绘简简，之后“二月繁霜杀桃李”，美好戛然而止。诗人以外人口吻劝慰她的父母，用“彩云”和“琉璃”两个意象加强视觉冲击，更让人产生对美好事物逝去的惋惜之情。

二、古诗原文

简 简 吟

苏家小女名简简，
芙蓉花腮柳叶眼。
十一把镜学点妆，
十二抽针能绣裳。
十三行坐事调品，
不肯迷头白地藏。
玲珑云髻生花样，
飘飖风袖蔷薇香。
殊姿异态不可状，

忽忽转动如有光。
二月繁霜杀桃李，
明年欲嫁今年死。
丈人阿母勿悲啼，
此女不是凡夫妻。
恐是天仙谪人世，
只合人间十三岁。
大都好物不坚牢，
彩云易散琉璃脆。

三、古诗译文

A Chant[1] of Chienchien

The Sus' have a girl, with Chienchien her style;
Rosy her face, her willow-leaf eyes smile.
At eleven, she'd make up, glass in hand;
At twelve, brocading[2] she could well command.
At thirteen now, no tunes she's left untried;
She would not veil[3] her head, as she won't hide.
She can design various styles of her bun[4];
From her sleeves there's rose fragrance flowing on.
Her graceful bearing[5] one can hardly tell,
Turning and turning like a charming spell.
The second moon, frost does peach and plum sear[6];
She's died this year ere[7] her marriage next year.
Father, mother, do not wail, do not squall[8];
This girl won't be a mundane[9] wife at all.
She's Goddess exiled[10] to this world, I fear;
She's been destined to go the thirteenth year.
In a large sense, good things one can't hold fast[11];

Glass is fragile[12], and rainbows won't long last.

(赵彦春　译)

◎ 注释

1. chant：a short musical passage in two or more phrases used for singing unmetrical words；a psalm or canticle sung to such music. 吟
2. brocade：a rich fabric woven with a raised pattern，typically with gold or silver thread. 绣
3. veil：cover with a veil. 迷头
4. bun：a hairstyle in which the hair is drawn back into a tight coil at the back of the head. 云髻
5. bearing：a person's way of standing or moving. 姿、态
6. sear：burn or scorch the surface of（something）with a sudden，intense heat. 杀
7. ere：before. 欲
8. squall：（of a baby or small child）cry noisily and continuously. 啼
9. mundane：of this earthly world rather than a heavenly or spiritual one. 凡
10. exile：expel and bar（someone）from their native country，typically for political or punitive reasons. 谪
11. hold fast：so as to be hard to move；securely. 坚牢
12. fragile：（of an object）easily broken or damaged. 脆

四、译文赏析

1. 苏家小女名简简，芙蓉花腮柳叶眼。

译文： The Sus' have a girl，with Chienchien her style；
Rosy her face，her willow-leaf eyes smile.

赏析： 诗人开篇不设铺垫直入主题，用两个比喻勾勒出苏家小女的美丽容貌和灵动的表情。由于文化差异，用芙蓉和柳叶描写女子的容貌很难让西方读者产生情感上的共鸣，因此译者将"芙蓉花腮"译为 rosy face 而非字面的 hibiscus(芙蓉花)，符合英语对美丽女子容貌的描写习惯；将"柳叶眼"译为 willow-leaf eyes 但同时增译 smile 一词，有助于西方读者建立本体和喻体之间的联系。原文为七言新乐府诗歌，每联句尾押尾韵，首联押尾韵 ɑn，译者全诗也沿用了同样的尾韵特点，首联两句押尾韵/aɪl/，为此，第一句中的"名"译为 style。

2. 十一把镜学点妆，十二抽针能绣裳。
十三行坐事调品，不肯迷头白地藏。
……
殊姿异态不可状，忽忽转动如有光。

译文：At eleven, she'd make up, glass in hand;
At twelve, brocading she could well command.
At thirteen now, no tunes she's left untried;
She would not veil her head, as she won't hide.
…
Her graceful bearing one can hardly tell,
Turning and turning like a charming spell.

赏析：这三联描写了简简的成长过程和良好修养。简简不仅天生丽质，而且努力提升自我，自小琴棋书画样样精通。译者将"行坐事调品"正说反译，译为 no tunes she's left untried，与本联的后一句 would not veil her head 均为否定句，两句构成对仗，十分巧妙。"调品"即调丝品竹，即演奏弦乐和管乐，译者笼统地译为 tunes，简单明了。"殊姿异态"即特殊的姿态，译者更确切地译为 graceful(优雅的) bearing，与后面的 charming(迷人的) spell 相互呼应，使得译文自然顺畅、浑然一体。除了每联两句句尾互押尾韵外，译文第五联的 bearing，turning 和 charming 几个词构成句内押韵，且采用 ing 的词尾结构。

3. 恐是天仙谪人世，只合人间十三岁。
大都好物不坚牢，彩云易散琉璃脆。

译文：She's Goddess exiled to this world, I fear;
She's been destined to go the thirteenth year.
In a large sense, good things one can't hold fast;
Glass is fragile, and rainbows won't long last.

赏析：这里诗人以外人的口吻劝慰简简的父母，用天仙、彩云和琉璃这些美好的事物作比，既是感叹世事无常，也是留给父母一份美好的念想。译者将"天仙"和"彩云"译为 Goddess 和 rainbows，保留了原诗的喻体，但将"琉璃"这一文化色彩较浓的意象译为 glass(玻璃)。两者虽有一定的差别，但玻璃在烧制方法以及易碎、晶莹等特点上与琉璃非常近似，译为 glass 有助于西方读者的理解。

第三节　真娘墓

一、诗歌背景

这是一首杂言古诗。杂言古诗属古体诗的一种，句式长短不一，节奏变化较多。真娘生活在唐代，自幼父母双亡，被骗入青楼后因貌美擅舞成为苏州名噪一时的歌妓。但她人品高洁，守身如玉，为反抗鸨母的压迫而投缳自尽，葬在虎丘寺侧。唐敬宗宝历元年(825年)，白居易担任苏州刺史时曾凭吊真娘墓。诗人从真娘墓的凭吊入手，广用譬喻：用桃李、莲荷形容美人风姿；用霜摧桃李、风折莲荷来比喻美人逝去；用塞北花、江南雪比喻美人生命的短暂，抒发了对真娘美貌的赞赏和珍惜，以及对美好事物容易消逝的感伤。白居易的不少诗作都反映了封建社会妇女的不幸遭遇，诗人对她们的悲惨命运寄予了深切的同情。

二、古诗原文

真娘墓

真娘墓，虎丘道。
不识真娘镜中面，
唯见真娘墓头草。
霜摧桃李风折莲，
真娘死时犹少年。
脂肤荑手不牢固，
世间尤物难留连。
难留连，易销歇，
塞北花，江南雪。

三、古诗译文

There Lady Virtue's Tomb

There Lady Virtue's tomb,

At Tiger Knoll[1] does loom.
You can't see Lady Virtue in the glass,
Only her tomb o'er there in the deep grass.
Frost bites peach and plum, lotus blown aside;
Lady Virtue was still young when she died.
A creamy tender hand you can't hold fast;
A stunner[2] on earth cannot so long last.
It can't so long last, so inclined[3] to go;
Like northern[4] flowers, like southern light snow.

（赵彦春　译）

◎ **注释**

1. Tiger Knoll: also called Huqiu, a small hill or mound located in the northwest of Suzhou City, Jiangsu Province, and is also known as Haichong Mountain. It is said that King Helv of Wu was buried here. On it there are famous monuments such as Huqiu Pagoda, Yunyan Temple, Sword Pond and Thousand People Stone. 虎丘
2. stunner: a strikingly beautiful or impressive person or thing. 尤物
3. inclined: having a tendency to do something. 易
4. northern: the area to the north of the Great Wall, which was the historical dividing line between the Han ethnic group and the nomadic tribes of the north. The location of Saibei varies from period to period. 塞北

四、译文赏析

1.　真娘墓

真娘墓，虎丘道。

译文：There Lady Virtue's Tomb

There Lady Virtue's tomb,
At Tiger Knoll does loom.

赏析：本诗为杂言古诗，句式长短交错。第一行和最后两行均为两个三言，其他为六个七言。译者将三言句译为 5 个或 6 个音节的短句，七言译为 10 个音节的句子，体现出

句子长短节奏的变化，并使开篇两个短句押尾韵/uːm/。出于音节和押韵的考虑，译者根据上下文在“真娘墓”一句中增译了 There 一词，“虎丘道”一句增译了 loom 一词。与古乐府诗歌类似，本诗题目即第一句话，因此诗题中的 There 一词也予以保留。

2. 霜摧桃李风折莲，
真娘死时犹少年。

译文：Frost bites peach and plum, lotus blown aside;
Lady Virtue was still young when she died.

赏析：诗人以桃花、李花、荷花比喻真娘的锦瑟年华，以“霜”“风”比喻那些摧残真娘的邪恶势力。译者译出了这些比喻意象，特别是将“霜摧”译为 frost bites，该词来自英语的 frostbite 一词，含有类似的比喻，十分贴切。原文这两句七言押尾韵 iɑn，译文也互押尾韵/ɑɪd/。

3. 脂肤荑手不牢固，
世间尤物难留连。

译文：A creamy tender hand you can't hold fast;
A stunner on earth cannot so long last.

赏析：脂肤荑手来自《诗经·卫风·硕人》：“手如柔荑，肤如凝脂。”柔荑指植物初生的叶芽，旧时多用来比喻女子柔嫩洁白的手；凝脂指凝冻了的油脂，比喻光洁白润的皮肤。这两个比喻文化色彩较为浓厚，可能对西方读者造成理解障碍，因此译者译为 creamy 和 tender，便于读者的理解。译者将手和皮肤的“牢固”转译为 hold fast，fast 与后一句的 last 押尾韵。

4. 难留连，易销歇，
塞北花，江南雪。

译文：It can't so long last, so inclined to go;
Like northern flowers, like southern light snow.

赏析：最后诗人发出感叹，用“难”与“易”的对比，“塞北花，江南雪”的比喻感叹真娘美好生命的短暂。译者将这两组三言句译为对仗的两组 5 个音节的短句，用两个 so 和两个 like 使两个短句两两对仗，与原文形式、结构对等，且两组的句尾 go 和 snow 互押尾韵/əʊ/。

参考文献

1. 白居易. 白居易集[M]. 济南：山东文艺出版社，2021.
2. 白寿彝. 中国史学史(第三版)[M]. 北京：北京师范大学出版社，2016.
3. 晁旭. 论白居易江州诗歌的悲秋主题[J]. 连云港师范高等专科学校学报，2020，37(2)：55-58.
4. 陈伯海，等. 唐诗汇评[M]. 上海：上海古籍出版社，2015.
5. 陈建国. 江州司马白居易[M]. 南昌：江西高校出版社，2014.
6. 邓诗萍. 唐诗鉴赏大典[M]. 长春：吉林大学出版社，2009.
7. 杜学霞. 白居易“中隐”思想探析[J]. 河南社会科学，2017，25(12)：77-81.
8. 冯宇. 全唐诗广选新注集评(七)[M]. 沈阳：辽宁人民出版社，1994.
9. 霍松林. 霍松林古诗今译集[M]. 西安：陕西师范大学出版社，2018.
10. 贾文昭，等. 唐诗鉴赏辞典[M]. 上海：上海辞书出版社，1983.
11. 蹇长春. 白居易评传[M]. 南京：南京大学出版社，2002.
12. 姜红红. 白居易诗歌中关于“闲”的美学思想[D]. 金华：浙江师范大学，2015.
13. 姜树景. 白居易洛阳时期的“中隐”思想与诗歌创作研究[D]. 西安：陕西师范大学，2013.
14. 蒋建平. 唐诗宋词中的风雅与时尚[M]. 上海：文汇出版社，2010.
15. 刘叶秋. 历代笔记概述[M]. 北京：中华书局，1980.
16. 鲁迅. 中国小说史略[M]. 北京：人民文学出版社，1981.
17. 潘镛. 隋唐时期的运河和漕运[M]. 西安：三秦出版社，1987.
18. 彭定求，等. 全唐诗(下)[M]. 上海：上海古籍出版社，1986.
19. 汪翔，张金铣. 论白居易的致仕观念[J]. 河南科技大学学报(社会科学版)，2022，40(1)：95-100.
20. 王晓磊. 六神磊磊读唐诗[M]. 北京：北京十月文艺出版社，2022.
21. 吴大奎，马秀娟. 元稹白居易诗选译[M]. 成都：巴蜀书社，1991.

22. 夏昆. 在唐诗里孤独漫步[M]. 厦门：鹭江出版社，2015.
23. 萧涤非，程千帆，马茂元，等. 唐诗鉴赏辞典[M]. 上海：上海辞书出版社，1999.
24. 肖剑. 唐诗鉴赏大典[M]. 北京：长征出版社，1999.
25. 谢思炜. 白居易诗选[M]. 北京：中华书局，2005.
26. 于海娣，等. 唐诗鉴赏大全集[M]. 北京：中国华侨出版社，2010.
27. 袁行霈. 中国文学史(第三版)(第一卷)[M]. 北京：高等教育出版社，2014.
28. 詹杭伦，陈文新. 唐代科举与试赋[M]. 武汉：武汉大学出版社，2015.
29. 中国社会科学院语言研究所词典编辑室. 现代汉语词典[M]. 北京：商务印书馆，2016.
30. 赵超，郭聪颖. 凝视与塑造：白居易服饰书写中的自我形象透视[J]. 海南大学学报(人文社会科学版)，2021，39(1)：88-95.
31. 赵彦春. 白居易诗歌英译[M]. 上海：上海大学出版社，2021.
32. 周静敏. 贬途与心路——白居易被贬江州思想转折时间再考[J]. 九江学院学报(社会科学版)，2022，41(3)：36-43.
33. https://baike.baidu.com/reference/11001093/6deb0EA5gp_wYjjClfAeXxaU_vo2qZOMM6lInllPdK8WZbpib4JFcPqmQXWjqBuR85XuV5qxlDWsB3U_P7Ljr8K5x12nyrXB1qtTYPRR.
34. https://baike.baidu.com/reference/11001093/88abMENYSKe9_Wk1TfLvzwzeHkcyn3PN3DTmLXtZgzVbK9BvpOKtb6OxFWgblbmEu7Xpcd-1c1gSYiLCaFOx81Jm6pX_rR_AQpeAejdy.
35. https://baike.baidu.com/item/%E5%95%86%E5%B1%B1%E5%9B%9B%E7%9A%93/4575986.
36. https://zhidao.baidu.com/question/42561471.html?fr=search&word=%C7%EF%BD%AD%CB%CD%BF%CD%B5%C4%D0%B4%D7%F7%B1%B3%BE%B0%CA%C7%CA%B2%C3%B4&ie=gbk.
37. http://www.aisixiang.com/data/86007.html.